Published by: Cinnabar Moth Publishing LLC
Santa Fe, New Mexico

Cover Design by: Ira Geneve

ISBN-13: 978-1-962308-13-7
Library of Congress Control Number: 2024933841

The Path of Revenge

TOM HAWARD

For Gemma, whose love made my path one of healing.

Content Notes:

The Path of Revenge deals with many difficult topics that may be triggering for some readers.

Drug use (explicit)
Explicit language
Child abuse (non-sexual, explicit)
Medical trauma (explicit)
Genitalia mutilation (implied)
Homophobia (explicit)

1

The Kingdom of Askå: 2031

Bjorn Askå picked a bit of meat out from between his teeth, which had been bugging him for about half an hour. He sucked his teeth to make sure there wasn't a stray stringy bit.

"That was good," he said to himself. "Very tasty."

He picked up the remains of his meal and sucked some more meat off the bone, enjoying the rich, gamey flavour. The television was on, and it was streaming Grand Protector Faust's speech. Askå had seen the speech numerous times but enjoyed watching it. He liked Faust. He could see the deception in the Grand Protector's eyes, and he felt a kindred spirit with the man. But it wasn't his liking of Faust that had motivated him to watch the speech on repeat for the past few months. No, it was the message within the speech: Emperor Nero is dead. Those words caressed his mind and he smiled at the screen.

Faust's speech hailed Maximus Nero as the new Emperor Maximus II, who would be coronated in due course, but Askå's intel knew Maximus was a vegetable and probably couldn't even rule his own bowels, let alone an Empire. The Grand Protector also thanked the Emperor and the Senate for his newly formed role and promised to bring to justice those who had tried to bring down the Roman Empire.

"How didn't Maverick manage to kill him?" Askå was genuinely puzzled. "It's not a rhetorical question," said Askå to a man in the room with him.

The man was in the corner, sobbing, but eventually responded, stumbling over the words. "Who? K-kill wh-who?"

"Maximus. The man is a weasel. I have child fighters who would have been able to kill him in seconds, and yet Maverick couldn't. I've fought Maverick. There's no way he failed to kill Maximus by accident. He held back. Why would he hold back?"

The man in the corner sniffled but also sighed, as if exasperated by the questions, because it was clear Askå was having a conversation with himself. Askå picked up on the annoyance. "Apologies, am I boring you?"

The man stiffened and shook his head.

Bjorn pushed his chair back, and the heavy legs scraped the granite floor. He stood and arched his back. The chair he sat in was carved out of Britannia oak and weighed over 40 kilos. It had been made to be extremely uncomfortable, to his specification. He used the chair to discipline himself. He had pushed the chair back with ease. When Bjorn stood up, the man in the room noticed how it seemed to make the room appear smaller due to the size of the Aestii man. Bjorn Askå was over seven feet tall, his shoulders so broad he could carry a cross on each, his legs long and lanky, his platted golden hair the length of his back. Askå was also clean shaven, which was unusual: most men in the region grew beards to help combat the cold. It was another form of endurance the giant man put upon himself. He walked over to the man in the corner of the room, covering the large distance in a couple of strides.

The man in the room couldn't help but cower in the presence of such an intimidating person. "You're not boring me, I just don't have the answers you're looking for. Please, I'm of no use to you."

"But you must have met Maverick. Or even fought him?"

The man shook his head again. He shook it hard, almost like he was trying to shake away his reality.

"Curious." Aská looked down at the cowering man, intrigued by him. "I find it strange how you had all that power and responsibility, and yet you never encountered Maverick. Did you not try to hunt him? Smoke him out? Publicly challenge him?" Aská laughed to himself. "Of course you didn't challenge him. If you had then you wouldn't be here. You know, I used to stream all of Maverick's bouts when he was a gladiator. It was wonderful spectacle. I felt a sense of pride watching him. Seeing him dispatch people with a lackadaisical ease. He was always my greatest achievement." Aská crouched down so he was almost at the same level as his scared guest. "Where do you think he is?"

The man shook his head again. He shook it hard. Maybe the nightmare would end. "I don't know. Fuck. I honestly don't know."

The man tried to move to a more comfortable position, but his arms were tied behind his back. The position meant he couldn't feel his left arm at all because it was so numb. Aská stroked the man's hair. The man froze at the affectionate gesture. "I believe you, Titus, I believe you," Aská said. He stopped stroking Titus's hair and moved his hand to the Roman's arm, where he resumed the stroking with his thumb. "You know, there's a theory that people who lie and deceive and create a toxic environment for others end up tainting not only their soul, but their body too. They become rotten to the core, spiritually and physically. Look at that

3

piece of shit who was your Emperor. He was like rancid meat." Aská spat on the floor, as if he had actually eaten something rotten. He continued to stroke Titus's arm with his thumb. "You though, *Commander,* you're not rancid or toxic. A coward, yes, but rotten? No, you're an opportunist. Unfortunately, for you, the opportunity you thought you had bought was never going to match the budget I have at my disposal."

And that was the problem for Titus, the former Commander of Britannia: he had underestimated how much someone like him was worth to enemies of the Empire. Titus had bribed his way out of London, believing he was going to be executed by Emperor Nero II. The rebel effort against the Empire had increased in ferocity, killing a top Centurion and seeing many soldiers dying on the streets of London as well as many abandoning the Empire for the rebel effort. Boatman King, the rebel leader in London, had shredded Titus's reputation as a commander able to bring peace and stability. Titus believed it was inevitable that Nero would have him crucified on London Bridge, live streamed to the nation as an example of failure. In fact, if he had held his nerve and waited it out for a matter of days, then he would have seen Nero executed and possibly himself promoted to Grand Protector of Rome. His paranoia got the better of him though, and he thought he had bought a ticket out of Britannia and to the possible safety of the Republic of Indigenous America via a fishing boat with a greedy skipper. Unbeknownst to Titus, the greedy skipper was already in the pocket of Bjorn Aská and ferried the traitorous Roman directly into the Aestii's hands.

Something wasn't adding up for Titus: Bjorn Aská ruled the Kingdom of Rome and Aská. There was an alliance, a truce. Aská's kingdom was vast, but it was still a partnership with the Empire.

Soldiers and funds were sent regularly as goodwill. In return, the Aestii behemoth provided manpower, protection and intel. The relationship worked and everyone benefited. Aská spoke like Rome was the enemy and he had no access to information. It made no sense to abduct a soldier. An AWOL Commander would also be worth a lot of gold, so it didn't seem logical for Aská to have Titus locked away like this, doing these things to him.

Titus tried to express his confusion, in-between the sobs and pleading. Aská stopped stroking. "My dear man. I'm sorry for the confusion. I don't think you understand our purpose together. I haven't brought you here for information or Empire secrets. I asked you about Maverick because I'm a huge fan of him. I want to see him again and hoped you might be able to help. Your use to me isn't Empire-related at all. I thought I made it clear a moment ago when I was talking about how some people are rotten and some are not, like you. You're not tainted. That's good."

Bjorn cut the cable ties keeping Titus's arms behind his back. "See? I find you the opposite of rotten."

For a moment, Titus thought his captor's words related to releasing him, as he had just freed his arms, but as the Roman brought his arms in front of him and tried to rub his left wrist to ease the ache, he found there was no left hand or wrist available to rub. Just a white bandage covering a stump. Aská's words carried on calmly, as if everything was normal, about how people who are not toxic are not tainted and therefore taste the sweetest. Titus tasted as sweet and exotic as Aská had tasted in many years.

Before the Roman fainted from the shock, he glanced at the table Aská had been sitting at and saw the skeletal remains of his left hand on a plate. Titus then realised what meat had been stuck between Aská's teeth.

2

Maximus called for the nurse. Well, called was a rather generous word for the animalistic noise that his mouth emitted. Ever since his head had been caved in by a hammer, he wasn't able to vocalise much that made any sense. In his head, though, in his head, everything made sense and the words that bounced around his brain were as clear as the hatred that bubbled in his gut. The hatred was centred on Maverick Kirabo, the man who had wielded the hammer that had left a permanent dent in Maximus's skull.

It had been eleven months since Max had one minute been enjoying crucifying Olivia King, feeling the butterflies in his belly as he smashed nails through her wrists, and the next minute waking up in this gods-forsaken room, fluorescent lights causing splinters of pain in his skull and tubes sprouting from his body like a plastic porcupine.

Maximus made a guttural noise again to try and get the nurse's attention. Eventually she appeared; she tried to conceal a look of disgust, but she was either a poor actor or disinterested in trying. Maximus had assumed his face was a picture of horror from his injuries, which it was, but the nurse's disgust didn't come from the patient's wounds but from the patient's personality.

Maximus Nero was infamous for his sadism. He made no secret of the pleasure he derived from other people's pain. It was that pleasure that had motivated him to travel to Britannia to track down Olivia King. Olivia King, the wife of Boatman King, the rebel leader who'd caused Max's father, Emperor Nero II, endless frustration and anger. The British were an easy people to conquer and subdue, apathy about who their leaders were far outweighing any outrage about Roman rule. Boatman King had changed that though, inspiring people to resist. Resistance was one thing. The Romans were used to resistance. But information was leaking from deep within Roman ranks and no-one was able to understand how Boatman was learning of Roman plans. Nero's top commander in Britannia, Titus, had crucified countless soldiers he suspected of treason but to no avail. It seemed no-one was willingly divulging information to the rebels. And that was the key word: willingly. Maybe information was leaking unwittingly instead.

Before becoming Grand Protector of Rome, Faust was a soldier many believed to be the most intelligent man in the Empire and also the person the soldier Maximus felt should be leading Britannia instead of Titus. Faust focused on how information might have been accidentally leaked to the rebels and circled in on therapists and priests. Both these professions relied on confession, whether it be catharsis for the soul or for the mind. It was entirely possible soldiers were divulging Empire secrets to atone themselves and inadvertently feeding that information to a rebel.

Faust had dismissed priests as the leak because there were only five God-Carpenter churches in London and the priests of each church frequently begged the Empire for funding to keep their minuscule cult going. The Empire entertained followers of the God Carpenter because a former Emperor, Constantine, had become enamoured with the teachings of Jesus the Christ. Constantine had been assassinated before he was able to inspire many into following the path he had taken, but his passion left enough of an echo that the small religion kept smatterings of followers throughout the world.

No, the priests of the city weren't divulging secrets of the Empire, they had too much to lose and also any Roman of any importance wasn't wasting their time on a whimsical cult. Any Roman with information worth a damn believed they were in the favour of the Roman gods. The superstition ran deep, and Romans who had found success in the Empire made sure those superstitions were adhered to.

Apart from Faust.

Faust found most belief systems to be primitive nonsense. Not that he ever admitted such a thing. Most thought Faust was the most superstitious soldier they had ever met.

With priests eliminated from suspicion, it came down to therapists. The Empire didn't like its soldiers going for therapy, but after Nero's accession, it seemed the only fair thing to do. Nero's lust for fear and pain meant it wasn't only those who opposed him who were riddled with fear. Many Roman soldiers were also constantly anxious, fearing the Emperor would punish them for any mistakes. A lot of Romans in outposts like Britannia needed someone to confide in. It made sense to Faust that someone was exploiting that confidential privilege. Once that connection was explored, Olivia King's identity was quickly established. To Faust's dismay, Maximus Nero learned of the therapist's involvement in helping the rebellion and ordered everyone to stand down until he arrived in London and could personally crucify the "disrespectful bitch" himself. Faust warned Titus that Max's involvement was a terrible idea, but Titus wasn't going to interfere with Max's plans. He wasn't that stupid.

No Roman soldiers were going to argue with the Emperor's son, but unfortunately for Max, Maverick Kirabo was certainly going to disagree with Max's decision to personally crucify Olivia King. Olivia was a friend. Olivia was a hero. Olivia was not deserving of being treated with such depravity. Maverick took pleasure in attempting to take Max's head clean off when he swung the hammer.

Somehow, Max survived.

Even though his skull was now the shape of a half-deflated football, Max lived. And not only did he live, but he recovered. So, although the sounds that came out of his mouth were gibberish, Max's brain was working as efficiently as it ever had been and he was formulating how he would not only kill Maverick but make the man suffer and suffer.

He fumbled for his phone and wrote a note for the nurse to read. She continued to be blatant in her disgust. Maximus typed another note and passed his phone to her. Her disgust turned to fear. She nodded, dropped the phone on the Emperor's bed and left the room. Maximus picked up the phone and read the note he had typed.

Look at me in that way again and I will order your child to be flayed in front of you.

He sighed. By the gods, people were pathetic. Here he was, a voiceless retard, typing threatening messages on his phone and the fucking nurse scurried out of the room instead of doing what any good person would do: ram his damn phone down his throat.

He opened his messages app and typed out another message. He wasn't expecting a response as he hadn't had one for the previous four months, but hope sprang eternal. It marked itself as delivered, so at least he knew it had been received. He then video called his bodyguard, who answered immediately. The bodyguard knew by now to answer and not say anything. He knew what the Emperor needed. The bodyguard held the phone up so Maximus could see the bodyguard descend the staircase of the Emperor's palace, walk along the underground corridor to a door at the end and open it. The bodyguard walked inside, and the phone's resolution took a moment to adjust to the change in light. When the phone caught up the screen showed a large black man lying on a small bed.

"Damba," said the bodyguard, "the Emperor is on the phone."

Damba Kirabo, Maverick Kirabo's brother, had his hands behind his head and his eyes were closed. He eventually opened them and turned to face the phone. "Hail, Caesar."

Emperor Maximus typed, and his phone verbalised his words through the bodyguard's phone's speaker: *How are you feeling?*

"Fine, my Lord."

Any contact?

"No, my Lord."

He believes it's actually you?

"Yes, my Lord."

Why wouldn't he respond?

"He's not stupid. My Lord."

Maximus cut the call. He twirled his phone in his hands, thinking. He typed out another message: *Damba is working for me.* His phone pinged with a reply almost immediately: *I know.* The screen showed there was another message being typed. *You should make that hospital room feel more like home because I'm going to cave the other side of your skull in. Soon.*

3

Boatman lugged the basket of oysters across the mud flats and put them down by his small boat, which was beached.

The flats were tidal, so Boatman had beached the boat on ebb tides, and it would float again when the tide came back in.

He took a breath and then fished a large mesh nylon-string net from inside the boat. He tipped the oysters into the net and pulled the rope attached to the top, pulling the net closed, and tied a knot. He took a few steps to the water's edge and swished the net in the water to wash the mud and silt off the oysters. He threw the net into the boat; it landed with a heavy thud on top of a dozen or so nets, also filled with oysters. He picked the basket up and surveyed the mud flats. There were thousands of oysters scattered for acres and still plenty of time to keep picking them up as the tide wasn't coming in for another half an hour.

It was a chilly Autumn morning with barely a breath of wind. He gazed over to the other side of the channel to see a seal lazing on the mud. A heron landed a few metres away from Boatman, unperturbed by the man's presence. It only took ten minutes to leave shore and get to the oyster beds by boat, but it felt like a wilderness.

For a moment, Boatman felt like the trauma and stress of the past few months had evaporated, out here in this tiny wilderness.

"I definitely prefer hitting a Roman in the face to this." Tobias's words brought Boatman back to reality.

"Being out here is good for the soul," said Boatman.

"What the fuck happened to your soul? It's muddy, wet and cold. If I wanted that combination, I would have gone to fight in the Aestii region."

"You need an open mind, Tobias."

"No, I need to be somewhere hot. I used to have a gorgeous, golden tan. Do you remember that? Do you remember my tan? I looked good." Tobias looked down at himself, mud splattered up his oilskin overalls, "Now I look like a pale hobo."

"Did Maverick know where your off switch was? Because it would be really handy right now."

"I came out here with you. Voluntarily."

"Only because Bella didn't want you."

"I'm offended she didn't want me to go with her."

"She's hunting birds. It needs to be done quietly. As in, no constant talking," said Boatman.

"It just seems weird to want to do anything in complete silence."

"Tobias, having spent many times out here, alone with you, I understand why Bella wants complete silence."

"For the man who killed the Emperor, you're not very mature," said Tobias, and he squelched off to find some more oysters before the tide came back in.

Man who killed the Emperor. Boatman thought about that moment and how it had led to him standing on a remote bit of mud hiding from the Empire. After killing Nero and barely escaping with his life, because of a confrontation with former Centurion Faust,

Boatman evacuated London with his wife Olivia, Bella, Tobias and little Molly, an orphan he felt he owed a debt to. The only place he could go was where he had been raised when he'd been adopted forty years previously.

The Empire knew next to nothing about Boatman's past. They certainly didn't know about his life before becoming a rebel leader. Boatman's mother had been raped by a Roman soldier, leaving her injured and traumatised. The trauma never left her, and she died shortly after giving birth to him. A priest had cared for Boatman in his first days alive, but knew the little boy needed somewhere safe. It was an open secret that any child born a bastard to a Roman soldier would likely be disposed of to save the risk of having to fund the child's upbringing. The priest also feared repercussions for supporting the little boy, so he found a family who would love and care for him. The priest had made it very clear the boy should know exactly how he came to be in the world, because the gods would want to exert justice and possibly use Boatman as the weapon.

The priest knew a couple who were desperate to raise a child but couldn't conceive. They lived in a remote settlement on the coast of Britannia, only seventy miles away from London. It was an inconsequential place where oysters were grown to be sold to London, but not much else happened there. Families rarely moved away and instead carried on the traditions of their ancestors. Political figureheads or bastard children of the Empire seeking asylum weren't obvious residents of such a settlement. In fact, most of the small population couldn't recall whether they had ever seen a Roman solider. The settlement was only accessible by boat, and when a visitor arrived they would find little to do apart from being given a basket to go and catch oysters. Boatman was adopted into this settlement and until the day he decided to leave to avenge his mother, he too had never seen a Roman.

Then, for nearly a decade all he ever saw were Roman soldiers and the blood of Roman soldiers. All he saw were crucifixions and torture. All he felt was rage and vengeance and desire to wipe every Roman from the planet. Then he killed the Emperor, and for a fleeting moment thought it was all over and he wouldn't need to stomach Romans ever again. But that was only ever a fleeting moment because before the Emperor's body had turned cold, new powers forged to replace him and seek to cause Boatman more pain. So Boatman retreated to where he knew Rome had failed to influence and touch: home.

And so he stood on the mud flats that surrounded his adopted home of Meresig and realised he hadn't seen a Roman for almost a year. He hadn't shed any blood or cracked any skulls. The only things he had cracked were oysters as he knocked them apart so they were ready to be sold. He felt resentment that he was likely harvesting a product that Grand Protector Faust would eat, but his parents needed the money and couldn't be picky about who ate their molluscs.

He watched as Tobias bent over, dropping oysters into his basket, and felt regret. He had believed Tobias and Maverick were going to be the ultimate weapon against the Empire and, in many ways, they were, but now Maverick was missing, on his own mission of vengeance and Tobias was left wondering where his boyfriend was.

Boatman's phone rang, and he fumbled through his layers of clothes to answer it. It was Olivia. "We might have a problem."

"I'm listening."

"A couple have walked into the pub for a drink, saying they're oyster lovers and wanted to see where they're grown."

16

"Okay," said Boatman.

"They look like they're part of Faust's B-Unit."

"I'm guessing Bella agrees."

"She's been watching them and agrees. Faust's stooges always stick out. Especially in a place like this," said Olivia.

"Are they asking questions?"

"Not yet."

"They're probably trying to appear normal." Boatman took a moment. He looked over at the seal lazing on the mud. He was jealous of that damn seal, without a care in the world. "When you say Bella's watching them?"

Olivia paused. "She is, but not like that." Olivia knew her husband. She knew his thought processes, and she knew he was wondering whether Bella watching meant Bella had a clear shot with her bow and arrow.

"That's a shame," said Boatman.

"Maybe," said Olivia. "But them dying would most likely bring Faust to us."

"Maybe," said Boatman, repeating his wife's words. "But maybe that would be a good thing."

"Maybe," said Olivia again and then the line went dead.

Boatman watched as the seal flopped about and then glided into the water, leaving barely a ripple.

So obvious and yet so stealthy.

He wondered if that was how to win the war against Rome.

He called Tobias back over to the boat, saying they'd caught enough and it was time to head in. He also filled Tobias in on his call with Olivia.

As the boat got close to shore, Boatman cut the outboard and tilted it. The boat glided in and scraped along the stones as it came

17

to a halt. Tobias climbed out, and Boatman passed the nets to him one by one as Tobias loaded them onto an old Roman chariot. The Romans tended to give old chariots away as they upgraded their technology, and Meresig oyster farmers found them perfect for transporting oysters from their boats to where they would be processing their catch on land.

Before Tobias climbed into the chariot to take the morning's harvest to be processed, he said, "What are we going to do?"

"We're going to have to come out from hiding. There's no way we can stay hidden anymore."

"What if it isn't anyone from the B-Unit?"

"We can't take that risk. We have to assume it is."

"If they are Faust's spies, then we should just kill them."

"And bring a Roman army here in the process."

"I don't understand. What, then? We just run?" Tobias looked frustrated at the idea of running from any Romans again. He was angry that they'd been forced to retreat with their tails between their legs nearly a year ago and now they were potentially doing it again.

Tobias had been almost killed by Faust, stabbed from behind. A coward's way to attack, and he was aggrieved to have been caught out in a such a way. He was now fully recovered, and the last thing he wanted to do was feel like Faust was winning yet again. He was also surprised at Boatman's apparent willingness to retreat without a fight. Boatman had garnered a fearsome reputation in London, where he was almost a bogeyman in Roman consciousness. Part of the reason why Boatman almost toppled the Empire was the myth surrounding him. He was a story more than a person. He made soldiers afraid of their patrols at night. He killed a seasoned Centurion and fatally stabbed an Emperor. He showed how to make the Empire look weak. It brought Tobias confidence in the cause and made him believe anything was possible for the future. It made him believe there was a future without chariots and crosses.

But now they were here, talking about running from the Romans again. Running from Faust. Faust, who had nearly killed him. It seemed weak and fearful, and he didn't get it.

"Tobias, where are our resources? How would we form any attack against Faust?"

Tobias was angry. "Who needs resources? Does Maverick? He's prowling near Rome as we speak, about to pounce on Maximus."

Boatman went to say something back in anger, but shook his head instead, rubbed his face with his hands in frustration and said, "I'm going to take the boat home and talk with Olivia. Bella is keeping an eye on our guests, and we'll meet later to plan our next steps. You okay to sort this lot?" Boatman was looking at their morning's harvest. Tobias said it was fine and would speak later. "Oh, and grab your earpiece; we need to get back in the game."

Tobias gave the boat a shove. Boatman put the outboard's propellor back into the water, pulled the starter chord and steered toward his waterside home further up one of the creeks. Boatman eased off the throttle and looked back to see Tobias fire up the chariot loaded with oysters and drive off into the distance. The rebel leader felt a knot in his stomach. A knot of anxiety. He loved his childhood home. He loved being in nature and the sense of satisfaction it brought.

But.

But it was just hiding. It was causing him to be in limbo. He was avoiding his destiny. He was avoiding the path he should be taking.

4

Boatman pulled his boat up alongside the jetty attached to his home. He tied up and stepped onto the jetty. He walked along it to a veranda where there was a set of outside sofas. Olivia was curled up on one, wrapped up in a blanket and holding a cup of coffee. Boatman sat down next to his wife. "You okay?"

Olivia sipped her coffee. "Yeah, just enjoying the view in case it's the last time."

"We don't know it's Faust."

Olivia looked at her husband and felt a sadness. It was a sadness that hadn't really left her since she had been crucified. Maybe sadness wasn't accurate enough a word, she thought. It was grief. She grieved her relationship with Boatman. She also grieved the love she had once felt. It wasn't that she didn't love her husband anymore. It was that the love she did feel didn't burn brightly like it did before. That was painful. To look at the man she used to be besotted with and realise that, at times, there was resentment. Resentment because of how she had been captured by Maximus. Resentment because the man who instilled fear into Romans across Britannia had failed to even save his wife.

5

When, back in London, Boatman had been informed that there was chatter on the streets that therapists might be suspected as informants to the rebellion by filtering confidential information given to them from soldiers, Boatman wasn't convinced by this rumour. Or, at least, he didn't want to believe the rumour, because Olivia was in a very privileged position. She had built quite a client list, with one being Centurion Sulla, who oversaw patrols of the city limits. Sulla would regularly moan about how he wasn't taken seriously enough by Titus and how Titus didn't understand how vital Sulla was to keeping the city safe from rebels. Olivia would never ask direct questions about Sulla's operations, only about his feelings and perception of the world around him. Even so, because life and work for a Roman Centurion were so interwoven, he would share confidential operational tactics with Olivia because he was making a point about how no-one listened to him on how to improve their tactics. Olivia would then feed this back to Boatman.

In Boatman's eyes, if Olivia was in danger, then this Centurion Sulla would have walked into his next therapy session and arrested her. Boatman was also doubtful that any of the city's therapists would have been connected to any leaked information. Boatman instructed them, for their safety, to never share too much, only vague details that he could then untangle and use for the rebellion effort. If Rome did start digging, then therapists certainly wouldn't be considered, and the patients wouldn't suspect their confidentiality was being breached. In a relationship like therapist and patient, the trust given over is so instant, as soon as you walk into that room. No, Boatman thought, Olivia would not be suspected.

"How can you be sure?"

"Titus is weak. He worries about making everyone happy in London. He's always putting out fires each day. He doesn't have time to dig any deeper than superficial problems in the city. Honestly, Liv, there's no way therapists are under suspicion."

"What about the rumour? That doesn't come from nowhere."

Boatman pulled his wife in close to him. "I don't know. Maybe Mikey misheard." Mikey was a homeless guy who was paid by the rebellion to keep his ear to the ground. The Romans tended to give Mikey a wide berth simply to avoid getting their legs humped by Gordon, Mikey's amorous Cockapoo.

"I'm not comfortable seeing Sulla again."

"I need you to see him one more time, Liv. Look, Titus is on the back foot. Soldiers are scared to do their patrols. We just need a bit more information, and then I will pull you out."

Olivia drew away from her husband. "*We* need or *you* need? And I'm the one getting the information whilst you hide underground." Olivia put on her jacket and left for her office without saying goodbye.

―――――――

Olivia was in her office, sitting in her armchair, waiting for Sulla to arrive. There was a knock at the door and Olivia got up and answered it. Instead of Centurion Sulla standing there looking flustered as always, Olivia was faced with a man who looked like the personification of toxic. She stepped back, not to let the man in but because she could almost *smell* the badness emanating from him. He was about her height and looked unwell. Maybe he *was* unwell and had somehow stumbled across her door, Olivia thought at first. His skin looked almost waxy, like he never stopped sweating. In fact, if Olivia had seen this man asleep, she would have assumed he had been embalmed. She gathered herself and kept some bile back. "Can I help?"

"Hello, Olivia."

"I'm sorry, have we met?"

The man laughed. It sounded strange coming out of his mouth. Unnatural. "Surely I don't need to introduce myself?"

There's a thing about context. You could work in a store and serve a customer once a week for a year and then see them one time in your local pub and register that you knew them but struggle to know where from. Olivia was trying to quickly work through her own context struggle. She knew she recognised this toxic man but couldn't work out where from. She was guessing he was a patient of a fellow therapist but amazed she couldn't recall. No, that wasn't it.

"I thought I was more famous than that," the man said and sighed. "Anyway," he said to himself and pushed past Olivia into her office and plonked himself down on her chair. He sat there, feet firmly planted on the floor and his arms on the armrests. He sat there like it was a throne, and that's when it hit Olivia, that's when she knew who he was. She held on to the door to steady herself. *Run*, her brain told her, but her feet felt heavy.

"I wouldn't run, my soldiers have been told to kill you if you run."

Olivia stammered, but managed to say, "What do you want?"

"What do I want?" Maximus laughed that unnatural laugh again,

"It's *who* I want, not what."

"I don't understand."

Maximus tutted and wagged his finger at Olivia. "Let's not play this little game, hey?" Olivia was still holding onto the open door. "Close the door, Olivia. You'll die if you go out there. I'm your only chance to stay alive now." Maximus smirked. "Boatman won't be able to save you." At the mention of her husband's name, Olivia closed the door and took the seat opposite the Roman.

"Good girl." Maximus looked around the room. "So, how does this work?"

"What?" Olivia tried to maintain eye contact. She wasn't going to let him intimidate her.

"This whole therapy thing." He waved an arm. "What do we do?"

Olivia already knew the answer but had to ask. "Where's Paul?"

"Who?"

"Centurion Sulla. Where is he?"

"His name was Paul? Huh, how bizarre. You know, I'm only now realising I never got his first name. Even whilst I tortured him earlier." Maximus adjusted his position in his seat and crossed his legs. "But that's irrelevant. I want to know what's so good about therapy with you. Do I have to start talking about issues I have with my father or the fact that I want to fuck my mother?"

Olivia tried to process her situation and that she needed to keep this man in the office for as long as possible because Boatman would be here any minute. "Do you want to fuck your mother?"

The pause to think about her question was disturbing for Olivia. "I don't think so. I mean, if I ever met her, then I might think differently."

"If you find that question tricky, then I would humbly suggest you need intensive therapy." Olivia tried to look bored by the situation and looked at her watch. "My Lord, I hope you were only joking about torturing Sulla and that he will be here soon, but I'm extremely busy so, with all due respect, what is it you want? An appointment?"

Maximus leant forward and then slowly started to clap. "You're very good. I know why I'm here. You know why I'm here. And yet here we are with you masking the situation beautifully."

"I'm not masking anything," said Olivia. Her hands were trembling. "I am asking you to leave."

The heir to the Empire stood up and wandered over to Olivia's desk. He thumbed a psychology magazine and stopped on an article about leadership and sociopathic behaviour. He picked up the magazine and turned to face Olivia. "Can I keep this? I think my Dad needs to read it." He looked at his watch. "Well, it's time to go."

"Call ahead next time."

Maximus gently placed his hand on Olivia's shoulder and said, "I don't think you're understanding what I'm saying." He squeezed her arm, hard. "You're coming with me."

Boatman had taught Olivia how to protect herself. He had also taught her that the simplest form of attack was also the most effective. So she kicked him in the balls. Maximus crumpled whilst clutching what he held most dear. She hoped Boatman would be arriving any moment and rushed over to her desk. She opened a drawer and pulled out a taser. Boatman had insisted she had a gun in her drawer, but she had no intention of ever firing a gun on someone. When she turned around, Maximus was on her. She tried to aim the taser in his direction and fire, but he smacked her hand away and then punched her in the stomach. She bent over, wheezing, and fell to her knees. Maximus grabbed her hair and pulled. Olivia cried out. Maximus made his unnatural laugh again.

"Like I said, you're coming with me." Olivia tried to break free and as she did so some of her hair came out in Maximus's hands and she sprawled on the floor. Maximus stared down at the therapist, enjoying her pain. "You know, if you hadn't fought me or resisted, then we could have strolled out of here peacefully. But now, well, now you're lying on the floor, looking like a slut and maybe it's time to be treated like a slut."

Maximus kicked Olivia in the gut and then Olivia's hell began. And all the time Maximus raped her, she hoped Boatman would turn up and save her from the nightmare. Even as Maximus drove nails into her wrists while crucifying her, she thought, *Boatman will be here soon.* He never came.

6

Olivia sat on the sofa on the veranda of her waterside house and tried not to flinch when Boatman leaned in and kissed her forehead. Boatman noticed. "What's wrong?"

"Nothing."

Boatman rubbed his face and said, "It's always nothing." He sighed and stood up. "It's always nothing," he said again. "I need you to talk to me instead of pretending you're okay."

Olivia didn't expect the words to come out so quickly, but nevertheless they did. "I wouldn't need to pretend to be okay if you had been the man you were meant to be."

"What does that mean?"

"It's obvious, isn't it?"

"What?" Boatman paced around the veranda. "Just say it."

"You left me to the mercy of that animal."

"I got to your office too late. I went there. You'd already gone."

Olivia laughed. "Oh, I'm sorry for being raped and kidnapped too quickly for you." Olivia stood up, kicking her blanket off, and threw her coffee cup across the veranda. It made a plop as it hit the water. "You were meant to save me from that monster."

"You were safe. There was no reason to think anyone was after you."

"Tell that to my fucking wrists, Boatman." Olivia bared her wrists to her husband. Her right one showed the scar from a nail having been hammered through it into a cross. It was wrinkled and discoloured from the graft needed to repair the damage.

"You should have been there." She slumped back on the sofa, exhausted from feeling like she was saying the obvious. It wasn't only the exhaustion from feeling resentment for not being saved by the only person she trusted to keep her safe, it was the exhaustion that Boatman just didn't get it.

"You can't keep punishing me," said Boatman. "It's all been for something more. You took that risk when being with me. It was about destroying the Empire."

Olivia laughed. "And how's that working out for you?"

"Nero's dead, isn't he?"

Olivia stood up and walked into the house, "And it feels like our marriage is, too."

7

The only pub in Meresig, The Victorium, was situated on the waterfront area of the settlement. It was in the centre of the working area, where fishing, oyster farming, boat building and maintenance took place. The Victorium was a black, wood-clad building on stilts to protect it from when Spring tides were particularly high and could cause flooding. It wasn't a big building, but inside there was enough room to have a hundred people inside make it feel full but not cramped. The inside was very much in keeping with the waterfront, with fishing nets, pictures of local work boats, oil lantern lights and driftwood-clad walls. The landlord kept the place clean, served great beer and served even better seafood. Although the locals had no choice to go anywhere else, they genuinely loved The Victorium. There was always someone in there to share a drink with and talk about anything and everything. Because Meresig was only accessible by boat and its economy was mainly to export its produce to the Empire, the village didn't get many visitors. If there were visitors, the village knew about it before the guests had taken a step from the boat.

So the couple sitting in The Victorium having drinks had been scrutinised for hours already, and that's why Bella had set up a table in the pub to watch and listen. Bella was able to sit at a table near the couple without much worry because her involvement in the rebellion was more mystery than solid information. Bella had been involved in a passionate affair with Faust's wife, Alypia, but the affair had never become public knowledge. If it had, then Alypia would certainly have been crucified on London Bridge with the execution streamed across the globe. Alypia was a superstar, so her betrayal of Faust would have been used as the ultimate deterrent to betraying the Empire. As it stood, many months later, Alypia was still alive and continuing to wow the crowds with her glamour and charm. No, Bella was positive Faust had no knowledge of the affair and therefore no information about who she was and what she looked like. She kept watch over the strangers in the pub, confident that they, if they were hunting on behalf of Faust, would not be suspicious of her at all.

She continued to pretend to read her book whilst eavesdropping on the couple. She would let Boatman know if there was any reason to suspect Faust had found them. In some ways, she hoped he had because Boatman had lost his edge. He had lost his fight. This situation might force him to fight again.

8

The couple being watched were named Delilah and Sebastian and Bella was right, they were Faust's personal hunters. They were part of the B-Unit, which Delilah found crass, but Faust didn't care about crass. The Boatman-Unit was a clearly defined name for the people hunting Boatman and his crew. Delilah sipped her drink and looked at her surroundings. She grimaced and wasn't sure if it was the drink or the pub that made her scowl. It was probably both. The wine was some locally produced swill and tasted like vinegar. The Empire subsidised wine production in Britannia and even churned out marketing praising what was, in Delilah's mind, complete garbage. They did it to polish the egos of the British, to make them feel like they were producing a superior product and effectively make them apathetic about their subservience to the Empire. It was an obvious and almost infantile ploy, but it worked. The small vineyards that grew below average wines were happy to praise the Empire as long as they were getting rather generous subsidies for what they were producing. Grand Protector Faust had instigated more and more of these subsidies for a range of industries, and it subdued a large portion of the populous. Delilah was passionate about the now-dead Emperor Nero's belief in fear as a means of mass compliance, so she found Faust's rather coddling approach quite sickening, but it wasn't for her to judge how her leaders ruled.

It was her job to hunt.

Delilah took another sip of her wine, just to appear normal. She wrinkled her nose at the taste and took in the smell of the pub. It was fusty. The wooden building standing next to the sea for this many years meant the wood had absorbed a staleness. The smell was alien to her. In fact, ever since she had arrived in Meresig, she had been bombarded by alien smells. Salt. Mud. Seaweed. She was used to fumes from chariots and the sweet, metallic odour of blood. She very much hoped she would be enjoying the odour of blood in the coming days.

Sebastian took Delilah away from her thoughts. "What do you think?"

"I think Faust hates us," she said.

Sebastian swigged the last of his beer and smacked his lips. "I like this place. The beer's good."

Delilah looked at her brother and said, "You're a heathen. Mother brought us up on the finest things and you guzzle that crap beer like an orphan who hasn't had a drink in days."

Sebastian got up to order another beer and said, "You need to realise that simply emulating Mother's uptight ways doesn't mean she'll ever like you."

Delilah gave Sebastian the finger. He gave her a grin in return and went to the bar.

"Do you get any busier than this?"

The landlord barely looked up from pouring Sebastian's drink, "It picks up later in the day when people come ashore." The beer was dumped on the bar and the landlord said, "It's a weird place, Meresig, for tourists to come to."

Sebastian took a swig of his fresh glass of beer and said, "We like doing weird when it comes to holidays."

"Oh, you're a couple who likes something unusual?"

Sebastian nodded. "Something like that."

"Well you're in the right place," said the landlord, "the locals are very unusual. Where's your friend?"

"He's having a nap. Speaking of locals, do you know someone called Boatman?"

The landlord shook his head, "Boatman? Like the guy who was on the news a few months ago? No, doesn't ring a bell. I would know a local by that name. Everyone would know a local by that name and tell him to change it," he said and walked off to serve another customer.

Sebastian walked back to his table and glanced around. There was a table of locals who must have finished work early, laughing loudly at each other's jokes. An older couple were sitting at a small table in the corner. They were sharing a large bowl of mussels, slurping the molluscs and barely saying a word to each other. A young woman was sitting on her own reading a book. It was all rather innocuous.

"Did the landlord share anything worth knowing?"

"No, nothing." Sebastian drummed his fingers on the table. "Are you sure that intel was reliable?"

Delilah was twisting her rancid glass of wine in her hands. "Of course I'm not sure. That's the whole point of intel, Sebastian."

"Well, if this place is hiding the most dangerous man in Britannia, they're all pretty fucking relaxed about it."

"Mother would hate hearing such foul language."

"Mother can suck it." Sebastian looked over at the bar, watching the landlord pottering about. "What do you think about him?"

Delilah looked over at the bar and then looked at her brother. "I'm not interested in your sexual proclivities, brother. But I highly doubt he will be interested in you."

Sebastian snorted. "When does that matter?"

Delilah rolled her eyes. "At least wait until our objective is complete before indulging in extracurricular activities."

"Sis, you need to loosen up every now and then.

"It's hard to 'loosen up' when I'm the one cleaning up your mess after you've got carried away." Delilah told Sebastian to finish his drink as they needed to get back to their room. The Victorium had a couple of cabins to its rear, which were mainly used by the landlord when he had family to stay, but he had agreed to hire one out to Sebastian and Delilah.

They unlocked their room and stared at the bed. The figure on the bed stared back. Delilah walked over to the bed and said. "Your intel seems flawed." The man on the bed shook his head, sweat beading his forehead. As he shook his head, the tape wrapped around his head, covering his mouth, chafed on the bed covers. Delilah sat on the bed and wiped the man's brow. He flinched at her touch. "If the man who killed an Emperor is hiding out in this gods-forsaken place, then everyone seems mightily relaxed." Delilah pulled the tape from the man's mouth. "So?"

"I was told he had come here." The man was on the verge of a panic attack, "I swear."

Delilah put her face close to the man's and whispered in his ear, "I believe you. I believe you." She gently kissed his cheek, "But we have a problem, don't we?" The man just looked at Delilah, confused. "If Boatman isn't here, then either you lied to me or someone lied to you. But, either way, it makes me look stupid and, therefore, makes the Empire look stupid." The man shook his head again.

"Listen," he started to say, "'I'm not lying, I…'" Delilah put her hand on the man's mouth.

"I've got to be honest. I don't really care. If Boatman isn't here, then we look like idiots and you are worthless But if Boatman is here, then you've served your purpose. Either way, I'm not sure we have any other use for you."

"Then why the fuck did we bring him here?" Sebastian spoke up. The man on the bed glanced over to Sebastian.

"Because, darling brother, when it comes to betraying the Empire, the dead serve as much purpose as the living." The man's eyes widened, and Delilah pulled the tape back over his mouth. She then grabbed a roll of gaffer tape from the bedside table and tore a piece off. She stuck it over the man's nose and said, "The gods thank you for your service." The man tried to thrash his head around to loosen the tape, but Delilah jabbed him in the throat, making him gasp and try to suck in air. The tape stopped him from being able to catch his breath and the man arched his body in panic. His arms and legs were tied to the bed, making it impossible to escape. Delilah stood and watched as the man panicked and tried to stop death coming for him. She always found it fascinating to observe how different people approached their impending annihilation. Some people, like the man in front of her, were consumed by panic. Like they had never contemplated that death would ever find them. The arrogance of youth and feeling invincible carrying into adulthood. Others approached death with relief, like it was a blessing for someone to put them out of their misery. Some met death with anger. Anger directed at death itself and not the person acting as death's agent. Whatever the reaction to death, their fate was all the same.

Oblivion.

Delilah stood by her brother and as they watched the man die, she caressed the back of Sebastian's neck. Sebastian put his arm round his sister's waist and pulled her in close. "How come you get all the fun?"

"We won't be here for much longer. You can go play with that landlord when we're finished."

"What makes you think we won't be much longer?"

"If Boatman is here, then his own spies will have told him about us."

Sebastian broke free of his sister and glanced out the window. "Then surely we're not safe?"

"Probably not," said Delilah. But that was part of the game, wasn't it? The chase, the hunt. That's why Faust called upon them. Wasn't it? Delilah adored her brother but was frustrated with his jitteriness whenever Boatman was mentioned. "No wonder Mother called you Scaredy Sue."

Sebastian sat on the bed, next to the now-dead man, and looked at the floor, his arms resting on his thighs. "You know Doctor V said no-one should use that name anymore."

Delilah walked over to her brother, and he looked up. She slapped him hard across the face. "Then stop acting like a Scaredy Sue."

Sebastian sniffled a bit and then calmed himself down. He knew not to give his sister an excuse to hit him again. He looked over at the body. "What are we going to do with him?"

"He doesn't matter. Leave him there. We're going to take a stroll."

Sebastian hesitated but didn't object and got up from the bed. He wanted to question whether walking around an area that was potentially Boatman's backyard might be asking for trouble. He wanted to point out to his sister that he knew a couple of guys who had crossed Boatman and now they were six feet under. He wanted to point out that agreeing to be part of Faust's B-Unit was a stupid idea and they would be much happier back in London pulling the fanboys of Boatman off the street, instead of potentially having their necks snapped by the actual Boatman. Of course, he didn't say any of this because he didn't want to be slapped again. Instead they did as Delilah asked and took a stroll.

9

Meresig had a thriving oyster industry and sold millions of oysters to the Empire every year. For two thousand years, the Empire had sought after oysters from this tiny speck of place on the coast of Britannia, and as much as many bemoaned Roman rule, the oyster industry would never have flourished if it wasn't for Emperor Domitian in the First Century having such a craving for the mollusc. Further along the waterfront, a five-minute walk from the Victorium, were half a dozen wood-clad huts. Each one was owned by a different family, all of whom farmed and processed oysters. The families all owned various areas of seabed where their oysters grew. Once brought ashore, the oysters were processed and packed into crates to be sent to London or to Rome. The Senate in Rome had such an addiction to Meresig oysters they were rumoured to eat hundreds in a day whilst debating legislature.

Sebastian and Delilah walked past the oyster sheds, which were all teeming with activity. The sounds and smells were almost overwhelming for the brother and sister from London: jet washers cleaning mud from shells, full nets being tipped, mud spraying, machines counting. They walked past three sheds that all had teams of people working until they came to the fourth, which had a lone man hand-sorting his catch. They made a beeline for him so they could question him.

"Excuse me," said Sebastian. "Could we ask you something?"

The man didn't turn around or stop sorting, "We don't offer tours this time of year. You'll have to come back in the summer."

"It's not about having a tour, we wanted to ask about someone who might live here."

The man stopped sorting and turned around. He was tanned and lanky and had a bushy, brown beard. He had a woollen hat on pulled far down and a hood over the hat for extra protection against the cold. "I'm only a seasonal worker so don't know many people here, if I can help it."

"We're looking for this man." Delilah held out her phone, which showed a photo of an artist's impression of Boatman. There were no photos of Boatman in the public domain. Hardly any Roman survived their encounters with him to get a shot. One of the few Romans who had engaged with Boatman and lived was Faust. Faust was famous for having an eerily accurate memory of details and provided the B-Unit with an artist's impression, but how accurate it was after nearly a year was debatable.

The worker looked at the drawing, looked up at the couple and squinted. "Piss off, you're having me on. Why are you showing me a picture of him? He obviously isn't local."

"Have you seen Boatman on Meresig?"

"Oh, definitely. I see Boatman all the time. I'm meeting him for a beer later, then going for a trip to London to kill some Romans." The man eyed them both and said, "Why are you asking anyway? Are you soldiers?"

"Not as such," said Delilah. "Thanks for your help." She went to

42

put her phone away and then thought twice and pulled up another image. "Tell me, have you seen this guy?" The man looked at the image and shook his head. "Okay, thanks anyway," said Delilah and the man went back to sorting his oysters.

Once Delilah and Sebastian were out of sight, the man tapped his ear and said, "It is Faust's B-Unit."

"Did they speak to you?"

"Speak to me? They asked me if I knew you. They even showed me a picture of myself from my gladiator days. I looked good back then."

"You're sure they didn't recognise you?"

"I was smooth-skinned and tanned back then. Now I'm pale, hairy and haggard. I don't even recognise me," said Tobias. Boatman sighed into Tobias's ear. "So, what do you want to do?"

"We should say hello," said Boatman.

"Really?"

"Really."

"Why?"

"Because in a place this small, what else are we going to do?"

10

Olivia had been clear she didn't want to see or talk to Boatman, so he had climbed back into his boat and cruised back to shore to confront Faust's B-Unit stooges. She sat at the kitchen table, drinking another coffee from a different mug, as her other mug was sitting on the seabed. For almost a year, she had felt a sense of peace. Until now. She didn't know exactly what it was, but from a young age she'd felt a tremor in the universe itself. For many years, she could only describe it as a buzzing, like bees in her brain. As she grew accustomed to the buzzing, she learned it was more like a vibration indicating when something was wrong. A deep empathy for not just people close to her, but for the world around her when bad things happened. But, more specifically, the tremors in her brain became most active when a particular type of badness was occurring or present.

She had tried to talk to Boatman about it, but never found the words to adequately describe what she experienced. She also didn't know if Boatman would understand, because however she described what she experienced it sounded like something religious, which he branded as superstitious and irrelevant. But now the tremors were back, and they were strong.

The first ones came earlier in the day, and from the frequency of the vibrations she knew a man had died. He had died badly. Now the buzzing in her brain was incessant with warnings about the two spies sent by Faust. The silence had been beautiful, and now it was over. She knew it meant there was no way they could stay in Meresig. Their lives were no longer hidden. She felt another type of sadness, different to the grief about her marriage. This was a sadness that she would always be bombarded by the pain of others.

Molly walked into the kitchen. She saw Olivia sitting at the kitchen table with her head bowed. "What's wrong?"

"Nothing, sweetie. Just thinking. Are you okay?"

"Yeah." She grabbed biscuit from the biscuit tin and said, "I didn't have any bad dreams last night."

"That's wonderful, Molly."

Molly had been saved by Maverick and Tobias when Emperor Nero attempted to assassinate her and her mother as a lesson to her father, who had defected to the rebellion effort. Now, though, she was an orphan, her father executed and her mother having killed herself. She was eleven but to Olivia seemed like someone thirty years older with a cynicism beyond her years. Olivia wasn't particularly surprised by Molly's emotional maturity considering all she had experienced, but it was tough to watch an eleven-year-old girl never truly know the innocence that being that age should bring.

Olivia had found Sam, Molly's mother, dead and Molly had been in the room next door when the suicide happened. It was horrific and even to this day, Olivia couldn't fathom how someone could be so engulfed by the darkness that they would kill themselves whilst their daughter was in the same apartment. Olivia and Boatman had taken Molly under their wings, and although Molly adored Olivia she exhibited near hostility toward Boatman. In a rare outburst, Molly had said that Boatman had killed her parents.

Boatman was inured to death, destruction and people's anger aimed at him, but hearing such venom from the mouth of a child rocked him. He left the house that day solemn, immediately after Molly's angry words, and didn't return home until it was dark and Molly had gone to bed. Olivia had tried to get her husband to open up about it but to no avail. Olivia was confused by Molly's accusation because Kevin, Molly's father, had been killed by Roman soldiers. But then, something had never sat right with Olivia about that. She had always felt Boatman hadn't been completely honest about the circumstances of his death.

Olivia had also picked up deep tremors from Molly. Tremors of anger and resentment, and they were aimed at Boatman. Being on the run from the Empire and having no choice, Molly fled London with Boatman, Olivia, Bella and Tobias. The thing was, it didn't mean she was grateful for it. She appeared to tolerate Boatman and had warmed to Olivia like a mother, but Olivia sensed a darkness that was growing. Even after almost a year of living with Boatman, that darkness had not diminished and Olivia worried what that would do to a child.

"I don't hate him."

Molly dragged Olivia away from her thoughts and raised her head, "Sorry, Sweetie?"

"You don't need to worry that I hate Boatman, I don't."

"That's a strong word to use, Molly. You're just a child, you shouldn't hate anyone."

"And I don't. That's what I'm saying. I don't hate Boatman for killing mum and dad." Molly was sitting at the kitchen table, turning the biscuit from the tin over in her hands.

Olivia reached out to Molly and rested her hand on Molly's arm. "Sweetie, Boatman didn't kill your mum and dad. He tried his best to save them."

Molly took a bite of her biscuit, mulling Olivia's words. "Maybe," she said, "but if Boatman had never met them, they would still be alive." She got down from the table and said she was going outside to sit on the jetty with her fishing rod.

Olivia realised that was what the darkness growing was; there was a coldness to Molly's resentment. Children speak with such clarity and honesty, and she was telling the truth that she didn't hate Boatman. She was becoming indifferent to him and that was possibly even worse.

11

Molly sat down at the end of the jetty and cast her fishing line. She looked over her shoulder and couldn't see any sign of Olivia, so pulled out her phone.

She had a notification that she had a message and opened it: *Are you there?* Molly typed back that she was. *Are you okay?* She typed that she was fine.

Are you being looked after okay still?

I'm fine

We can't wait to meet you!

I don't want to get into trouble

You won't.

But he might get mad

You will be happier with us.

I hope so

Molly heard Olivia coming out of the house and quickly put her phone away. She reeled in her fishing line and recast it. The creek that their house sat on was quite narrow and lots of tide ran through it each day. It caused quite a concentration of food sources for marine life and usually meant lots of mullet swam near the jetty. It rarely took Molly very long to hook something. Olivia turned her nose up at mullet, saying they tasted too muddy, but that was one thing Molly and Boatman saw eye to eye on. They enjoyed the dense flavour of mullet, especially served with some buttery, salty samphire grass.

"No joy yet?"

Molly shook her head at Olivia's question.

"If you manage to catch something other than mullet, that would be nice."

"I'll try," said Molly.

"A bass would be nice."

Molly looked over her shoulder at Olivia and smiled. Olivia smiled back and walked back into the house. Molly pulled her phone out again and read the reply: *We know so!* She put her phone back in her pocket and wondered if her text friend was right and life would be better away from Boatman and Olivia. She loved Olivia, but Boatman had made her mummy so sad she didn't want to live anymore. And she was sure Boatman had killed her daddy. She could go somewhere with other children and maybe not think about her mummy and daddy anymore.

12

Boatman and Tobias walked into The Victorium. Delilah and Sebastian were sitting at a table in the corner. The rebels sat down across from the Romans. Delilah looked at Boatman and then looked at Tobias. "Have you remembered something or is this the locals welcoming visitors?"

Tobias frowned, looked at Boatman and then looked back at Delilah. "For an elite unit, you're not very bright."

"I didn't say anything about being part of a unit."

"We worked it out."

Delilah arched an eyebrow. "What are you, part-time detectives when you're not washing oysters?"

Tobias carried on frowning, looking puzzled. Boatman verbalised what Tobias was thinking. "We're the reason you're here. Check your phone."

Delilah stared hard at Boatman whilst Sebastian pulled out his phone and checked the artist's impression of Boatman. It was amazing how some subtle changes to an appearance, like contact lenses and a hair cut, could make someone look completely different. The artist's impression of Boatman had a man with longer hair, dark brown eyes and a close-shaven beard. The man sitting at the table had short hair, blue eyes and a big, bushy beard. Delilah spoke up. "It is you."

Sebastian's eyes widened when he realised he was sitting opposite Boatman King. He went for his gun, holstered inside his jacket. He didn't manage to get his hand off the table.

One of the many stories that floated through barracks about Boatman was his superhuman reflexes and how it seemed impossible that he could move that quickly when fighting. Sebastian had spoken with a soldier who had watched Boatman fighting Faust and couldn't comprehend how the rebel moved so effortlessly. Sebastian thought the soldier was using hyperbole and that the mythos around Boatman exaggerated the abilities of a normal man. Sebastian now back-pedalled on his cynicism because as he had gone to lift his hand to reach into his jacket and retrieve his gun, he found his fingers bent back on his right hand without seeing even a blur of movement from Boatman. Tobias had also produced a gun and was pointing it at Delilah. Boatman looked almost bored at the minimal effort it took him to incapacitate Sebastian and said to Delilah, "Yes, it is me."

Delilah glanced at the gun and then back at Boatman. "I guess I need to ask what you want."

"It's simple, really, just leave Meresig and pretend you never saw us."

Tobias cleared his throat. "Without wanting to point out the damn obvious, but considering no-one recognised us, they would have left without having to pretend they never saw us."

Delilah laughed, "I don't understand how idiots like you caused the Empire so much hassle. Our intel about Meresig was strong. We would have eventually flushed you out. Dodgy beards wouldn't have lasted very long as disguises. We always flush people out."

"They fooled you," said Tobias.

Boatman ignored Tobias's comment. "What intel?" Boatman bent Sebastian's fingers back further. "What intel?" Sebastian whimpered.

Delilah sighed. "You know, most people aren't as strong as they think they are. Most people break just with a hint of a threat. No, actually, most people break because their ego can't help but blurt any information that is deemed a secret." She took a swig of her wine. "Even if it's their own children."

"What? What do you mean by that?"

Delilah's phone was on the table, and she picked it up and scrolled to a photo. She turned the screen to face Boatman. Boatman faltered when he saw the image and released his grip on Sebastian. "How did you find her?"

"Like I said, we always flush people out."

Sebastian was rubbing his hand, but the relief was short-lived. Before he knew what was happening his fingers were being bent back again. "*How* did you find her?"

Delilah had put her phone on the table, the photo still on the screen. "I think a better question is: what will your wife have to say?"

"Tobias, shoot her," said Boatman.

Tobias glanced at the phone and then at Boatman. "What?"

"Shoot her."

"Some context would be really, bloody helpful right now."

"Forget the fucking context. I said shoot her."

"Boatman, I'm not shooting her in here. Especially as I have no idea what the hell is going on. Who's that?" Tobias pointed at the photo.

"That there is someone who will die if you shoot me, Tobias," Sebastian said.

Boatman lost his cool, punched Sebastian hard in the face, making the Roman crumple, snatched the gun from Tobias, stood up and pressed it against Delilah's head. It all happened with such speed it took Tobias a moment to realise he was no longer holding the weapon. "You're bluffing, she won't die."

Delilah tried not to flinch at the gun. "But what would your wife say if she knew you would casually discard her mother like that?"

Boatman hesitated. "What do you want?"

"I'm not telling you anything whilst there's a gun in my face."

Boatman took a moment. His anger was clouding his judgement. The audacity of this woman, here in his home settlement, dictating a situation. It made him want to pull the trigger. He lowered the gun. "I'll ask again, what do you want?"

"It's not really what I want. I'm just the messenger."

Boatman raised his gun again. "So it won't matter if I shoot the messenger."

Delilah spoke up quickly. "It's what Faust wants."

"And what does he want?"

"You." Delilah looked Boatman square in the eyes. "What else would he want? He specifically said he wants you and doesn't care about anyone else."

"Bullshit," said Boatman. Nevertheless, he still lowered the gun again.

"C'mon, don't be naïve. Faust doesn't bullshit. He wants you."

"I could kill you and still walk into London, surrendering."

"You could. But your wife's mother dies if I, sorry, *we* don't return to London. With you."

"When?"

Delilah picked up her phone and looked at the screen. "No time like the present."

"Seriously?" Tobias laughed. "Boatman, you should give me the gun back and I will shoot her. You can't just leave with them. How the hell do you even know that's definitely Olivia's mum, or that she's even alive if it is?"

"Trust me, she's alive," said Delilah.

"Oh, that's fine then. The psycho Roman has just said we should trust her." Delilah pulled another photo up showing Olivia's mother holding a newspaper dated the day previously. "Well that shuts me up," said Tobias.

Boatman sat back down. He felt impotent. He had a choice and it seemed like history was repeating itself. It felt like time was circular for him and situations were happening again and again, just with subtle differences. This moment, this situation, felt like he was back in London watching Molly's father Kevin die and then having to lie to Molly about the circumstances. Boatman felt this way because he had decided Kevin had to die to protect a greater purpose.

He now faced the thought of killing Olivia's mother to save the greater purpose of getting to Faust. Seeing these people hunting him down, it had energised him. It had invigorated him to become the hunter again and finish what he had started. Unfortunately, that's also why he felt impotent. If he killed these stooges from the B-Unit he would be killing Olivia's mother. If he sacrificed himself, he would be saving a life but crucifying himself and never getting to fulfil his goal. His mother had been killed by the Empire and he had almost got his revenge before Faust outmanoeuvred him. And here he was again, outmanoeuvred again. He also faced the awful realisation that his wife was drifting farther and further away and if she ever discovered that he had sentenced her mother to death for his own cause, she would be lost to him forever.

"There needs to be live-streamed proof Olivia's mother is safe before I go with you. A photo can be easily doctored."

Delilah was about to say no but then changed her mind. "That's fine. I'll make a call."

"And I need to say goodbye to my wife."

This time Delilah laughed. "You think this is some cliché soap opera where you can have an emotional goodbye to your family before the villains take you away?" Delilah looked at the time. "You have an hour to meet me at the foot ferry." Delilah got up to leave and Tobias piped up. "Aren't you forgetting something?" Delilah shook her head, so Tobias continued. "What about him?" Tobias jerked his thumb at the unconscious figure of Sebastian. Delilah was walking away from the table and said, "If my idiot brother wakes up in time, then he can meet me at the ferry too. If he doesn't, well, he'll have to deal with the locals."

"You said if both of you don't make it back to London, then Olivia's mum dies."

"And you believe everything someone tells you?" Delilah scoffed and left the pub.

13

Tobias grabbed the glass of unfinished wine Delilah had been drinking, knelt in front of Sebastian, who was sat unconscious on the floor, and then threw the wine over him. Sebastian jerked awake. He tried to get up, but Tobias clamped his hand on the Roman's shoulder and forced him to the floor again. "Not so fast."

"Get your fucking hand off me. Do you know who you're dealing with?"

"Well," said Tobias and looked at his watch, "according to my watch, I'm dealing with a dead man in about fifty minutes."

Sebastian was confused, very confused. One minute he had been trying not to cry because of the pain Boatman was inflicting on him, the next minute he was soaked in wine and wondering where his sister was. Tobias was squeezing his shoulder causing a sharp pain to fizz through his body. He tried to move again but Tobias was strong. Very strong. He decided the pain wasn't worth it. He tried to scan the pub, looking for his sister but couldn't see her. In fact, those who were in the pub tried their very best to pretend there wasn't a man being held against his will in the corner of the room. He knew it, he had always known it; his sister didn't give a shit about him. He was discarded as soon as he was deemed unnecessary, which was how she had always been. He remembered when they were barely teenagers and Delilah had convinced him to sneak out of their house one night for an adventure. The adventure had been to see if they could hop over the fences of as many gardens as possible without getting caught by any homeowners. Seb hated garden hopping as he wasn't particularly athletic as a child and struggled to get over fences without making a racket. Delilah always mocked him if he showed any trepidation, so he never felt like he had a choice.

This particular evening went as well as he had expected and three gardens in, he tripped over and fell into a pond. It wasn't Delilah who pulled him out but the angry owner of the property. The owner didn't even wait to question Sebastian on what he was doing, almost drowning, but beat the hell out of him and then dumped him on the street. Delilah had watched Sebastian being dragged into the street and instead of helping her brother had rushed home, climbed into bed and acted as surprised as everyone else when soldiers brought her brother home. Sebastian had never uttered a word about his sister's involvement because if he had, then the beating he had received from the homeowner would have been nothing compared to the torture his depraved sister would have bestowed upon him.

So Sebastian was sitting awkwardly on the floor of the pub comprehending that his sister was content with discarding him like a toy she had grown bored with. "Where's my sister?"

"On her way home," said Tobias. Sebastian's eyes widened. "You should shit yourself. Your sister offered you up like a sacrificial lamb to the locals." Sebastian glanced around the room again and the locals still appeared to be disinterested in him.

"How?"

"How?"

"Yes, how has my sister offered me up?"

"Because," said Tobias, "she said that if you don't wake up soon then we can feed you to the locals."

Sebastian frowned. "But I am awake."

Tobias smiled. "She doesn't know that."

Boatman looked at his watch and said, "Stop fucking around, Tobias, I need to go."

Tobias squeezed Sebastian's shoulder and told him not to move a muscle. He stood up and sat next to Boatman, who was nursing a glass of beer. "We have a bargaining chip. A skinny, scared bargaining chip."

Boatman picked up the glass of beer like he was considering drinking it and then placed the glass on the table again, rubbed his eyes and then pinched the bridge of his nose. "Look at him, he's not much of anything, let alone a bargaining chip."

"C'mon, he was chosen to come here to find the infamous Boatman."

"Chosen or dragged?" Boatman decided to have a swig of his beer. It was warm and he grimaced. "Look, there's no way he means enough to Faust to be of any use to us."

"We should dump him in the sea then," said Tobias.

"Why?"

"One less Roman to worry about."

"They like dumping bodies with no care. Let's not copy them."

"I seem to remember us leaving a lot of dead bodies back in London," said Tobias.

"Bodies of Romans who fought back. Not bodies of trembling prisoners."

Tobias shrugged. "They're all the same to me."

Boatman stood up. "I need to go." He looked at Sebastian. "Get up, we're going to see your sister. Tobias, please go and see Olivia and tell her what's going on. I'll phone her too, to explain, but you need to tell her that I've gone back to London."

Tobias didn't attempt to hide his frustration. "We have a Roman prisoner, we can do an exchange! I don't get why you're acting the martyr."

Boatman grabbed Sebastian, pulled him to his feet and then said to Tobias, "No wonder Maverick decided to leave. Just shut up and go and tell Olivia what's going on."

"What about Olivia's mum?"

"What about her?"

"What do I say?"

"Don't say anything until I have proof of life," said Boatman. "It would devastate her to have hope about her mum and then find out the worst." He and Sebastian then exited the pub, leaving Tobias wondering what the hell was going on.

14

"He's what?" Olivia thought her anger toward her husband was at its limit in regard to his abandonment of her in London, but now he was abandoning her again.

"He's going to phone you soon, to explain, Olivia, but he feels he has no choice."

"Ah, yes, Boatman's classic fallback, having no choice so he can be the martyr."

Tobias was about to say *ditto* but thought it inappropriate. Instead he repeated that Boatman was going to call her to explain.

Olivia eyed Tobias, who was doing his best to avoid eye contact. "What are you not telling me?"

"Nothing," said Tobias. "Look, you need to get your stuff together and we need to get away from here. The Empire might still come for us even though they have Boatman."

"Fuck you, Tobias. Always covering for him." Tobias had no response to that and said he would be back as soon as possible.

After Tobias left, Olivia went and found Molly to tell her that they were going to have to leave. "Where are we going?"

"I'm not sure, sweetheart, but it's not safe for us here anymore."

"Where's Boatman?"

"I'm not sure about that either."

"So it might be safer for us if he's not with us, then." It wasn't a question and Olivia was starting to feel Molly had a point about how toxic her husband was to be around.

Molly and Olivia packed up as much as necessary and then Tobias picked them up and ferried them to shore. "The foot ferry leaves in about thirty minutes, and I have a taxi waiting for us."

"Where are we going?"

"Where we should have gone from the very start."

Once they were safely in the taxi Tobias said, "I'm going to get some shut eye. We won't be there for a while. I'd suggest you do the same."

The taxi was an old chariot, no longer needed for military purposes and converted to be a comfortable ride for six passengers. Tobias was stretched out at the front, behind the driver, Olivia was in the row behind and Molly was curled up in the corner at the back. Olivia craned her neck to look at Molly and said, "Try to have a nap, Molly." Molly just nodded her head and stretched out on the long seat. Olivia turned back round and said to Tobias, "I thought I was getting a call?"

Tobias had his arm over his face, trying to nod off. "He'll call. He said he would. C'mon, Liv, he's trying to draw Faust's stooges away from you. He's their prisoner now; he'll call when they let him."

"Tobias?"

"Yeah?"

"Don't call me Liv."

Molly had pulled her phone out and was texting again:

We r leaving Meresig

Where are you going?

I don't know

Find out. I can meet you there

K

Molly asked Olivia where they were going, and Olivia realised she hadn't got to the bottom of that. She went to ask Tobias but he was snoring. Olivia asked the driver where they were going but he shrugged and said the drop off was somewhere remote and he had never been there before. "Sorry, sweetheart, we'll have to wait and see," said Olivia and swore under her breath at her husband for putting them in this position.

Molly sent a message letting her anonymous friend know she would tell them her location as soon as she found out.

15

Boatman sat in the chariot sent to collect him, Delilah and Sebastian. They were only just over an hour from London, so Boatman didn't have long to work out how to turn this situation around. Before he agreed to get in the chariot, he reiterated the need to see proof of life of Olivia's mother. Delilah had looked at the soldier driving for potential backup if Boatman caused trouble, but his face indicated he would rather have been crucified than try to stop Boatman doing anything. Sebastian also looked like he would have preferred to remain unconscious than spend another minute with Boatman, so she realised she had little choice but to honour Boatman's request and show proof of life.

Boatman's infamy continued to intimidate soldiers throughout London, even after a year of him being underground. Scores of soldiers had died through Boatman's actions. He had been a myth, a bogeyman whispered through garrisons. In fact, the number of soldiers who had died from personally meeting Boatman was minimal. The *thought* of Boatman was enough to trigger fear. Boatman was dangerous, and Grand Protector Faust had experienced that firsthand and survived, barely. Delilah had only glimpsed Boatman's potential lethality with the speed at which he disarmed Tobias and immobilised Sebastian, but in that moment she understood why Faust was desperate to find this man and bring him back to London. She also understood why the soldier driving them back looked so pale. Delilah herself, though, wasn't as scared. Men always had a weakness, and she was always very good at finding it.

Either Delilah and Sebastian didn't care, or they assumed Boatman wouldn't have been so prepared, but neither of them showed any signs of knowing Boatman still had his earpiece in. He had heard from Tobias that Olivia and Molly were out of Meresig and on their way to a new location, and he was currently listening to Bella telling him some very bad news.

"I know you can't respond to what I'm saying, but it's bad, Boatman. I'm not sure your sacrifice really means anything judging by what I'm looking at right now."

Boatman touched his ear to activate the two-way signal and turned to face Delilah, "What would I be looking at?"

Delilah tilted her head in a question. Bella spoke in Boatman's ear. "He's been suffocated. Judging by the marks on his wrists he died in a panic."

"Can you expand on what you mean?" Delilah squinted, dubious about Boatman's question.

"Will I be recognised afterwards or just be a dead stranger?"

"It's no stranger. I'm sorry," said Bella.

"Oh, Boatman, I never realised you were so vain. Your death will be celebrated throughout the Empire. You will not be a faceless stranger on a cross," said Delilah.

"I'm guessing my family will be involved in this."

"Sorry, yes. It's Olivia's father," said Bella.

"That's up to Faust," said Delilah. "And how satisfied your death will make him."

"Fuck," said Boatman and he slumped forward, head in hands.

"Sorry," said Bella, "Where do you want me?"

"I don't know," said Boatman.

"What was that?" said Delilah.

"I'm thinking out loud," said Boatman.

Bella signed off as she knew Boatman needed time and it would get dangerous communicating with him. She looked at the dead body of Olivia's father, tied to the bed in the room Delilah and Sebastian had rented at The Victorium. She wanted to weep at the carnage and pain that had been wreaked on Olivia, all to get at Boatman. Boatman's family history was so vague the Empire had nothing they could use to get to him directly. The Empire, though, they weren't worried about being direct when they could be indirect and cause even more pain and division. And division was going to rip though Boatman's life as Olivia was faced with yet another reason why knowing him caused such destruction.

Bella loved Boatman and was loyal to the cause to find a way to cripple the Empire, but she understood why Olivia was struggling so much about the worthiness of the rebellion. And when Olivia discovered her father had died to flush out Boatman, Bella doubted Olivia would be able to look her husband in the eye ever again.

16

"We're here," said the taxi driver.

Tobias stretched and said, "Already?" He yawned and then said, "Have you seen anyone?"

"Nope, not a soul in sight."

Tobias sat up and looked out of the chariot's window, scanning the woodland, just to make sure he trusted the taxi driver. Satisfied, he woke up Olivia and Molly. "We're getting out here, stay close to me."

"When you say *we're here,* where exactly is *here?*

"We're close to the Caledonia Kingdom border."

"Sorry?"

"I don't think I need to repeat it."

"Tobias, they'll kill us," said Olivia.

"Maybe, maybe not."

"Maybe? Tobias, we're poison."

"You don't know that."

"Don't I? How long were we travelling?"

"About eight hours."

"So basically a lifetime," said Olivia. "Our images are probably plastered all over Empire streams."

"I was told that Boatman going with them would mean we would be left alone."

"By the gods, Tobias, you actually believed that?"

Tobias blushed. He was naïve and had always been naïve.

When he had been a gladiator, he believed that if he fought well enough and survived enough bouts the Empire would eventually have pity and reward him with freedom for his service. And then after what seemed like an endless number of blood-thirsty fights, a senator came to him. The senator congratulated Tobias on his exemplary performance, saying the Emperor himself was always so wonderfully entertained by Tobias's showmanship. Here it comes, thought Tobias, the golden ticket to freedom. A pass, at last, from the sweat, blood, shit and sobbing as yet another gladiator had their insides splattered on the arena floor for millions to see as it was streamed throughout the world.

That golden ticket didn't come. Instead, after the senator congratulated Tobias and praised him for his fighting abilities, the senator told Tobias that he was going to be involved in the fight of the century. Tobias had asked the senator to repeat what he said, and the senator had indeed repeated that Tobias would be involved in the bout of the century. Now, Tobias didn't know much, since he had been a gladiator since he was a teenager, but one thing he did know: a fight of the century would need to involve Maverick 'The Beast' Kirabo. And if it involved Maverick Kirabo, then Tobias knew for a fact that he wasn't being greeted by a senator to be rewarded. He was being greeted by this senator to be given a death sentence.

Maverick Kirabo was the most feared gladiator throughout the Empire, and for good reason. Tobias was famous for his endurance and gritty wins. Maverick was famous for obliterating every single person who came into contact with him. Tobias might have sweated and grimaced through his bouts, but Maverick was known for barely breaking a sweat before killing his opponents. Tobias, like every other gladiator, was terrified of the thought of facing Maverick. Like many hoped they never bumped into Death and found their time was up, gladiators prayed to the God-Carpenter, Zeus or Jupiter (or all three at the same time) that they would never have to face Maverick. Unfortunately, the world of gladiators was relatively small and eventually the odds stacked against you. It seemed, for Tobias, the odds had finally turned against him and although he was confident in his skills as a killer, he knew that would probably extend his life by about thirty seconds between having a sword and not having a sword.

There had been one other problem for Tobias. He was madly in love with Maverick. He adored him. He had not only watched Maverick fight, he had watched Maverick in the times they had been cooling off and wiping the blood off their chests. To fight Maverick was an honour, but to love Maverick and never have the chance to tell him, well, that was far more torturous. He wondered if it would be possible to somehow get Maverick to show him mercy if he knew how much Tobias loved him.

Or at least have a swift death as a gesture of kindness to a love-sick puppy.

It appeared Tobias was at least going to have the chance to plead for a swift death. He would be sharing a suite with Maverick for a couple of days before their contest. The Empire wanted to film the two fighters, documenting their time together like a voyeuristic wet dream, before the gladiators spilled blood for millions to see.

Tobias guessed he had pissed one of the gods off in this life or another because his final hours were going to be filmed chatting about the weather with the guy who would be decapitating him. As it turned out, Tobias had managed to be in the right place at the right time, and his time in the suite coincided with Maverick's plan to finally escape the Empire and no longer be entertainment for bloodthirsty masses. Reluctantly, Maverick allowed Tobias to tag along. "Once we're out of here, we go our separate ways," said Maverick.

Tobias blushed, disappointed.

Maverick frowned. "Have I said something wrong?"

"I just thought maybe we could get to know each other."

"Get to know each other? You know we're going to be on the run from the Empire, not having a vacation, right, whatever your name is?"

Tobias went a deeper shade of red, disappointed Maverick didn't know his name. "It's Tobias."

"Okay, well, Tobias, I'm not really one for doing some sort of best buddy adventure. I'll help you get out of here and then you're on your own."

As it transpired, they never did go their separate ways, and love had blossomed between them. It didn't stop Maverick from regularly rolling his eyes at things Tobias said, but the men formed a love that saved them both.

Now, though, now he wasn't with Maverick and didn't know where his partner was. He was trying to keep Olivia and Molly safe, but here they were, in the middle of nowhere and he didn't know how safe he could keep himself, let alone anyone with him. He had to trust his abilities and the plan Boatman had put together in case something like this happened.

"Olivia, I need you to trust me. We can get there. We have supporters who sympathise with us and what we have done."

"I'll believe it when I see it." Olivia took Molly's hand and said, "We'll be safe soon, sweetheart."

Tobias opened a navigation app on his phone and said, "The safe house is just over the border, about an hour's walk."

So they started walking.

17

After nearly an hour and a half, they reached the safe house. They had travelled along country lanes and fields to avoid too much contact with anyone. The house was made of stone, a door in the very centre and a chimney on each end of the house. The front door was set off by a veranda. Tobias wondered why architects decided to design houses to look haunted and whether cliché was part of the curriculum. He knocked on the door, turned to tell Olivia and Molly to stay back until he had spoken with his contact, turned back and found a shotgun in his face. He knew he should have expected it, because the house was a cliché but he didn't *actually* think the whole shotgun through a gap in the door thing was done by people.

Tobias raised his hands and stepped back, the gun followed him and attached to the gun was a woman, tall, with long jet-black hair, very angry. "Who are you?"

Tobias kept his hands up. "Tobias. Boatman should have told you we were coming."

"I haven't heard anything from Boatman." She stepped forward and pressed the gun to Tobias's chest.

Tobias swallowed hard. "Even if you haven't heard from him, you know him?"

"So?"

"So, he must have told you to be prepared for random people turning up."

"He did." She didn't ease the pressure of the gun.

"So, maybe you want to stop being the angry loner with a gun?"

"Maybe you want to think about who's holding the gun," said the woman.

"Maybe," said Tobias and then grabbed the gun and pulled it toward him, knocking the woman off balance and loosing her grip on it. In a moment, Tobias was holding the gun and pointing it at the angry woman. "Then again, maybe you want to think about who's holding the gun." Tobias looked over his shoulder and said to Molly and Olivia that everything was okay and looked back to find another gun in his face. Arrogant error on his behalf.

"Drop the shotgun or I will make your face disappear," said the woman. Tobias obliged. "I don't give a shit about Boatman and his preordained plans."

Tobias was missing Maverick; his presence tended to make people much more willing to talk because they were usually scared of him as soon as they saw him. "Look, we won't trouble you for long, we just need one night here and then we'll be gone. Boatman said he sent money to cover an intrusion like this."

"That was before Boatman killed the fucking Emperor. If I get caught helping you, crucifixion will seem like a holiday." Olivia stepped forward and the woman warned her not to come any closer. Olivia listened, but still spoke. "Please... sorry, what's your name?"

"Kiera." She didn't take her eyes off Tobias.

"Kiera, please. We're begging you."

Kiera looked at Olivia. "Are you Olivia?"

Olivia nodded.

"Sorry about what happened to you."

"Thanks. If it wasn't for Tobias," she nodded her head in his direction, "I wouldn't be here at all. We're just trying to get to safety, Kiera. We mean no trouble and won't cause you any trouble."

Kiera thought for a moment and then let the gun drop to her side. She motioned them to come inside the house and said one night was all she could do. It was too dangerous otherwise. Tobias was about to be the last through the door when a gunshot stopped him in his tracks. He turned around, the shotgun he had swiped from Kiera no longer by his side but tense in his hands. What the gun was aimed at was a group of ten men, all aiming guns right back. "Fuck," muttered Tobias.

"So much for causing me no trouble," said Kiera and stood alongside Tobias, her gun also raised.

"Stay inside the house," Olivia told Molly and stepped out on to the veranda, also holding a shotgun.

"Where'd you get that from?"

"We're at the house of an angry loner, Tobias, there's guns everywhere."

"I'm standing right here," said Kiera. She dismissed the jibe though and called out to the armed men, "What do you want?"

The men had made a semicircle and the one in the centre stepped forward, "Just the girl. We just want the girl."

Kiera glanced at Tobias and Olivia, confused, and they too had similar looks of confusion on their faces. "The girl?"

"That's right. Give us Molly and we leave peacefully."

"You must be confusing this house with that other stone house ten miles up the road," said Tobias. "There's no Molly here. It might be worth doing a bit of door to door. All the houses round here look the same."

The man in the centre laughed. "You're a funny guy. Funny doesn't change anything, give us the girl."

"Why the hell would they want Molly?" Tobias said and stepped down the steps from the veranda. "What do you want with Molly?"

"None of your business," said one of the men in the group and fired his gun. The shot hit Tobias square in the chest, and he went down.

The man in the centre, without hesitation, turned his gun on the man who had fired and shot him in the head. He turned his back on Olivia and Kiera and said to the group, "No-one fires, you hear? No-one! The girl comes with us, alive." He turned back to Olivia and Kiera and said, "I'm sorry about your friend, but I promise, if you give us Molly then you both will walk away unharmed."

"No fucking chance," said Olivia, "Leave now and tell Faust he can go fuck himself."

The man in the centre laughed again, "Faust? Seriously? You think Faust sent us?" The man brushed an imaginary speck from his shoulder, "I'd like more credit than that. Faust is pathetic."

"Then who are you working for?"

The man ignored the question and fired his gun multiple times. Kiera was hit and went down. Olivia was hit too, crumpling to the floor. The man walked up the steps of the veranda, over the bodies of the two women and into the house.

Olivia heard a muffled scream and then the world went silent.

18

Kiera woke with what felt like the worst hangover she had ever experienced. It took her a moment to get her bearings and then she realised she wasn't on the veranda, where she last remembered being, but on the floor of her lounge. She got to her feet and her head pounded so much she had to sit down and wait until at least she didn't want to open her skull and rip her brain out. When she felt close to human, she shuffled into the kitchen and there she found Olivia with her head in her hands.

"Are you okay?"

Olivia didn't raise her head. "No, not really."

"What happened? Everything's a blur."

"You were hit by some powerful tranquilliser darts," said a voice from behind. Kiera turned to see Tobias standing at the kitchen doorway.

"I saw you getting shot."

"I was caught off guard a little while back." Tobias tapped his chest and then lifted his shirt to reveal a protective vest. "Not happening again."

Olivia stood up. "What about Molly?" Her head pounded and

she tried not to vomit. "Where's Molly?"

Tobias shook his head. "She's gone."

Olivia slumped back in her chair. "Why did they want her?" No-one had the answer to that question. "Why would the Romans want her?" She started to cry. "That poor girl has been through hell and now she has to go through more." Tobias went over to Olivia and held her.

"Who says it was the Romans?" Kiera managed to sip some water and keep it down.

"Because who else could it be?"

"It's not the Romans' style," said Tobias.

"What's not?" Kiera asked.

"Leaving people alive," said Tobias, "It's not really their style."

"Faust let you live," said Olivia, "Maybe he was sending a message with taking Molly."

"It just doesn't make sense to me that they would come all this way to take Molly and leave us alone and alive."

"Since when did the Romans make sense?"

"I don't know, it just seems really off."

"Everything's off, Tobias. All the time. When it involves us, it's always off."

Tobias huffed in agreement. Kiera took another sip of water, hoping not to bring it back up and said, "It feels like you're both avoiding the obvious." Kiera took their blank faces as permission to continue, "Who knew you were bringing Molly here?"

"No-one," said Tobias.

"No-one?"

"Absolutely. We kept it as close to our chests as possible."

"Our chests?"

"Sorry, Kiera, I'm clearly being a dumb twat right now and

not getting your point, even if it is, in your eyes, as subtle as a sledgehammer. Why don't you just explain it to me like a four-year-old, because I'm feeling your pain."

"You keep saying no-one knew you were coming here, but then you're saying *we* at the same time. All I want to know is, who knew you were coming here, apart from the people in this room?"

"Well, apart from us, there was Boatman and Bella. But that's it."

"But that's not it," said Kiera, "The only way anyone found you here was someone saying something, so if it wasn't either of you then it had to be Bella or Boatman."

Olivia laughed, "As much as I currently find it hard to say a good word about my husband, it makes no sense that he, or Bella for that matter, would want to reveal to the Romans where we are. What's the point of arranging this safe house in the first place?"

"Why does it have to be that he wanted to? He's a Roman prisoner now. He could have told them under duress."

"Trust me, Boatman would give nothing up." Olivia looked Kiera square in the eye, "He would make them think he was enjoying the pain."

"So that leaves Bella," said Kiera.

Tobias shook his head. "No way." Kiera tilted her head in doubt. Tobias looked at Kiera and then looked at Olivia. "No fucking way was it Bella."

Tobias was protective of Bella and found it insulting her name was even mentioned when discussing a potential betrayal. He had seen the love she had for another woman and the pain of betrayal from that same woman, and she had still remained loyal. Bella had entered into an affair with Alypia, the wife of Faust, and Alypia had discarded her when she discovered her underground identity. Bella had the chance to use the affair as ammunition but never did.

Even in betrayal she exhibited loyalty, so Tobias knew there was no chance she would have betrayed them to the Romans. It served no purpose to Bella and Bella wanted the same as them all: to drive the Empire from Britannia's shores.

"Well then, who was it?"

The question hung in the air, and it wasn't easily answered. One thing they did know was that they had to get away from the safe house as fast as possible. If someone had come for them already, then it was likely more would follow.

"We need to get to our rendezvous point," said Tobias. He looked at Kiera, "And it seems like we now have a spare space."

"Considering how awful it's been knowing you both for this short time, I'm not convinced I want to spend any more time with you."

"It's not safe at all for you, Kiera, you need to come with us," said Olivia. "This place is compromised." Olivia noticed Kiera's face drop and corrected herself. "Your home is compromised and I'm sorry we did that to you. Honestly, I'm truly sorry."

Kiera didn't respond for a minute, but took another sip of water, trying to fight back the nausea of the tranquilliser dart. She sipped again, slowly swallowed and said, "I see it in one way, really. You coming here, in the amateurish manner that you have, means I'm more than likely dead if I stay in this house and I'm more than likely dead if I leave this house." Tobias went to defend himself and explain how safe Kiera would be with him, but Kiera raised her hand, her face reddening in annoyance, so Tobias kept his mouth shut and Kiera continued, "God knows how you were involved in the killing of an Emperor, but I don't have any faith in taking a journey with you. You had a vulnerable little girl with you, and she's been abducted. All I can say is that I will feel much safer here, on my own, than going anywhere with you two. So, please, get the fuck off my property."

19

Boatman found himself in a much more comfortable room than he anticipated when he arrived in London. Delilah and Sebastian had escorted him into the HoC, the Roman HQ in London, and barely a word was spoken other than Sebastian promising to Boatman that he wouldn't get caught off guard next time and that Boatman better watch out. Boatman had nodded in agreement with Sebastian's sentiments before punching Sebastian square in the face and knocking him out cold.

Boatman looked around his room and noticed the Empire had barely updated the decor. It was still a homage to Britannia's former days of glory. A photo of Winston Churchill in the early 1960s, with his infamous outstretched arm and open-palm hand salute as a marker of victory. Churchill was always vague about his famous hand gesture and its origins, but many believed it was a deliberate attempt to enrage the Roman Empire, and particularly the Emperor. Some works of art depicted Romans saluting in a similar fashion, but the Empire never endorsed or recorded such a type of salute and even banned its use. One reason for banning its use was its association with cultural cleansing. As brutal as the

Roman Empire was, it prided itself on diverse cultures to keep it in power. The thought of certain cultures or races being wiped out because of a misguided belief of superiority was unacceptable. Churchill's gesture, therefore, seemed to be on the surface a blatant defiance of Rome like a mockery. To some, there was a darker underbelly to Churchill's salute, and that was maybe he also actually believed some races and cultures to be inferior.

Boatman had never particularly given much thought what Churchill had believed. He was yet another politician who said one thing but did the opposite behind doors they expected no-one to open. Boatman was a product of Roman disregard for life, his mother ultimately not surviving being raped by a Centurion. Although Boatman had a stable life growing up in Meresig, with guardians who took care of all his needs, he wasn't nostalgic about his childhood or the Britannia that once was, which they would sometimes talk about. Nostalgia was like a drug to inject into your eyes for that rose tint and into your brain for that fuzzy feeling that so many people were yearning for but was, in Boatman's eyes, just a form of mass delusion.

He got it, though. Nostalgia was a powerful propaganda tool. It kept people in line and manipulated public opinion. If you kept convincing people that the past was amazing and the reason for their current woes was the collapse of modern society, well, the population would lap it up. Boatman had seen it happen with his own efforts to expose and overthrow the Empire. He thought by killing Nero in Britannia, it would cause an uprising and rejection of Roman occupation. In fact, it did the opposite. Nero's death meant the Romans dragged hundreds of people out of their homes and crucified them for even the most tenuous link to the rebellion. The Crucifixion Channel was streaming flagellations and crucifixions all day and night. What that caused was a rejection of Boatman's efforts and the good they were trying to bring. People connected Boatman executing the Emperor to their loved ones being executed. Boatman had thought that when they had fled the city they would be returning to London within days, weeks at the most, once news of Nero's death circulated and the public realised the Caesar was mortal. He assumed people would form an insurrection, knowing they didn't have to bend to the whims of a man who was just like them.

That just didn't happen, though. It turned out people were angry their subservient way of life had been ruptured. People were angry because Boatman's rebellion had been a thorn in the Empire's side but there had been a fragile yet intact harmony between Roman occupation and the population of London. Even though rebels were crucified on London Bridge as a deterrent, polls always suggested Boatman's efforts were well supported. When Nero died, though, Faust was brutal in his revenge against the rebellion and indiscriminate in his killings. Boatman's polling figures tumbled, and Faust used this as the opportunity to bombard the public with propaganda about how life was good before Boatman killed the Emperor. It didn't take long for people to deliberately ignore the daily crucifixions and torture and believe Boatman was the cause of their ills.

Boatman felt like his mission had not only failed but gone backwards by years. And now he was in the HoC staring at nostalgic imagery, harking back to days that never were. He was staring at a photo of a meeting between a contender for the position of Prime Minister of Britannia and Emperor Augustus II in the early 1960s. Boatman had to look at the caption to remember his name: Alexander Johnson. Apparently Johnson had travelled to Rome to promise the world to Augustus in return for peace. Johnson believed he would win the next election and showed his confidence by risking a meeting with Rome. The photo on the wall showed a laughing Johnson and a smirking Augustus.

The photo displayed wasn't a true reflection of the events that played out. Johnson had promised a lot to Augustus if he should win and borrowed a lot of money to fulfil his promises. Johnson didn't win; Churchill trounced him in the election. Johnson had bet a lot of borrowed money on himself winning and therefore lost a lot of money. It was rumoured the people he had borrowed money from didn't take kindly to Johnson's catastrophic failure and wanted their money back immediately. Johnson was said to have asked for time to retrieve it and went looking to borrow more money to pay his debtors. What happened after that was conjecture, but Johnson's body was found bloated and floating in the Thames a few days after the election. It looked like he hadn't been able to pay his debts. The official story released by Government, though, was an accidental death, and a homage to Johnson's life was played out through the usual propaganda mechanisms.

Boatman found the photo vulgar, but no surprise considering how desperate governments were to manage their image. The door to his ostentatious prison cell was unlocked and in walked a man who had, in Boatman's mind, been in the military for a long time. He had a shaven head, a thick neck and shoulders as broad as Boatman's. "The Grand Protector would like to meet you for dinner this evening."

"The Grand Protector? So Faust is still up his own arse, then." Boatman looked the man up and down. "Have we met?"

The man bristled to the question, which Boatman found weird. "No. But if we had, then you wouldn't be standing here."

Boatman guessed he must have been spending too much time

with Tobias because he was about to say to the angry man that he wasn't in the mood for a dick-measuring contest. Instead he said, "Well, I am standing here."

The man stepped into the room, red-faced, his neck almost pulsating because of the stress causing his veins to throb. "You killed my brother, Aloysius. I promised Faust I could keep my cool seeing you, but I lied."

"I would rethink that lie if I were you."

"I'm not scared of you. I'm looking forward to shitting on that myth about fearing you."

Boatman put some distance between himself and Aloysius's brother. "Being scared of me isn't the thing you need to be focusing on. I can imagine that you've been told that if I get hurt, then you'll be facing severe consequences."

"I don't care."

"Really? Because, knowing Faust, it won't just be you that the threat of harm is against if you do anything to me." Aloysius's brother hesitated. Boatman guessed someone he loved was flashing through his mind. Faust really did have something big planned if soldiers' loved ones were in danger if Boatman was harmed. "If it's any consolation, you can spit on my corpse when it's all over."

The Roman gave Boatman a rude hand gesture and told the rebel leader someone would be back in an hour to collect him. Just before he slammed the door, he said, "We know you would be able to escape from here if you really tried, but remember who would die if you did a runner."

"You?" Boatman said. "Because if it meant you being crucified then I'll climb out the window now."

Aloysius's brother went red in the face again and left the room. Boatman was sure he heard a wall being punched.

20

When the evening came, Boatman was collected by a soldier and taken to Faust's private dining room. Faust was sitting at a long table. He was engrossed in cracking the claws of a lobster and sucking the meat out. Faust saw Boatman enter the room and stopped eating. He wiped his mouth and gestured for Boatman to take a seat at the opposite end of the table. Boatman sat down, aware of two soldiers flanking him, just behind his chair. Faust picked a stringy piece of lobster meat from between his teeth and said, "I'm shocked."

"About?"

"How easy it was to get you here."

"It's easy to get anyone to do anything when you threaten their family," said Boatman.

"You know the game," said Faust. "Don't get all self-righteous on me."

"I do know the game," said Boatman. "And now I'm in the same room as you." Boatman looked over his shoulder at the two guards. "And by the looks of it, you don't have anything in place to stop me snapping your neck."

"I'd keep your mother-in-law and your wife at the forefront of your mind, if I were you."

"Their sacrifice is worth it if it gets rid of you. I should have done it when I had the chance."

"Don't be whimsical, Boatman, life is just a series of trade-offs. Like you just did with your wife, which I'm sure she would be thrilled about if she knew."

Boatman stiffened. "She's always known the risks."

Faust took a swig of beer and then squinted. "Hmm, I'm not so sure she would agree with you on that. If you tell me where she is, I'll spare her."

"She's where being spared isn't an option, so your offer is pointless." Boatman rubbed his face. "There's not much point threatening a man with nothing to lose." He put his head in his hands and said, "I'm on my own from this point on."

Faust held the bottle up, asking if Boatman would like one. Boatman shrugged, indicating he would and Faust nodded for a soldier to bring the rebel a beer. Once Boatman had taken a swig, Faust continued the conversation. "I'm curious, did you truly think killing Nero would get rid of us?"

"No," Boatman thought for a second, "I just wanted to prove emperors bleed just like the rest of us."

Faust laughed. "Oh, he did indeed bleed. When I found him, at first I thought he had fallen asleep and poured a whole bottle of wine on the floor."

Boatman gulped his beer, wiped his beard and said, "As much as I enjoy these chats, what do you want?"

"I wanted to thank you."

"For?"

"Making me the most powerful man in the world."

Boatman squinted, "Unless I'm missing something, you're not the emperor."

"I might as well be. Maximus is a vegetable. He won't recover. Your actions made me king." Faust raised his beer, "Cheers."

"You didn't get me here to thank me for your ego getting massaged."

"No, I didn't. I actually wanted a favour."

It was Boatman's turn to laugh. "What makes you think I would give you anything?"

"Call it professional courtesy."

"I seem to recall the last time professional courtesy was associated with you, my good friend ended up in hospital."

"How is he?"

"Let's not piss around with banal, piss-poor small talk. What do you want?"

Faust smiled briefly, but then his face darkened. "It must be obvious that you will die in the near future. There can't be any other outcome for the man who killed an emperor." Boatman nodded. Faust continued. "But before we make an example of you, I'd like you to broadcast a message to the few supporters you have, who are making life difficult for our operations."

"A message?"

"Yes. Only something brief."

"What kind of message?"

"Basically telling your followers to stop. To retire even. Telling them their efforts are futile because your cause is over and you want to die knowing no-one else will be hurt."

"Let me get this straight, you want me to abandon everything I stand for, publicly, to make your life that little bit easier?" Boatman rubbed his beard and laughed a little. "I always thought you were an intelligent man."

"My father always used to say that if you don't ask, you don't ever know the answer. Personally, I fucking hated that saying because if you can read people, then you usually do know the answer before having to open your mouth."

"Then why did you ask?"

Faust shrugged. "Sometimes when all is lost people give up caring."

"Who says all is lost?"

"And there's me thinking *you* were an intelligent man."

"Hope and intelligence aren't mutual."

"I would think it's naïve to have hope in this situation."

"Maybe."

"Well, gathering from intelligence coming from Rome, your trusty sidekick Maverick is about to walk into a trap, so he's not coming to your help. And Tobias never seemed quite as effective when he didn't have his boyfriend to hide behind." Boatman was good at not showing his emotions but Faust could read someone with the tiniest of tics. "Hmm, it's always nice to catch you off guard. You didn't know what was happening with Maverick." Boatman didn't bite. Faust waved his hand, dismissively, "Anyway, it's irrelevant to the current situation. As you said, you don't like banal small talk, so talking about the vagaries of Maverick's fate won't interest you or, I suspect, be something you want to talk about because you would never want to give anything away that would betray your most loyal puppy."

Boatman turned to one of the guards loitering behind him and held up his empty beer bottle, indicating he wanted another one. The guard glanced at Faust and Faust nodded. Once Boatman had a beer in his hand, he said, "This is the thing, you're not making any sense."

"Why?"

"Because you want me to betray everything I hold dear, to try and disenfranchise a few gutsy followers? But you know I wouldn't even give you a hint as to how I'm feeling about Maverick, just in case that would somehow betray him?"

Faust tipped his beer in Boatman's direction. "True." He took a gulp. "But you probably know that pathetic group of stragglers trying to do you proud."

"Probably," said Boatman. "But I sure as hell wouldn't give them up to you."

"I can torture you to do that broadcast."

"You can try." Boatman smiled. "Someone tried that once. Torture, that is. It didn't end well."

"Everyone breaks."

"They do." Boatman tipped his beer in Faust's direction this time, mimicking the Roman. "But do you want a broken torturer?"

Faust was trying to read Boatman, but struggled. "I doubt that very much."

"See, again, I thought you were an intelligent man, Augustus. I'm not a liar or a bullshitter. I would ask you to talk to Centurion Atticus about it, but, well…" Boatman let the sentence hang, as he had been the one who had blown Centurion Atticus to smithereens via a boobytrap. "I don't know if it's genetic, as I never knew my father, but it's harder to torture someone when they don't care about the pain."

Faust felt his stomach turn, because he knew who Boatman's father was. He knew Nero's father, Centurion Ira, who was banished to Askå's kingdom, was also Boatman's father. He didn't know what to do with that information and how he could manipulate Boatman, or even the Empire, so he preferred to push the knowledge into a box for another time.

93

"If I can't appeal to your charity, or your fears, then I will have to remind you that I still have Olivia's mother in my custody, and I will hurt her if you don't do the broadcast."

"I didn't think that was part of the deal. She was meant to be released."

Faust put his drink down, placed his hands palm down on the table and leaned forward, as if sharing a secret. "When it comes to you, and what this is, there is no deal. You killed an emperor. Rules don't apply, and if you were naïve enough to think what Sebastian and Delilah told you was somehow part of that noble Roman code, then you're really nowhere near as pragmatic as I gave you credit for."

In a move so fast there was barely time for anyone to register it, Boatman had stood up, swivelled round and grabbed one of the soldiers behind him by the throat. The soldier spluttered at the grip on him, and his hands were only midway up from being by his side when Boatman slammed him on to the floor. The impact knocked the soldier out cold. The second soldier in the room had been so stunned at the speed and ferocity of Boatman that he was only just getting himself alert enough to try and help his comrade. His good intentions were short-lived as Boatman, whilst still with his body turned away from the soldier, kicked the soldier in the stomach with such speed and force the man folded to the floor, desperately trying to catch any breath. Boatman stood and started walking toward Faust. "The only naïve person in this room is you, Augustus. I surrendered easily for a reason."

Faust didn't move. He wasn't scared. Boatman hesitated at this and swore, turning too late but just soon enough to see Sebastian at the door to the dining room, holding a gun. Sebastian fired and Boatman was struck in the temple, making him crash to the floor.

The shot didn't kill him, though. It was a rubber bullet, which was meant to incapacitate, not kill. Faust looked down at the unconscious figure of Boatman and said, "No, you were the naïve one." He looked at Sebastian. "Get him ready."

Faust left the dining room and made his way back to his office. He had hoped that maybe Boatman would fear for the safety of his supporters and decide his sacrifice was worth it if it stopped anyone else getting harmed. He decided he was wrong. Yes, Boatman was naïve, but so was he. He was going to use Boatman as a pawn to kill Nero and ascend to the throne, but instead stood in the shadow of a man more depraved, whose skull resembled a dented tin can. Yes, naïvety was infectious.

21

Emperor Maximus looked out over Rome from the balcony of his palace. The cool morning air made it hard for him to breathe, and he spluttered as he got a lungful of misty air. After almost hacking up his lungs and taking a few minutes to compose himself, the monitors on his wheelchair eventually stopped frantically beeping. He wiped his mouth and looked back over the city; he despised the dreadful city known as the capital of the world. His father had loved Rome and all its pomp and grandeur. He had loved making any excuse to have a grand entrance into the city, with the crowds lining the streets, adoring him, with giant screens erected all over the city so that anyone and everyone could watch footage of their beloved Caesar. Nero had loved an audience and as much publicity as possible. He had even found amusement in bad publicity, enjoying watching videos online of people calling the emperor a false god and a tyrant. He enjoyed it because even in what they were saying, he was still the centre of attention. He had also enjoyed watching footage of those brave enough to criticise and abuse him, because he would play their footage back to them whilst torturing them after his spies had tracked them down. Yes,

Maximus thought, his father had loved Rome and the adulation that had come with it, but Maximus, he gazed at the city and wanted to see it burn.

Maximus had left Rome a year ago to go to London. He was fed up with being in a city that had become a subservient bore. His father had brutalised so many people of note within the city, and their families, that there was almost a quietude to a once-bustling place. Fear had not crept in through the population, like a toxin, but been like a searing light, ripping through eyeballs. Not that Maximus entirely minded his father's approach to leadership, because all the people being dragged into custody for treason meant there were plenty to choose from to experiment on.

Maximus was obsessed with genetics and how people were stitched together. He was particularly fascinated by gladiators and their physical construction. And that's how he saw them: constructions, like the Colosseum. Max wanted to pull the pieces apart and see how everything worked. He had found articles relating to genetics in the Senate library, written by two obscure Germanic scientists. Their research was focussed on twins and the possibility of how twins could unlock so many genetic mysteries.

The two scientists had been crucified by Max's grandfather, Caesar Augustus. They were part of a group Augustus found abhorrent and also a danger to the Empire's stability. Augustus believed their ideology to be poisonous and could never see a partnership. It was rumoured that Augustus's actions, killing these Germanics, diverted a potentially genocidal level of destruction being planned. Maximus had read the obscure articles, intrigued by the theories and also disappointed that his grandfather hadn't had the foresight to keep certain people alive as future research scientists. Maximus had decided that gladiators were his ideal species and would be most able to handle pressures on their bodies.

One specimen he was in particular awe of was Maverick 'The Beast' Kirabo. Maverick was undefeated as a gladiator and terrified most who fought him. Some weren't afraid and believed they would be the one to prove Maverick was fallible. It had never happened. Their blood smeared the floor of the gladiator ring and splattered Maverick's face on many occasions as a grim reminder of these fighters' arrogance in believing they could defeat The Beast. Maximus had watched one of Maverick's fights from a ringside seat and had felt his tummy flutter with pleasure watching this behemoth of a man obliterate his opponent.

He was gutted when Maverick had escaped from the Empire, as he had hoped his father would have allowed him to experiment on Maverick and unlock the key to being such a perfect specimen of a human. His disappointment had been short-lived, though, as he soon found out that Maverick's family originated from Uganda and Maverick had a younger brother. There was a way to unlock The Beast's genetics and it was through Damba Kirabo instead. He'd sent a team to Jinja, the Kirabo's hometown, abducted Damba and brought him back to Rome.

Damba had been a fantastic test subject, but for Maximus he still wasn't as good as the goal. Maximus had travelled to London to enjoy crucifying Olivia King, but in the back of his mind he had hoped he would draw out Maverick. The dent in his skull and the tubes protruding from his body, though, were not the outcomes he had planned. Now he was back in Rome, he still had Damba, and yet again he was drawing Maverick out of the shadows.

After the message he received from Maverick, he had ordered soldiers to move him from the hospital to somewhere secure. He couldn't be sure Maverick was bluffing. After all, anyone could have guessed the Emperor was in hospital, but he couldn't take that chance and wake up one night with The Beast standing over him. If The Beast was coming for him, then he wanted to it to be a little more stacked in his own favour. The palace was surrounded by legions of soldiers and his bodyguards swept the palace hour after hour. He guessed that at least gave him an extra five percent chance of survival.

His phone notified him that a soldier was at his living quarters door, so he wheeled off the balcony into his large and ostentatious living room. Max heard the doors beep and unlock and a guard opening them. A few muffled voices confirmed security clearances and in walked a soldier with Damba Kirabo close behind. Maximus typed into his phone and a robot voice from his phone told Damba to take a seat. When he had got out of hospital, he had been given a new phone, which verbalised everything he typed. Although it was as inhuman a voice as it could get, Max liked it. He liked how inhuman it made him because, really, he wasn't human. He was more than human. The voice continued, *have you heard from him yet?*

"No, nothing."

Try him again.

"I've tried many times."

Is he in the city?

Damba huffed in frustration. "How would I know?"

He's your brother. What is he planning?

"How many times do I have to repeat myself? I haven't seen him in years. I barely know him. I don't know what he's planning."

Damba was sitting on a sofa upholstered with depictions of the now-dead emperor Nero as a muscled adonis. The new emperor wheeled in close to Damba. The Ugandan turned his head to the side in submission. He winced at the robotic voice of Caesar. *I see*

100

that defiant trait of the Kirabo family still lingers.

Damba kept his face turned away and shook his head.

Good. The emperor kept his chair close to Damba. *So, I will ask again: what is your brother planning?*

Damba didn't respond for a moment but then he turned to face Maximus. "Revenge," he said quietly and matter-of-factly.

Maximus stared at Damba for a moment and then laughed. Well, laugh would be an exaggeration of what happened. A sound from Maximus's throat, combined with a snuffle sound from his nose is what Damba heard. The emperor typed into his phone, *Revenge?* The robotic voice couldn't express incredulity, but the emperor's animated face made up for it. *What? For bringing you to Rome? For taking you away from your shitty village? For giving you a better life?*

Maverick's brother shook his head again. "No. It won't be for that."

Then what?

"If he's the same as when we grew up together, he will be coming for revenge against you for damaging his ego." Confusion replaced the emperor's expression of incredulity.

Revenge? I'm the one wearing nappies and I sound like a low-budget robot from that shitty film studio my cousin set up.

"And that's why he wants revenge," said Damba and looked at the emperor square in the eyes. "You dared to have the audacity to survive."

22

The Emperor had dismissed Damba back to his living quarters and wheeled back outside onto the balcony. Not only did he have a view of the city he despised, he also had view of a courtyard. Because he was in a wheelchair, Max had instructed the balcony to be altered to ensure he had an unhindered view. Instead of traditional stonework creating the balcony frontage, it had been replaced with clear glass so Max could wheel to the edge and still see everything below. He sent a message to his cousin, Felix, the owner of the low-budget film studio that Max had financed, indicating that he was ready for the show. Felix replied that it would be starting in fifteen minutes, and he would be with Max in five.

Five minutes later, Felix was standing beside Maximus and said, "Are you ready, my lord?" Maximus nodded that he was. If Max still had use of his legs, they would have been jittering with excitement. If he had any functions of his body below the waist then his trousers would have been twitching. Felix shouted, "Action!"

The courtyard was enclosed by extensions of the palace. Before Max had travelled to London to crucify Olivia King, he had requested the courtyard be built, along with the various rooms and spaces he was now looking at. Some of those rooms were living quarters and some were cells for prisoners. Some were also large, empty spaces for Max to make sure his special shows could be produced. Special shows like the one beginning for him. His original plan had been to crucify Olivia King, stream it via the Empire Network and then do similar live streams from the comfort of his own home. A hammer crushing his skull had put that plan on hold. Until now.

At the far-left corner of the courtyard were large double doors. They opened outwards and four soldiers appeared, carrying a metal crucifix and two saline drips. They got to the centre of the courtyard and placed the crucifix into a metal slot bolted into the ground. The slot had a long hydraulic arm attached to it, and the crucifix was bolted in place. A soldier pulled out a remote control and pressed a button. The crucifix began to lower down until it was flat against the ground. A solider touched his ear and spoke. Within a couple of minutes, two figures emerged from a doorway on the eastern side of the courtyard. One figure was a soldier, dressed like the emperor in a black suit and wearing a laurel wreath. He was dressed like Max had been on the day he'd travelled to London to crucify Olivia King. The other figure, being dragged by the soldier dressed like Maximus Nero, was a young woman in a beige suit. She was cable-tied round her wrists and there was a long silver chain attached to the cable ties. The woman was in-between being dragged and stumbling behind the soldier. She was shouting for help and screaming expletives at the soldier and anyone else in the vicinity. She looked just like Olivia King.

Max enjoyed the screaming. Again, if his lower body actually worked, then he was sure his trousers would have been twitching at the sound of her screams. Even though he wasn't able to get an erection anymore, and he could only gaze fondly back at the memory of how hard he got when he hammered that first nail into Olivia King's wrist, he still found himself giddy at looking at the scene before him. The woman did everything in her might to try and stop the soldiers from putting her on the metal cross. She kicked and squirmed and swore. The soldier who had been dragging her got frustrated and slapped her round the face. The blow shocked her, and she went silent.

Max raised his hand and a robotic voice commanded the man to stop. The soldier looked up, as did the woman, and Maximus's robotic voice sounded again, instructing the solider not to mark her face. The soldier lowered his hand and turned his attention back on his hostage. There was something about seeing Caesar and the instructions he gave that sucked all hope out of the woman. Seeing him on the balcony, observing the show, and realising all the cameras positioned around the courtyard were pointing at her, caused her to wilt both physically and mentally. Her life had been one of subservience to the Empire, a child growing up as a servant in the palace, who had eventually become as disposable as the nails used to crucify her.

Max's artificial voice bounced off the courtyard walls. *Soldier, remember what you rehearsed.* The soldier nodded and got into character as Felix kept the cameras rolling. What happened next was a complete reenactment of when Max crucified Olivia. The only difference being that this was a reenactment according to Max's fantasy, not his reality. His reality was not befitting of an emperor, but he was able to make this show something he would want to watch again and again, fantasising that it was how things had happened in London.

Felix had set up a screen showing the scene unfolding in the courtyard, as the soldier crucified the woman who was made to look like Olivia. Max reached out and stroked the screen as it showed a close-up of the woman's fear as her arms were stretched out over the T of the cross. The soldier playing the role of Max pulled out the nail gun and positioned it over the woman's left wrist. Max told him to stop before the trigger was pulled. The soldier looked up at the balcony, confused. The woman felt herself dare to have a glimmer of hope that the crucifixion wouldn't go ahead.

Use a hammer.

The soldier said, "Sorry, my Lord?"

I used a hammer, the way it used to be done. Use a hammer.

The soldier nodded and went to the toolbox and pulled out a club hammer. The woman fainted at the sight of it.

Max sat enraptured by the recreation of his time alone with Olivia. If he could have jumped out of his wheelchair and done a little dance, he would have. He was still disgusted with himself that he had been so sloppy and not noticed Maverick and Tobias sneak up on him a year ago. Any outside observer would have pointed out that no-one would have noticed Maverick and Tobias, because they were like ghosts that night. Max, though, believed he was a god made man, just like his father was. He had to be a god, because he was hit in the head, with a hammer, by The Beast. No mortal man would survive that. And if he had survived an assassination attempt like that, then the gods were smiling down on him. He dismissed his current physical state as part of the gods' sick jokes they liked to play. He guessed it had been the trickster Mercury who had allowed him to have his skull caved in, as that was Mercury's style. He also guessed that it was all part of a larger plan, devised by the gods, to allow him to implement his revenge on The Beast.

Max watched as the soldier grunted and sweated, hammering the nails through the wrists of the woman, and felt jealous of the soldier and also resentful. He resented the soldier for having the opportunity to do something so stimulating and sensual as crucifixion but treat it like it was a chore. Being able to look someone in the eyes as you were in control of their life was a gift from the gods.

This grunting soldier was not appreciating his gift and had barely looked at the woman whose life he had control over. It was disrespectful and brutish. Max was certainly going to enjoy watching the footage of the crucifixion and how it would take him back to when he got to be alone with Olivia, but the soldier wasn't worthy of such an honourable reenactment. Once the filming was over Max would order the soldier to be brought to his living quarters and then the emperor would make sure the soldier understood the magnitude of what he had just done. Max thought about what he would make the soldier do, and for the second time that day, if his lower body worked, his trousers would have twitched with excitement.

23

Damba sat in his living quarters and felt dirty for his interaction with the Emperor. He was relieved, though, that he had been dismissed before having to watch the show. Damba was six-foot-six, an inch taller than his older brother, long-legged and broad-chested. Maverick, although slightly shorter, appeared larger. Maverick was like a brick wall with limbs and made you feel smaller in his presence. Damba had only known his brother when they were young boys and they were regularly spearing fish on the shoreline of Nnalubaale. Their father had taught them how to fish by net and by spear. Netting was for money; spearing was for fun. Most days the boys enjoyed spearing. Damba always remembered how he was faster than his brother, but Mav was so much stronger. Damba could throw a spear with more whip, but Maverick could snap a spear with the power of his throw. Even as a boy of only twelve, Mav was able to spear a fish and then it was a struggle to remove the spear from the seabed.

The most notable time Damba had seen the extent of his older brother's power was when two men approached the brothers while they were fishing. The men were dressed in army fatigues, which were only associated with guerrilla groups, who were scattered around the jungles of east Africa. The men had drawn guns on Maverick and Damba with the belief they would scare the boys into submission. The men were there, recruiting children to take to the northern Uganda. A man named Joseph, who believed the gods had ordained him to build an army in preparation for the end of the world, was sending his soldiers throughout the country to recruit the Lord's Fighters. The recruitment side of things actually meant being forced by gun point back to Joseph's base camp. So, the young Ugandan brothers were faced with that prospect and were staring down the barrel of two guns.

There's something pure about being young and carefree; fear and foreboding aren't part of your psyche. Fun and innocence are your friends and anything outside of that is alien. Mav and Damba had spent their morning enjoying the simplicity of spear fishing and swimming in the cool waters of Nnalubaale. When the Lord's Fighters arrived, with their guns aimed at the brothers, the brothers reacted as they would if a predator came at them from deep within the jungle: on instinct. Damba's reactions were proven, at that moment, to be faster than his older brother's because he had raised and thrown his spear before Maverick had even reacted. Unfortunately, for one of the soldiers, he was also far slower than Damba and before his trigger finger could move to the trigger, it was twitching in a dead spasm as he lay on the floor with a spear in his chest. The second soldier, who had watched an eleven-year-old boy throw a spear with such skill, also didn't have much time to be impressed, because as he turned his head from the twitching body of his comrade back in the direction of the brothers, all he saw was a flash of colour coming from Maverick's hands. Then everything went black as a spear hit his chest. That was then proof that although Damba was faster, Maverick was stronger, because the spear had entered the soldier's chest and pierced through bone and tissue to protrude from his back.

Maverick and Damba had stared at the bodies of the guerrillas they had killed and, like close siblings do, simultaneously wondered if they were really looking at actual dead bodies. They had killed numerous fish. They had speared a handful of wild hogs. They had almost speared each other by accident once or twice, but they had certainly never seen a dead human before. It took them a while to process the severity of the situation before them, because they were only young boys, but when it dawned on them what they had done, they didn't hesitate to find their parents.

Their mother and father had rushed to them and as soon as they saw the bodies, they had instructed the boys to start digging graves. No-one was going to know the soldiers were missing and no-one was going to miss the soldiers. Also, the Lord's Fighters, controlled by Jospeh Kony, were expendable. Kony would never have searched for them because he took it as part of the plan to have collateral damage across the country. Kony worked on the odds: recruit more children than the men who die recruiting the children. The two soldiers killed by Maverick and Damba were forgotten as soon as they left Kony's base camp. After the bodies had been buried, the Kirabo family never spoke of the incident again. It wasn't a good idea to speak aloud when the Roman gods might hear.

When the Romans came to Jinja a year later, though, and dragged Maverick away, Damba wondered whether the gods had seen what they had done. When the swarm of soldiers arrived in their village, Damba had picked up his hunting spear to give the Empire a similar treatment to the soldiers on the shore of

Nnalubaale, but Damba's father had ripped his spear away. He told his boisterous son that killing a soldier would not compensate for their entire village being razed to the ground. A legion of soldiers had come for the strongest boys in the village, to take them away and train them as gladiators for the Emperor's pleasure. Maverick was by far the strongest boy in the entire village, and Damba had wanted to protect his older brother, like they had a year earlier when the Lord's Fighters had been pointing guns at them both on the shore of the lake.

The thing was, this time, if Damba killed a soldier, a legion of soldiers would have killed his family. It took Damba's father to make the young boy realise that innocence didn't exist anymore. As Damba had watched his brother be dragged away, and dragged away was the literal description because it took four soldiers to carry Maverick away and one of those soldiers received a broken arm in the process of trying, Damba also watched the final shred of his childhood being dragged away.

Damba tried to remember his brother's face from when they were children and struggled to visualise anything but a vague generic form. He was living in the Emperor's Palace, a prisoner and a medical guinea pig, and all he could see when he pictured his brother were the images of Maverick in promos for his next gladiator match. Damba had no idea what his brother was like now. He remembered the boy who laughed a lot and grinned every time he speared a fish. He was confident that easy-smiling boy was a distant memory, even in Maverick's mind. He got up from the sofa. Even though he was a prisoner who was on call to the Emperor's every whim, at least he had a fridge fully stocked with beer. He walked into the kitchen, a large open-plan kitchen with a large island in the centre. Damba liked to sit at the island and drink a beer, pretending that maybe he was living a mundane life. Tonight, he wasn't going to sit at his stall, drinking a beer, pretending to be a normal man with a boring life, because his stall was occupied by someone else drinking one of his beers. Maverick cracked open another and slid it across the island top.

"We need to talk."

24

Damba believed he was beyond being surprised, having scars from the countless tests performed on him since being abducted by Caesar Maximus, but he was wrong. Seeing his older brother, one of the most wanted men in the Empire, casually drinking a beer in a kitchen that belonged to the Emperor, well, that managed to elicit surprise. He'd known Maverick would come for him, but to see his brother for the first time in six years in such a vanilla setting seemed surreal. Six years ago, he had only briefly seen his brother before being taken away by soldiers. Maverick had appeared, back in Uganda, as if he was going to save the day. He had thought Maverick was going to stop the abduction, but instead, his brother and Tobias had fled the scene and left Damba to Max's every despicable whim. At the time, Damba had known Maverick had little choice, but it didn't stop the feeling in the pit of his stomach, a feeling of resentment, that his brother had abandoned him. Maverick was one of the most feared men in the world and arguably the best fighter who had ever lived, so Damba went to sleep on many an occasion with a niggling sense of abandonment.

Six years later and his brother had come for him, but a lot of pain had passed through Damba's body in that time. The pain he had experienced was etched on his skin. Just as Maverick was no longer the quick-to-laugh child from Jinja, Damba was no longer a carefree boy.

"How did you get in here?"

"It's good to see you too, brother."

"You can't be here."

"It's a bit late for that." Maverick swigged his beer. "By the gods, take a seat, you're making me uncomfortable."

"*I'm* making *you* uncomfortable? Soldiers could walk in here any moment," said Damba.

Maverick laughed a little as he drank more of his beer. "I doubt that. They'll be clearing up whatever mess Max is currently making."

"The show's over."

Maverick looked at his brother. "I'm talking about the mess being made in Max's living quarters." Maverick looked back at the bottle he was holding, "The soldiers guarding your door aren't going to be thinking about what you're up to for the rest of the night." Damba instinctively rubbed the grafts on his right arm, remembering being left to Max's depravities, and knew Maverick was talking sense. He took a seat opposite his brother.

"Even so, you still can't be here. You'll be killed."

"I won't. You know I won't."

"What do you want, then?"

"To walk out the palace doors, with you next to me."

"That's impossible," said Damba.

"I caved in the skull of the Emperor-to-be. Nothing's impossible."

"Still impossible to kill, it seems."

"Boatman would disagree," said Maverick. "But that's not the point. I promised to come back for you, little brother."

Damba shook his head and said quietly, "Little brother. Maverick, we barely know each other. We're acquaintances. You've come back for me, but you don't know me. You don't know who you've come back for."

"I know you've been through a lot."

Damba held his hand up. "Let's not do a long-lost-brother therapy session, okay?" Damba stood and went to the fridge. He pulled out another beer. He didn't offer Maverick one. "Max did horrible things to me. The Empire did horrible things to you. There's a big difference between us, though."

"How so?"

"You grew to hate the Empire. I grew to love it."

It was Maverick's turn to be surprised. He looked over at his brother, trying to gauge if he was joking or not. "I'm sorry?"

"Why are you so surprised?"

"Because I was taken away when we were kids, and you were abducted by a maniac. Damba, I know you have been through a lot since you've been in Rome, it's surely a reason to hate everything about the Empire."

Damba closed the fridge and leaned back against it. Maverick may not have known his brother anymore, but he still knew people and how they behaved, and the way Damba was trying to appear nonchalant was telling Maverick that his younger brother was the opposite of that. "Remember what it was like back home?"

"I thought we weren't doing a long-lost-brother therapy session."

"Just go with it."

"I remember fishing by the lake with you most days. I remember being happy."

"I don't," said Damba. "I don't remember being happy. I

remember our parents mourning you, and me living in the shadow of you for my entire life."

Maverick was confused. "Even if that was the case, surely that was better than what Max has done to you?"

Damba absently rubbed his arm. "At least with Max I was finally seen." Damba had been staring at his shoes and looked up at Maverick. "I was in your shadow as a child and then you became this rock star gladiator with posters of you throughout Uganda. When Max took me and tested me to find out why I'm made up the way I am, well, I was pleased someone was interested in me."

"You're fucking serious?" Maverick laughed. "Being tortured by Maximus Nero made you feel wanted." He carried on laughing. "You're right, I clearly don't know you." Maverick stood up. "We need to go."

Damba shook his head. "No. I've been seen, it's not possible to leave."

"I got in here, Damba, it's easy to get us out."

"That's not what I meant."

Maverick had spent more than two decades in a gladiator ring and therefore sensed a shift in someone's behaviour, like a primal detection alarm. Most times, before Maverick's brain had processed that danger was imminent into a conscious thought, his body was already responding. Maverick had got up from his stool, the primal part of his brain sending pulses of warning. Even with all those years of training, Maverick's instincts having kept him alive all this time, there was one inalienable truth he couldn't hide from: his little brother was always faster than him. The tranquilliser dart hit Maverick in the chest before he was able to even register Damba had pulled out the gun. Maverick went to step forward, his brain telling him to get to Damba and throttle his deceptive little brother, but his legs failed to get the memo and he collapsed.

Damba waited to be sure his brother was out cold and then bent down beside him. "That's not what I meant at all. It's time for you to be in my shadow."

25

Olivia took a seat on a fallen tree and tried to suck in some air. They had been walking for five hours, skirting around main roads and traversing the hills and deep woodland that southern Caledonia offered. "Tell me we're close to somewhere we can rest for the night."

"Just another hour and we'll be there," said Tobias.

"You make that sound like good news." Olivia was breathing hard, trying to replenish her lungs. "What about Molly?"

Tobias pulled out his phone and opened the tracking app. He had installed a tracking application on his and Molly's phone without Molly's knowledge but at Olivia's behest. Tobias had been reluctant because he felt Molly should know. He wasn't experienced with children, but he felt children were his equal so should be informed of any decision like an adult would be. Olivia disagreed. She had said to Tobias that Molly had seen her parents torn from her in the space of days and needed as much protection as possible. The tracker was a simple element of protection, in case anything happened to her. Tobias hated to admit that Olivia was right, because here they were, trekking through far too much greenery for Tobias's liking, trying to work out who had abducted Molly and why on earth they wanted her.

Tobias pinched the screen of his phone to get a better context of where Molly was in comparison to their location. "She's in a settlement, east of where we're heading."

"How far east?"

"Olivia, we can't go after her. They'll kill us."

"What happened to you, Tobias?"

"I almost died, that's what happened to me."

"You were a gladiator, Tobias. I'm sure you almost died a number of times."

"Not like that," said Tobias.

"Like what?"

Tobias waved his hand. "It doesn't matter. Liv, I can't take the risk of you getting injured," he said. "Or worse."

"Molly needs us, though. I can feel it." And she was telling the truth. She could feel it. She was sensing Molly's emotional vibrations, and it was like a nervous buzzing. She had felt it when Molly's dad and mum had died. She had felt similar vibrations moments before Max strolled into her office and took her away to be crucified. She had felt it in the night in a different way. Vibrations from Molly were connected to fear and confusion. The vibrations in the night were connected to depravity and she knew those sensations came all the way from Rome, where Maximus was. She knew she was never going to be able to escape him. Being crucified by him and violated by him, she knew that a part of him would always corrupt every inch of her being. She hated that his toxic nature had infected her mind and body and that she would feel his presence on occasions like these. She didn't tell Tobias, but in the night, she had sensed depraved glee coming from Rome. Although she didn't know what it was specifically about, she prayed to the God-Carpenter it had nothing to do with Maverick.

Tobias brought Olivia away from her vibrations and said, "You might feel it, but we're not equipped to do anything about saving her."

"Why not?"

"You saw how easy they took us out back at Kiera's."

"They caught us out. We will have the surprise element this time."

Tobias laughed. "I think you're overestimating our abilities."

"Why?"

Tobias paused, a one-word question was very hard to answer. "We just don't have the resources. Or the backup."

"You and Maverick didn't have the backup when you saved me."

Tobias's mind flashed back to the raw brutality of Maverick on London Bridge when they saved Olivia. "That's true. I'm pretty sure you can't rip a man's jaw off the way Mav can, though. That's the difference."

Olivia didn't have an answer to that. She stood up. "I can't force you, Tobias, and I think we can still help her, but I'm too tired to fight you." She started walking on, aiming for the settlement closest to them. "Let's get moving," she said, over her shoulder.

Tobias didn't argue; he was tired too and his side was hurting. The doctors had said there was no permanent damage from Faust's stab wound, but it didn't change how some days Tobias prayed his organs weren't failing. And that was the real truth: a year ago he would have agreed with Olivia and regardless of the odds he would have stormed into the settlement where Molly was being held and tried to tear someone's jaw off, like his lover would have done. Now he was scared of getting hurt and scared of dying before seeing Maverick again. He missed his partner and he felt frail without the love of his life by his side. He was ashamed, too, because he couldn't even tell Olivia how he was feeling and out of anyone in his life, she was the one who would have completely understood. Tobias caught up with Olivia and they set off for the settlement only two miles away. With the steep terrain and the wide berth they were giving the main roads, it was going to take them an hour to get there.

Tobias was right, and the rebels arrived at the settlement just under an hour later. It was a small settlement consisting of one main street, lined with drinking houses, a food store, a butcher, a fishmonger and, from what Tobias could tell, not much else. Tobias also noted how very un-Roman it was. The Caledonians had experienced a brief rule by the Romans, but, depending on whose history you read, either the Romans couldn't handle trying to subdue the Caledonian people or they found very little benefit of ruling such a cold and gods-forsaken country.

The Empire tended to completely avoid the country nowadays, preferring to leave the boisterous country alone to govern itself and agreeing to trade with it for mutual benefit. Emperor Nero had once toyed with the idea of bringing Caledonia into the Empire again, subduing the nation through fear and awe, but after sending a couple of legions there to research what it would take to overcome the population, he decided against it when just the heads of the legions returned. It would be too expensive and time consuming trying to get Caledonian savages in line, and he needed his soldiers focusing their energy on finding and eliminating Boatman and his followers.

The Caledonians weren't naïve and knew there would always be a risk of another invasion, so they adapted their country to anticipate this. Settlements like the one Tobias and Olivia encountered were built as part of that anticipation. They were built on through-roads, acting as supply chains for the people of

Caledonia and allies visiting, but also acting as warning posts in case enemies travelled through. The biggest question Tobias had was whether the settlement would view them as allies or enemies.

It was early evening and dark already. On one side of the street was a pub and opposite was a hotel. Olivia headed straight for the pub, its windows showing an alluring orange glow, which must have been an open fire burning. Tobias didn't even think about objecting. He was gagging for a pint and somewhere to warm up. Olivia was already striding ahead of him and as he caught up, he winced from the pain of where he had been stabbed by Faust a year earlier. The colder conditions of Caledonia made his old wounds ache, so he was looking forward to sitting by a fire and drinking something to numb the pain.

They walked into the pub and it had the vibe of a local watering hole where everyone knows each other and everyone certainly knows any patrons who aren't local. Olivia found a seat near the fire and that convinced Tobias it was a good idea going there first, instead of the hotel. Tobias went to the bar and ordered two pints. There was a man standing at the bar, cradling a pint of beer. He spoke to Tobias, "We don't serve Romans here."

Tobias didn't look at the man. "Thanks for the info. I'll be sure to pass the message on if I bump into any Romans."

"No, I don't think you understood me."

Tobias turned to look at the man next to him, "No, I did understand you. You want me to tell any Romans that I might come across that they're not welcome here."

"Are you being belligerent, boy? I'm saying that you're not welcome here, because you look like a Roman to me."

Tobias snorted. "I look like a Roman? Wow, okay, that's interesting coming from a guy who looks like one of his parents possibly mated with a heifer."

"Don't you dare call my Ma a heifer."

Tobias held his hands up. "My friend, I just said one of your parents. If there's stuff you need to work through that makes you instantly think of your mum, well, that's your shit to deal with. In fact, my friend over there is a therapist. I could probably get you a discount on your first session." Tobias walked away from the bar carrying his two pints and sat down in a chair opposite Olivia, who was looking a bit drowsy from the warmth of the fire.

"You doing okay?"

Olivia nodded and took a swig of her beer. She glanced up and past Tobias. She raised her chin and Tobias looked over his shoulder. The anti-Roman from the bar was walking over to where Tobias and Olivia were. Tobias stood up. "Look, my friend, I'm not a Roman and we're having a quiet drink. Okay?"

"I know a Roman when I see one."

"Good for you. Let me know when one comes in the pub," said Tobias.

The man jabbed his finger at Tobias. "If you're not a Roman, you're one of their spies."

"Buddy, even if I was a spy for the Empire, you have nothing to worry about. A fat, sweaty, pathetic ginger man isn't the top of the list of Faust's worries."

The Caledonian stepped into Tobias's personal space, and Tobias wrinkled his nose at the smell of stale sweat coming from the man. "If you think I'm pathetic, how about I show you how pathetic you are by going outside."

"Going outside?" Tobias laughed, "What shitty films have you been watching? In my world, I'll beat the shit out of you here and then sit down and finish my beer. But it's good to know you agreed

126

that you're fat and sweaty as you seem only offended that I called you pathetic."

"This is my friend's pub. I'm not getting your blood on their carpet."

Tobias looked over his shoulder at Olivia and rolled his eyes, and then looked back at the Caledonian, whose breath was making him want to knock him out on that basis alone. Tobias shrugged and pushed past the man and went outside. The ginger Caledonian followed, along with Olivia close behind and a couple of the local man's friends. Tobias eyed the man up, like he would have done if he were still in a gladiator ring. It was second nature to look for weaknesses. Judging his opponent, there were a lot of weaknesses.

Tobias conceded that men from small settlements like this, although out of shape and usually half cut, could sometimes pose more danger than well trained athletes. They could be dirty fighters who weren't bothered about getting hit in the face. The thing was, even if this Caledonian was an intimidating street fighter in his local settlement, hardly anyone would have ever faced an experienced gladiator and survived. For Tobias, he had only feared two men in a fight and one of those had become his lover. "Shall we get this over with?" Tobias said.

The Caledonian was swinging his arms about, warming up. "You'll regret what you said about my Ma."

"You're right, I do regret it." Tobias stepped forward. "Because I'm tired, pissed off and I just want to drink my beer."

The Caledonian grunted. "You need to show some respect." He pulled out a knife. "And you need to show it now."

Tobias froze for a moment. He was surprised at his reaction as he had faced countless fighters who were well trained and ruthless. The Caledonian was holding a small knife that was puny compared to the swords and spears and guns Tobias had dealt with over the years. This was the first knife that had been pulled on him since he had been stabbed by Faust a year ago. Faust had done it stealthily and Tobias had barely registered the blade going into his side at the time. He only knew he had been stabbed when he had woken up in the hospital and experienced the excruciating pain of someone having defiled his insides with a blade.

Even though the Caledonian was inexperienced with professional fighting, he was still seasoned enough to register Tobias's hesitation. He took the hesitation as an opportunity and lunged at Tobias. Tobias was thankful for a small number of things in his life, and one of those was his natural instinct in dangerous situations. It was very true of the human condition that people, when in danger, fly, freeze or fight and Tobias was thankful that his preconditioned response to danger was to fight, even when a knife was coming at him.

The Caledonian lurched forward with the knife, aiming for Tobias's stomach. Tobias had been in a fighting stance, with his right foot in front of him, in line with his torso. As the knife came at him, he swivelled his hips, turned his body away from the blade and grabbed the wrist of the Caledonian. He then quite simply tugged the Caledonian's arm downwards. It completely threw the man off balance, and he stumbled forward. Tobias didn't let go of his wrist, though, so the man stumbled and then sprawled on the ground whilst being held by Tobias. Tobias then twisted the man's wrist and something made a cracking noise, which made the man cry out and drop the knife. Tobias let go of the man's wrist.

The man acted on instinct to protect his damaged hand. He pulled his arm in close, holding his wrist and shocked at the pain. He managed to get to his knees and looked up at Tobias, who was standing over him. Tobias didn't wait for a surrender or apology and punched the man hard in the temple. It was like a sledgehammer arcing through the cold, evening air and the man's head hit the ground, with his body taking a bit longer to catch up. One of the Caledonian's friends commented, a few weeks later in the pub, that at the time, when Tobias had punched his friend in the temple, his friend had resembled a Jack-in-the-Box in the way his head had hit the ground and it looked like his body was on some sort of spring the way it bent at first. The man was out cold, and Tobias turned to face the small group of locals watching on. He didn't need to say anything. The group silently filtered back into the pub.

Olivia stood next to Tobias and looked at the unconscious man, "Was that really necessary?"

"No."

"Then why do it?"

"You tell me. You're the therapist," said Tobias and went to walk back into the pub.

"Tobias, they're not going to serve you now."

"Then I'll make them. I just want a pint."

"I'm sure that's what every landlord wants to feel, to be fucking terrified of the patrons."

"Well go and sweet talk them, then. I'm gagging for a drink," said Tobias.

Olivia looked exhausted from the exchange. "What would Maverick say to you in this situation?"

"Probably that I punch like a sissy. Which is ironic."

"Why are you like this?"

"Again, you tell me."

"There's no real consensus on the origins of being a twat, Tobias."

"For a therapist, your bedside manner is very poor."

"You're thinking of a nurse and I'm pretty sure you pissed all of them off when you were in hospital last."

"They didn't get my humour."

"Tobias, no-one gets your humour."

"I was going to say that Maverick does, but he's buggered off and left me. You know—" Tobias stopped talking as the lights to the pub went out. "I have a feeling the lights being turned out even though there's a pub full of people is not a good sign."

"Tobias, we need to leave."

If Tobias had been with Maverick, he would have disagreed with Olivia about leaving, and he and his fiancé would have enjoyed waiting for whatever rabble emerged from the pub. Maverick wasn't with him, though, and his main concern was getting Olivia to the rendezvous point. They began to run down the street, looking for a parking lot or any means of transport to help them get to the next stage of their journey. Tobias felt his stomach lurch. He'd had the opportunity to try and get Olivia and Molly safely through Caledonia without too much drama and to where they needed to be, for their safety, but now they were running for their lives. Again.

Olivia was ahead of Tobias and turned a corner, seeing a sign indicating parking nearby. In the middle of the road stood a couple. Olivia slowed down to a stroll. Tobias caught up and they stopped about fifteen feet from the couple. The woman was on the phone, and when she saw Olivia and Tobias she hung up and said, "We haven't had trouble with Romans for decades. These two are the ones to break the truce?"

"We're not Romans, we're just passing through your settlement," said Olivia.

"I have a badly injured friend who disagrees that you're just passing through."

"You need to choose a better breed of friends then, because

that ginger twat deserved what he got," said Tobias.

The woman scowled and pulled out a knife. Tobias tipped his head back as if asking the gods for patience. "What is it with you lot and knives?"

He made a move toward the woman and Olivia stepped between them. "Please, no more violence tonight." She held her hand out at the woman, pleading.

"No more violence? We haven't had any violence until you showed up," said the woman. She slashed her knife at Olivia, catching Olivia off guard. Olivia instinctively put her hands up to protect herself and the knife slashed the palm of her hand. She gasped and fell to the ground, clutching her hand. Tobias ran forward and when the woman slashed at him, he caught the woman's wrist and punched her in the gut. She folded over, gasping for air.

Tobias turned to see the man pull a gun. He was about ten feet away and Tobias knew he wouldn't be able to disarm him if he fired. He also knew he had to make sure he kept Olivia alive. He had failed to protect her from being crucified and he wasn't going to fail her again. He ran at the man, guessing at least he created a barrier to any stray bullets hitting Olivia. The man raised his arm to fire, but Tobias heard no sound and saw no muzzle flash. All he saw was the man drop to the ground with an arrow protruding from his chest. Tobias turned around with the word *Bella* on his lips and thankful she had found them. Bella's name caught in his throat though as he saw not Bella standing there with a bow and arrow, but Kiera. "Let's get out of here," she shouted.

Tobias didn't hesitate. He picked Olivia up from the ground, and they jogged over to Kiera. She was standing by a truck and told them to get in. They duly obliged and Kiera climbed into the driver's side and sped away from the scene. She looked into her rear-view mirror and saw a blurry haze of figures running up the street, weapons in hand. A crack of gunfire went off in the distance and Kiera held her breath in case a window shattered or a tyre was taken out, but nothing happened and they rumbled along away from the settlement in peace.

26

"What compelled you to come find us?"

Kiera had been driving for nearly an hour before anyone had spoken. Olivia was asleep, her hand bandaged up, courtesy of the first-aid supplies kept in the truck. "Apart from complete stupidity, I had made a promise to Boatman. I never thought I would have to go through with that promise, but here we are."

"You knew him from a long time ago?"

"Yeah, I knew him before his London life. Before he became so serious." Kiera glanced in her mirror at Olivia, and Tobias saw it. He tried to imagine Boatman as anything but serious and couldn't do it, so he guessed Kiera must have known Boatman when either drunk as hell or tripping her tits off.

"It's a hell of a promise for you to have come and saved us."

"Not really, considering all he's done for me."

"I just find it weird that he's never mentioned you before."

Kiera looked in her mirror and frowned. "How long have you known Boatman for?"

"It feels like a week, but it's been an age. Or is it the other way?"

Kiera looked in her mirror. "What do you mean?"

"If you've known Boatman, I'd think it's obvious. It can feel like an age even when it has been a short while. When I met him, he beat the crap out of me, though, so that had an influence on how I view him."

"I feel like we're talking about different men," said Kiera. She rubbed her face, yawned and ran her hand through her hair, "but, knowing Boatman, he was always very good at throwing people off."

Tobias found her turn of phrase rather odd, but didn't pursue it. He was tired and stressed about Olivia. She wasn't badly injured, but it didn't take a psychiatrist to know that the injury she sustained, no matter how superficial, was enough to torment her and bring back memories of Max standing over her with a hammer.

"I know you made a promise to Boatman, but you didn't need to come find us. Also, how the hell did you find us? We could have gone a number of ways."

Kiera said, "I promised Boatman that when the time came, I would be there for him or whomever he wanted me to be there for. He planned this route to escape if it all went wrong and Rome won the war. I've traced this journey countless times in preparation, so unless you're completely useless at following a map, you were going to have to pass through that town."

"Thank you. You came at the right time."

"Honestly, I was expecting to arrive at the hotel and find you there. Having only known you for a few hours, though, it wasn't surprising to find you about to be killed by an angry mob."

"I have that effect on people."

"You're quite the catch."

"My fiancé would agree."

"Someone was deluded enough to agree to marry you?"

"He couldn't resist my searing wit."

"I assume you save that searing wit for when you're with him?"

"I think you've been living alone for too long," said Tobias, and Kiera narrowed her eyes at Tobias in the mirror.

"So, where is this obviously very forgiving and very patient fiancé of yours?"

"He's making amends."

"For what? Your failure?"

Tobias huffed. "You know what, you keep talking as if everything has gone wrong, but I seem to remember the news reporting a very dead emperor."

"And yet here you are," said Kiera.

Keira's comment killed the conversation and they drove in silence for the rest of the way. They arrived at their destination while it was still dark, in the early hours of the morning. Tobias had nodded off for a couple of hours and had woken up a few minutes before they reached the rendezvous point. Olivia was also awake, and when Tobias asked how she was feeling she just said she was fine without wanting to elaborate. Tobias pulled out some gold to give to Kiera but she waved it away, reiterating that she had made a promise to Boatman to help him when it was needed. Tobias thanked her for everything and made his way toward the small pteron-chariot waiting for them. Olivia climbed out of the truck, paused and turned to face Kiera, "How did you know my husband?"

"It was a long time ago when he was searching for possible allies. In the process of the search there was a moment where he saved my life."

"And after all this time you still feel like you owe him?"

"We only have one life, don't we? Didn't realise there was an expiration date on gratitude."

Olivia's head dropped and she sighed. "I'm sorry, you've been

135

very kind to us. And you clearly think a lot of my husband."

"No offence, but it seems like I'm one of the only people around here that thinks a lot of your husband. Mrs King, I haven't seen Boatman in many years but I'm finding it hard to understand the animosity toward someone who is so fiercely loyal and courageous."

Olivia didn't want to keep this conversation going, and Tobias was calling her, saying they had to go, creating a convenient escape. "Thanks again for helping us." She went to leave but then said, "You should come with us. Surely your house isn't safe anymore?"

"Thanks for the offer, but I'll be fine," said Kiera. "You need to go," she said and Olivia closed the door of the truck. Kiera drove off, the truck's rear lights leaving small, red pin pricks in the distance.

Olivia got to the pteron-chariot and, climbed the small ladder and was welcomed by a member of staff who showed her to her seat. The pteron-chariot had only 12 seats and Tobias and Olivia were the only passengers. As Olivia sat down, she heard Tobias ask a staff member if was definitely safe because a metal tube with wings didn't feel very safe. The member of staff assured him everything was fine but slipped him couple of pills and handed him a bottle of beer nonetheless, and said that if he took the pills he would be asleep in a matter of minutes and would wake up at their destination. Tobias didn't need telling twice, popped the pills and swigged the beer like his life depended on it. The pteron-chariot staff member asked Olivia if she too would like something to help her relax, and she said that a drink without the pills would do just fine. She did ask how long it would take to arrive and was told it would be five hours so to stretch out, relax and try to get some sleep. "Sorry, just one more thing," said Olivia, "Are you sure the Empire won't try to stop us whilst flying?"

"There's no need to worry. This is a diplomatic flight from the Kingdom of Caledonia. Rome has never interfered with a flight like this."

"There's always a first time," said Olivia.

The staff member chuckled. "That's very true, but Rome wouldn't risk it."

And she was right; Rome wouldn't risk interfering with a flight out of Caledonia because the consequences would be massive. When the Empire was driven out of Britannia the first time, the Caledonian Kingdom vowed to never be vulnerable to Roman invasion again and over generations created a form of insurance against any Caesar getting delusions about invading Caledonia again.

By the time the Romans had returned to British shores, there had been a number of clever protections created, which weren't fully understood by Rome until the Caledonians showed them. One was Caledonia's utilisation of the sea. Caledonia was surrounded by water, which was a source of great wealth through fishing, but it also meant the sea's power could be harnessed to not only power the kingdom but act as a weapon, if needed. Great dams were built at the south of the kingdom, which generated hydropower, but these dams also were a warning to anyone wishing to intimidate or attempt to bully the small kingdom. The dams were fitted with gates and if those literal flood gates were opened the devastation that would be caused on Britannia would be unfathomable. Britannia under water would not be a valuable asset and especially when the Empire viewed Britannia as a key to its bigger objectives of finding a way into the Republic of Indigenous America.

The dams also provided an extensive amount of power to northern parts of Britannia and the Senate, back in Rome, had regularly reminded Nero, when he was alive, that if Caledonia cut off power to parts of Britannia then his grip on the country would weaken considerably. Brits tended to be apathetic about authoritarian rule if it didn't interfere too much with beers after work, but there would definitely be riots if even those small pleasures were taken away.

Indeed, for a small nation, Caledonia wielded a lot of influence over the mighty Empire and emperor after emperor hated that fact. Brute force didn't always win the day and Grand Protector Faust understood this, which is why, after a year of ruling Britannia he had not lost any sleep over the Caledonia situation. In fact, he believed in killing people with kindness and maybe that was the way to subdue the overly confident leaders of the Caledonian Kingdom.

Faust had welcomed the current leader, James Hardie, to London to talk about their ongoing relationship and bestowed Hardie with the most extravagant of welcomes. Hardie wasn't easily impressed, being a staunch socialist who believed the Empire should maybe spread the wealth a lot more, but Faust knew everyone bends when their ego is being massaged. And Hardie did eventually bend. He wasn't hypnotised by Faust's generosity, but he certainly warmed up by the end of the weekend.

Hardie knew about compromise anyway; after all, he had conceded that Caledonia should remain being referred to as a Kingdom, even though it was a republic, because the Caledonian Kingdom was taken more seriously in regard to trading than the Caledonian Republic. Hardie knew it was petty and people shouldn't be so easily swayed by a name, but the human condition was that easily swayed, so he wasn't going to obsess over it. They had also recently struck a lucrative trade deal with members of the Aquitania region, so being pissed at a name felt rather pointless.

So the flight out of Caledonia in the small pteron-chariot was left in peace to fly over Empire-owned waters and onwards toward the Republic of Indigenous America. Tobias and Olivia weren't certain about who they were exactly meeting when they arrived in the RIA, but for all the chaos Boatman had caused, Olivia had to admit she was thankful for the safe route out of Britannia. The RIA was known as a nation that believed in peace over oppression and although they had never publicly criticised any emperor, it was an open secret that they welcomed anyone who opposed the Empire. Boatman's effort was not seen as ideal in his methods, but it was viewed as noble in his intention, and he had formed friends who would look after him and anyone close to him.

Olivia managed to fall asleep even though she was afraid of travelling to somewhere so unknown. The vibrations coming from Molly and the fear she was feeling also eased. Olivia thought that maybe she wasn't picking up on what Molly was feeling because of the distance being created between them, but something niggled in the back of her brain that maybe, just maybe, Molly was somewhere that was actually making her happy.

27

Faust was walking along London Bridge watching as some newly caught rebels were being crucified. Boatman had been chased out of London and the rebel effort was still trying to emulate his prior success, but it wasn't going too well for them. Faust admired their tenacity because he wasn't quite sure what endgame they thought they could achieve. Faust had seen Boatman's endgame and thought he could exploit it. He was impressed that Boatman had anticipated that insight and outmanoeuvred him, twice. Even so, after all the testosterone flying around and the dick-measuring that men do, Boatman was now on the verge of being crucified and all his efforts were pointless.

Faust walked up to a crucifixion point as a rebel was about to be put on the cross. The cross was attached to the hinge of a hollowed post, which was piled into the ground. On the back of the cross was a hydraulic arm that would hoist the cross when necessary. There was also a saline drip bag attached to a panel just below the T of the cross, ready for a drip to be inserted into the rebel in order to prolong the pain.

Faust was proud. History books over the centuries marvelled

at the Roman ability to kill and how, 2000 years ago, no-one killed much more efficiently than the Romans did. In order for an Empire to grow and remain in power, it had to not only carry on killing efficiently, it had to get better at it and also be a bit more terrifying with it. And that's why Faust was proud, because here he was, on London Bridge, in 2031, looking at one of the most brutal methods of killing and admiring the tweaks made to make it even more brutal.

The saline drip was, even for him, sadistic, but the camera mounted on each cross so people could alternate between victims whilst watching online was the next level in voyeurism and masochism. Even though he found it to be overkill and never really understood the attraction of watching someone slowly die, he also knew it was a powerful propaganda tool. It surprised him that even with bodies paraded on this bridge, with people walking past on their daily commute to work, rebels were still popping up every week. They had this naïve belief that they would be able to finish what Boatman started and even as they were crucified, they still thought maybe he would be there to save them. Which he wasn't.

Faust walked over to one of the crucifixion points as a rebel was having his arms pulled wide for the nails to go in. Another ingenious method to improve the speed and efficiency of the process was that straps were tied around the wrists of the victim and attached to pulleys on the ends of the cross where the arms were nailed. With a flick of a switch, the pulleys, which were connected to the same hydraulic system as the arm used to hoist the cross, slowly pulled the victim's arms outward until the wrists were in place for the nails to go through. The mechanical system also stopped the struggle some soldiers had, trying to pull the arms outward. Some people accepted their fate when being crucified and almost willingly stretched their arms out. Others, like the rebel in front of Faust, fought to the end. Instead of soldiers battling to pull the arms out, the straps easily pulled the arms out, ready for the nails. The man tried his hardest to resist, even as his shoulder popped.

The rebel on this particular cross was a man in his seventies. A soldier was about to fire nails through his wrists. Faust held his hand up and the soldier with the nail gun stepped back. Faust stood over the rebel. "What's your name?"

"Who wants to know?"

"I would think you know who I am."

"Sorry, I don't watch the reality show shite."

Faust laughed. "What makes you think I'm a reality show star?"

The rebel looked Faust up and down. "Because you don't look like you've done a hard day's work in your life. I assumed you're here for clicks or stars or whatever bullshit you lot chase after."

"You know, the last time I came here and spoke to a Boatman supporter, he roasted me. I do love the British wit."

"Let me stop you there, young man. Firstly, I'm not interested in banal small talk with you as if that makes your primitive brutality any less shitty. Secondly, I'm not here because of Boatman. I don't support Boatman."

Faust looked over at one of the soldiers who shrugged, indicating he was just the executioner. "What do you mean you don't support Boatman?"

"Boatman can get fucked for all I care," said the older man. "I had a good life before he killed Nero."

"Then why are you here?"

"Well, it seems you lot, if you are a soldier, only like it if you're doing the killing. I was in my local pub, having a beer, when one of Boatman's nutty supporters came in spouting bollocks about forming an uprising. I threw a glass at him, telling him to shut the fuck up and go find people who care. Well, the glass hit him, he fell and split his head open. And just my luck there was a bloody soldier standing there to watch it all."

"You're not serious?"

The older man eyed Faust. "Do I look like I'm joking?"

"It just seems a little far-fetched," said Faust.

"Oh, okay. Far-fetched, hey? Well it's pretty bloody far-fetched that you lot have managed to rule the world for two thousand years when dickheads like you seem more comfortable with a manicure than an angry mob, but here we are."

Faust laughed again. He realised he hadn't laughed properly in what seemed like an age and couldn't believe it was an old man on a cross who had changed that. "You know, considering you're not a follower of Boatman, I could let you go."

"By the gods, spare me from the benevolent crap and expecting me to beg for my life. Just tell that soldier over there, who doesn't look old enough to hold his own dick, let alone a nail gun, to come over here and get on with it."

"Fair enough," said Faust and instructed the young soldier (who did indeed look too young to do anything but piss his own pants) to proceed with the crucifixion. If the young soldier was affected by the older man's jibes, he didn't show it because he pulled the trigger on the nail gun like he'd done it a thousand times.

Faust stayed to watch as the older man was hoisted high on London Bridge for all to see. If the older man had entertained Faust for a split second and maybe kissed his ass slightly, then maybe he would never have been crucified. Then again, although Faust enjoyed the banter, which he seemed to encounter at crucifixions, he was having a shit time with his wife, Alypia, and he was the

Grand Protector of Britannia, and some unknown either didn't know who he was or pretended not to know and that alone was enough to deserve to be nailed high for London to see. He stood and watched the older man struggle to breathe and then looked at his watch. He did it so nonchalantly that the man on the cross would have found the casual gesture of wondering the time as existential agony. Faust smiled at the man's pain.

Faust saw the time, felt his anxiety heighten, stepped away from the cross and strode along London Bridge back toward his chariot, which would take him to the Castrum. He was running late so pulled out his phone and made the scheduled call. The screen came to life and Faust said, "Hail Caesar."

"Hello, Grand Protector," said Maximus. Or, more accurately, said the robotic voice speaking on behalf of Maximus. Even though the voice was artificial and therefore discerning tone was not possible, Faust still felt the mention of his official title was sarcastic.

"How are you, my Lord?"

"Only shit myself once today. How the fuck do you think I am?"

"You have the best medical team in the world, my Lord. You will recover soon, I am sure."

"Recover soon? You know, my father used to speak almost enviously about your intelligence, Grand Protector, but even a child would know I'll be soiling myself like one of those retards my father used to fuck. Did you know about that?"

"About what, my Lord."

"About my father's sexual proclivities."

"It was none of my business. A Caesar can do as he wishes. That's his divine right," said Faust.

"Humour me. I'll give you a divine pass and promise not to execute you for speaking ill of my father."

Faust knew Max's promises were worthless. "I kept away from gossip, my Lord."

"That's obvious."

"How so?"

"Because if you had listened to gossip you would have looked into that slut of a wife of yours."

"I'm sorry, my Lord, I'm not sure what you mean?" Faust did know what he meant. He knew very well, but playing ignorant would bore the young emperor and not spark his sadistic joy in other people's pain.

Maximus rolled his eyes. "Never mind. I don't have time or energy to explain. I hope you have some good news for me to make up for this god-awful video call."

"I have Boatman in custody."

"I'll need proof."

Faust switched to the photo application on his phone and sent Max a photo of Boatman in the Castrum. "I would like to schedule his crucifixion for a few days' time, to be streamed around the world."

"Well, well, well. I underestimated you, Grand Protector. And I have something very special for you." Max sent Faust a photo of Maverick, unconscious on a bed.

"Is he alive?"

"He is."

"Should we crucify them together?"

"No, I have a better idea. I will be in touch," said Max and cut the call.

The screen went black, and Faust put his phone away. He pulled his phone out again, to check the call had ended and then said to himself, "Fucking prick." Faust wasn't sentimental and didn't need praise to excel at his job, but Max's lack of enthusiasm about

Boatman's capture and condescending withholding of information about future plans made him wish Maverick had done the job properly and beaten the little shit's skull to a pulp.

28

Maverick woke up, strapped to a bed. He tried to break free, but the straps didn't budge. The bed whirred and the top half rose, putting Maverick into a sitting position. In the room with him was Emperor Maximus. Maverick took in the sight of the emperor's skull, which had been caved in on the right-hand side, and was still confused how anyone could survive that. Hair hadn't grown back properly on it, so there was an attempt at a comb-over using wispy strands of hair. Even though he hadn't managed to kill Max, Maverick was pleased it appeared he had made the Roman's life a misery. Looking at the wheelchair and various tubes protruding from the young Caesar, Maverick thought that maybe death would be a relief.

"You look like shit," said Maverick. "And someone needs to be straight with you and tell you that having your hair like that makes you look like an idiot."

Max started typing and his artificial voice said, "You can mock me all you want, I have you now."

Maverick squinted and then his booming laugh bounced off the walls. "That's how you speak now? I just need to put a blade in your hand and you'd be a mobile, talking can opener." Maverick laughed again. "You know, I came all this way to cave the other side of your skull in, because I was pissed off I didn't do it properly the first time, but I'm actually happy I did fail." He was still laughing.

"You won't be laughing soon."

"Sorry, can you turn the bass up a bit, you're coming across a little tinny."

"You think you're funny, swordsman, but humour won't save you," said Max.

"It doesn't matter what you say, that stupid robot voice of yours means I can't take it seriously. Tobias would have loved seeing this."

"Tobias? I'm afraid to tell you that he's no longer hiding away in Meresig." This time Maverick did stop laughing. "He ran away, like the coward he is, and left Boatman all alone."

"Bullshit."

"Is it?" Maximus pulled up a photo of Boatman in custody in the Castrum and turned his phone to face Maverick.

Maverick said, "That's a fake."

"I don't need to fake things when it comes to your pathetic rebellion."

"Pathetic? You won't be calling us pathetic when I'm caving your skull in."

"I doubt it will be my skull you'll be caving in based on what's in store for you in a few days."

"By the gods, can we not do the vague threat thing like you're creating some sort of dramatic effect? And please get straight to the point, because that robotic voice is already driving me insane."

Maximus went red faced and typed again. The voice said, "How about this, then." Maximus pulled up another app and bounced what was on his phone on to a screen in the room.

The screen on the wall, opposite Maverick, blinked into life and a video started to stream. It was a promotional video advertising *The Greatest Fight of the Century*. The video faded to black and a menacing tune began, with drums pounding. Maverick didn't need to see what was going to appear next, because he knew. Nevertheless, the video did continue and computer-generated images of Maverick and Boatman appeared on the screen with jumpy cuts of very old footage of when Maverick was a gladiator and CGI of Boatman in a gladiator ring. Maverick didn't look away from the screen. He wasn't going to give Maximus any indication that his anxiety was rising, and rising fast. Tobias would ask Maverick, when they were curled up in bed, if he ever got scared and Maverick would say that he did, and he got scared often. The thing was, it was impossible to tell with Maverick. Strapped to a bed, watching a trailer advertising his imminent gladiatorial combat with the man who killed an emperor, Maverick still didn't give off any sign that he was concerned. The truth was, he finally understood the fear his opponents felt when they knew they were going to face someone they couldn't beat.

"What do you think?" Maximus asked.

"I think you need to focus your energy on something else, like learning how to go to the toilet."

"I'm going to enjoy watching Boatman gut you."

"Boatman won't fight me," said Maverick, "And I won't fight him. You're going to have a lot of people pissed at watching two men refusing to fight each other."

"You will fight each other."

Maverick scoffed, "What are you going to do, round us up in your wheelchair, like sheep, and force us to fight?"

"I won't need to force you to fight." Maximus tapped his phone again and another stream was projected on to the screen. This time it was a live stream of Damba in the courtyard below Max's quarters. He was tied to a post and a soldier was whipping him. He was topless, and the leather whip was tearing through his skin. Damba's arms were tied together above his head and attached to a ring in the top of the post. His legs kept giving way, but he couldn't collapse.

"You sick fuck," said Maverick. "He betrayed me for you."

"I'm a sick fuck? Faust told me that on the day you did this to me," Max pointed to his head, "you also tore a soldier's jaw off. I would think you're screwed when it comes to taking the moral high ground. And Damba didn't betray you for me, he betrayed you for the Empire. Big difference."

"I promise, I will still cave the other side of your skull in. And rip your jaw off."

"I don't doubt your sincerity, swordsman, but it will have to be after you kill Boatman, because unless you fight him, I will keep having Damba whipped until his flesh is peeled from his bones. That's how I herd you. That's how I force you. Refuse to fight and Damba will be torn apart and he will be cursing you with every dying breath knowing it was you who had the power over his life."

"Boatman won't fight me."

"It doesn't matter if he does or doesn't. If he doesn't, well, it will be a quick death."

"I'm not killing a man who refuses to fight back."

"You did it easy enough with me."

"Clearly I didn't, because you're still talking," said Maverick. "Sort of."

"The more you mock a Caesar, the greater the punishment from the gods, Maverick. You should be aware of the anger you're brewing with the gods."

"What on earth did you do to the gods then? Because I can imagine only being able to speak in vowels because of what a black man did to you is the worst form of punishment possible."

Maximus ignored yet another jibe from Maverick and wheeled out of the room. He was going to enjoy watching Boatman slash that arrogant prick to bits. At the same time, he felt sad. He had adored Maverick since he was a child. He had waited up in the night to watch Maverick's fights and collected the Gladiator Top Fighter cards every season. Maverick had been a part of his life since he was a teenager, and he was enamoured of him. He felt angry having met Maverick and the man was such a savage. His grandfather had said it was foolish to meet your heroes, but Max thought that nonsense, until now. Maverick was obnoxious and Max was now wondering how he had ever looked at the man as anything but a tool for better ratings for his Empire TV channel.

Maximus got to his quarters and instructed all staff to leave. He needed to be alone. He needed to think about how he would make Maverick suffer. Heroes are only heroes when they do what you imagine them to do. Seeing Maverick made Maximus realise there's no such thing as a hero. If that was the case, then heroes were as fallible as the peasants starving on Roman streets. And if that was the case, then Maximus decided he was going to make sure Maverick knew what it was like to feel like a peasant.

29

Faust sat on the steps outside the Castrum and put a cigarette in his mouth. The Castrum was the main hub of all Roman operations in London. It was colloquially referred to as the HoC because of its previous incarnation when the British used it for democratic debate. That was nearly a hundred years ago, though, so democratic debate was one of those whimsical things people spoke about like when they believed their god would stop Roman invasion. The British were known for having delusions of grandeur and during the time Rome hadn't invaded thought they were somehow protected from invasion because they had gods more powerful than the Romans' gods. They thought they had been specially selected to show the Empire would eventually fall because the world around Britannia was collapsing and yet they were still resisting. That completely changed, though.

The Empire didn't fall, but the British arrogance did, and with that arrogance so did the cohesion Britannia enjoyed. When Roman troops stepped foot on the shores of Britannia again, the population divided over who was to blame. As Faust puffed his cigarette and watch Londoners walk by, he smiled to himself at how easy it was to manipulate people. Maybe he found it easy because of his memory palace, maybe it was because people were just that bloody easy to manipulate. Faust had arrived in London many years after Emperor Augustus II had swept through towns and cities, taking back control. What Faust had found, when he was assigned a post as a Centurion was that the Brits were pissed off at each other more than the Empire. They blamed each other for their lives not being what they believed they should be. It was like they refused to acknowledge they were being controlled by another force and the only reason they were in the mess they were in was because of other Brits not doing the right thing for the greater good of the nation.

As Faust smoked he took a stroll through his memory palace to dig out some history on when a nation's population turned on each other over their woes as to what was likely a force beyond them. The library of his palace was on the outskirts of it in the meadow area. Knowledge had to be an open, accessible thing, which made his world history library completely appropriate to be in a sunny, abundant meadow. The books weren't on shelves but acted like petals on thousands of flowers. When Faust plucked a book from a flower, it magnified in size and opened to where Faust needed it. The book he plucked analysed the history of scapegoating throughout cultures and history of humankind. It didn't appear to matter what race, religion or culture Faust read about, scapegoating was almost like a foundation of human history. Tribes and nations used scapegoating consciously and unconsciously to find a way to understand why bad things happened to them. Instead of looking for a solution through the good nature of humanity, a scapegoat was a much easier solution. If there's a drought, use a scapegoat. If there's a flood, use a scapegoat. Scapegoats were either literally sacrificed to the gods to try and appease them and bring balance to the people or, like Faust was seeing in Britannia, sacrificed figuratively. Faust's encounter with the older man on London Bridge highlighted that a bit of propaganda, a squeezing of people's liberties and the ones trying to help become the ones being blamed. Not all the public were turned against Boatman, but there was enough ill feeling toward the rebel leader, based on polls conducted, that Boatman's demise wouldn't cause too much unrest.

The whereabouts of Olivia King bothered Faust, though. And Boatman's nihilistic comment that she was somewhere dangerous didn't seem right. He went back into his memory palace and pulled up the conversation he had shared with Boatman and the words the rebel used: *where being spared isn't an option.* Maybe where she was meant there was no need to be spared because it was a safe place, and sparing or not sparing never entered into the equation.

Faust called Delilah and said that she and Sebastian needed to try and find Olivia. There would be a trail, and it needed to be followed. Delilah squealed at the prospect of another hunt. Faust grimaced at the sound. He was fully experienced in death and destruction and had enough blood on his hands to last an eternity, but the delight of tracking someone down to inflict misery was unpleasant, even for Faust. It was undeniable that she and her brother were the best at what they did and had justified the existence of the B-Unit.

Maybe Faust's analysis of Boatman's words was a dead end, but maybe, just maybe, it was yet another weapon to use and finally put the bastard rebel and his followers in the ground for good.

30

The Grand Protector of Britannia walked back into the Castrum and made his way to the medical wing. In an almost mirror image of Maverick in Rome, Boatman was strapped to a bed and in a sitting position. He too was awake, but he wasn't exhibiting Maverick's humour. The look he was giving though, made Faust pause for a moment to check Boatman was fully strapped to the bed.

"I have something to show you," said Faust.

"I'm not interested."

"You will be," said Faust and turned the television on in Boatman's room.

The same trailer Maverick had seen a few hours before now appeared and Boatman watched as the trailer advertising the fight between Maverick and Boatman was played. As usual, Boatman didn't react to what he was watching. He didn't hesitate to speak as soon as the trailer finished though. "You think you're going to be able to make me and Maverick fight?"

"That's the thing. I thought the same as you; that there's no way you two will fight each other. You both couldn't give a shit about our threats to your lives. But then Caesar reminded me that you both do care about other people and you'll do whatever you can to save them."

"There's only one person Maverick cares about and I know for a fact you don't know where he is."

"Really? Only one person he cares about?"

"Well, other than Tobias, there's Damba, but he's dea—" Boatman stopped in his tracks.

"Dead? No. No, not so much."

Boatman felt his confidence leave his body like a tyre losing air because of a massive puncture. He always felt like he had a way to get out of a situation but at every turn the options for success were becoming fewer and fewer. He had thought being presented to Faust like a sacrificial lamb was ideal to get close enough to kill Faust, but he was wrong. He had thought Maverick would have actually turned back from his mission in Rome and come to London, but he was wrong. He was fairly confident Tobias, Olivia and Molly had made their way to safety, but now he wasn't so sure and doubted they were even alive. If Maverick had been subdued, then maybe Olivia and Tobias weren't protected by the escape plan Boatman had put together. They had been strict in refusing to contact each other, so that the Empire couldn't intercept any communications and locate them, but in return for that, the uncertainty of anyone's safety intensified. And now he was hearing of Maverick's brother possibly still in Max's captivity.

"Even if Maverick was cornered, I know for a fact he wouldn't sacrifice his integrity and fight me."

"Integrity?" Faust chewed on that word. "You rebels like to think of yourselves as innocents."

"I seem to recall holding my wife as she was struggling to stay alive after being crucified."

160

"And I seem to remember picking up the pieces of one of my soldiers after you were done with him."

"He enjoyed killing. I'm not going to feel any sympathy."

"But you're the good guy."

"I'm not oppressing a nation."

Faust laughed. "Your ideological crap might have worked using some of your shitty leaflets a few years ago, but let's be honest, Mr King, the only difference between you and me is the fact that I happen to have the symbol of the oppressors who are winning."

"Like I said, I've never been an oppressor."

"By the gods, Boatman, for the leader of the most influential rebellion in a millennium you're either very naïve or deliberately ignorant."

"I've made difficult choices, but I'm not an oppressor."

"Yes, I'm sure the times you've executed my soldiers you have grappled with the existential conundrum of it."

"And I'm sure as you force me to fight Maverick to the death you're grappling with the existential crisis of that."

"There's no existential crisis when it comes to weeds."

"You see us as weeds?"

Faust had found a seat against the wall where the television was but hadn't been able to stay seated for long. He paced the room, impatient and frustrated. "You see yourself as something other than that?"

Boatman strained against his restraints. "Fuck you for even questioning that."

"Boatman, all you rebels have done is sprout up and try to suffocate what Rome is trying to achieve. Yes, we see you as weeds."

"There are plenty of people who see us as beautiful."

"Your country has plenty of beautiful weeds."

"I should have killed you when I had the chance," said Boatman.

"But you didn't. And here we are," smiled Faust. "But enough of the small talk you love so much." Faust pulled up an app on his phone and bounced what was on it onto the television screen. It was a video call, and when the call was answered it showed an image of Maverick in the same position as Boatman; strapped to a bed in a sitting position. Maverick and Boatman just stared at each other. "Well, come on, say hello. You must have missed each other."

The rebels didn't say anything for a minute or so, both trying to work out how the hell they had got into this situation and also how the hell they would get out.

"Are you okay?" Boatman broke the silence.

"No. Not one bit. Tobias was always right. I'm a fucking idiot when it comes to my brother."

"You've seen him? Damba?"

Maverick took a deep breath and said, "I've seen him. He's why I'm in this situation."

"I don't understand," said Boatman.

"Neither do I," said Maverick.

"Whatever happens," said Boatman, "remember our promise to always allow one of us to be free to fly in this world and to expose the bullshit of this Imperial bollocks."

Maverick nodded. "Will do, boss." Maverick smiled. "I'll see you in the ring."

Faust had sat down to watch the interaction between the two men but was bored by their sentimentality. "That's enough between you two," said Faust and before the rebels were even able to say goodbye, Faust cut the call.

Boatman didn't get angry; he was amazed he was given the opportunity to speak to Maverick. He thought Faust's arrogance has grown even more for him to have allowed the rebels to communicate with each other. There must have been confidence in their security to feel able to let Boatman and Maverick speak like that, but then Boatman wondered if Faust's arrogance was guiding his life right now. For Faust, he was holding all the cards, so there was no harm in letting the rebels have a video call before they met each other in the gladiator ring.

"I wonder," said Faust, "how will you kill The Beast when you meet him in the ring?"

"If I ever have to kill Maverick, you'll be long dead before that happens."

"Your romanticism will be your undoing, Boatman. You don't have any wriggle room on this. There's no silver bullet you can produce. If you don't fight Maverick, he will kill you to save his brother." Faust pulled his chair next to Boatman's bed, "Can you really stand there and let an inferior fighter cut you down?"

"I did with you."

Faust laughed, "And look where it got you." Faust stood up and said, "See you in the ring."

"What?"

"Come on, you didn't think after you kill The Beast, that would be the end of your challenge? If you want your freedom, then how better to earn it than defeat the Grand Protector of Britannia?"

"You're insane."

"Maybe," said Faust. "But it keeps the nation servile knowing there's going to be a fight between their leader and the former people's hero."

"Like I said, you're insane."

31

A year previously, Faust had been to the Britannia Colosseum in London to meet with Boatman and discuss a truce and deal to dethrone Emperor Nero II. Faust had watched as Boatman had arrived along with his little group of followers. It wasn't going to be a meeting, but an ambush, so Faust changed his plans and put Tobias in hospital. The new Colosseum had been shut for many years because of poor planning by the architects and builders, who didn't take into account the fact that London's riverside was covered in oyster shells. Most houses had foundations of oyster shells, so the Colosseum was no different. But when it was built, none of that was taken into consideration and the replica of Rome's famous building started to slide and was therefore unsafe for anyone to use. After Faust had been made Grand Protector, he decided it was an abomination to have the new Colosseum sit there empty and slowly rotting. It was an embarrassment and made the Empire look weak. Nero was dead and Maximus was a dribbling mess in hospital, so the Senate needed someone to bring balance.

Faust was the man. Faust drilled home to the Senate that if he were to bring balance to the Empire, then they needed to show it with their gold. Faust demanded that the Senate pour gold into the work needed to make the new Colosseum safe, as that venue would be the centrepiece of London entertainment. It would also be a powerful statement that Roman rule was not defeated by Boatman but made stronger in spite of Boatman. It had been built decades before, when Emperor Maximius's grandfather, Augustus II, ruled the Empire. When Nero came into power, he lost interest in trying to put the building right. Boatman's rebellion added to resources being siphoned elsewhere. To save some face, Legatus Titus would release a statement that the Colosseum remained closed because the threat of a terrorist attack from the rebels was too great and the Colosseum was a prime target.

After a year of intense and expensive work on the foundations of the Colosseum and huge investment in its structure, it was ready to be opened to the public. Faust thought having Boatman crucified in the middle of the Colosseum in front of a sold-out audience, streamed around the world, was the ideal event to mark its relaunch.

Maximus though, had other ideas and Faust, admittedly, thought it a better idea. A gladiator match between the world's best-ever gladiator and the world's most feared rebel. It would be a global sensation. Throw into the mix that Faust would fight the winner of The Beast versus Boatman… well, people would be so buzzed for it they would definitely forget the added oppression coming from the Empire.

Faust was correct in his assumption because on the day of the bout, which had been made a public holiday in Britannia, the streets were teeming with tourists and residents, eager to get as close to the action as possible. The schedule of the day's events had been advertised for months leading up to *Beast Vs Boatman*, including a procession through the streets of London, where Maverick and Boatman would be paraded in front of the public so people could get a glimpse of the fighter they were supporting. Both fighters were in separate, bullet-proof chariots that meandered through the streets on their way to the Britannia Colosseum. Faust didn't want to take any chances with such a public display of the fighters so not only were the chariots reinforced with bulletproof glass, they were flanked by a dozen soldiers each.

It was unlikely anyone would attempt to break the prisoners free, considering the abundance of security in the city, but Boatman and Maverick still had some dedicated followers willing to make a sacrifice to save their heroes. The online buzz for the fight had been fervent, with viral sharing of the event throughout sites such as Post-Me, the Empire approved community site. Viral videos were being shared in the millions of old footage of when Maverick was a gladiator and the most feared fighter in the world. Supercuts of Maverick's best kills were being shared by people of all ages. Maverick had been infamous throughout the Empire at the peak of his career. People were terrified of him, but there were also many who felt spurred by him. They wanted to prove Maverick wasn't the invincible fighter that everyone thought he was and show the world The Beast could easily be defeated. Those who had the gold paid to prove they could obliterate The Beast. Their blood spilled on the ring floor or their heads removed cleanly from their bodies proved otherwise.

As with humanity throughout time, history always repeated itself and now, with footage of Maverick surfacing again and a gladiator match about to commence, there were very rich men and women already bidding to fight Maverick if he survived the matches with Boatman and Faust. Maybe they thought they were better fighters than anyone who had been before them. Maybe they thought Maverick had been out of the gladiator game for so long he would be rusty enough to get an advantage over. Or maybe they wanted the fame. Whatever the reason, the Empire was seeing huge amounts of gold being spent in Britannia as a result of the match and huge amounts of gold being spent on adverting revenue. *Beast Vs Boatman* was not only helping grow the Empire's riches but was also a powerful propaganda tool.

Interspersed between footage of Maverick fighting, trailers advertising the fight and pundits giving their views on who would win the epic battle, there were also talking heads of random members of the public giving their views on the match. The Empire made a point of getting lots of footage of people who were usually against something as barbaric and archaic as a gladiator match, but how their opinion had changed considering how much the occasion was uniting the nation. And who doesn't love an extra national holiday in a year?

The Beast Vs Boatman was billed as the greatest gladiator match since Priscus Vs Verus in AD 80. The epic match, two thousand years ago, lasted for over three hours until both men surrendered to each other by laying down their weapons. The fight was of such a standard and brutal flair that Emperor Titus, who had been watching the match, gave both gladiators their freedom. A film had been made by the Empire's production company, dramatising the fight as the greatest duel in history. There had been a massive spike in views of the film since the announcement of the fight, as if people were getting themselves in the mood for the brutality.

Now the day had arrived, and Faust looked around the Britannia Colosseum at the eighty-thousand-strong crowd from the balcony inside the stadium. Emperor Maximus was with him, the beeps from the monitor attached to his wheelchair inaudible because of the cheers and roars of the eager crowd. Faust had been watching the polls online, curious as to who the public thought would win. Maverick seemed to be winning public opinion, but Faust suspected that was more because Boatman's abilities were a mystery to most. Only a handful of people were able to recount Boatman's almost supernatural fighting skills.

Faust was one of them. He had only survived an encounter with Boatman because he had analysed Boatman's skills from the luxury of his memory palace, which gave him insight into Boatman's fighting style. He had seen Boatman fight from some old CCTV footage when Boatman easily dispatched half a dozen soldiers and Faust revisited that footage again and again inside his memory palace. It gave him the skills he needed to face Boatman a year ago and almost win, and it gave him the skills he would need to defeat Boatman in the ring if need be.

The Britannia Colosseum was about to host its first ever gladiator match and that was history in the making. It was also about to be the setting for the Grand Protector of Britannia executing Boatman King, the rebel who killed an emperor. That? Well, that would go down as legend.

32

In the lower levels, beneath the Colosseum, Maverick and Boatman were waiting in separate areas. They could hear the noise of the crowd. Music was blaring throughout the stadium, exciting the crowd and getting them to sing and dance along until the main the event. The source of the music was a band on a main stage, singing classic anthems such as *We are the Empire* and *Eye of the Caesar.* The stamping of eighty-thousand feet made the lower levels tremor and Boatman clenched his jaw at how easily people were whipped into a frenzy. He was sure there were people in the crowd who, a year ago, would have been claiming they would do anything for Boatman and the rebellion. Now they were baying for blood.

Maverick, too, sat and listened to the music vibrating through the ceiling and assumed he would feel dread waiting below the arena, listening to the chants of the crowd. He assumed it would bring back only anger and resentment toward the life he once had. As he sat on a bench, tying the laces on his boots, he was surprised at the exhilaration he was feeling. The rush he felt before a fight was pumping through him.

Years before, when he had waited to be called, he felt the rush of knowing he was about to fight because he knew, whoever it was out there, he would beat them. Easily. This time though, he was feeling the rush because, for the second time in his life, he wasn't sure if he could win. And in some ways, that made him feel more alive than ever before. Maverick was used to being feared and people cowering in his presence. He was used to seeing that nervous look in their eyes, where they would subconsciously look around, hoping someone would come to their rescue, but then realising the hopelessness of the situation.

This time, though, when he would face Boatman, he wouldn't see that look of fear. He wouldn't see hopelessness or despair. He would see the same look he always had in the arena: assurance. The Beast was always assured of his skills and abilities, and he knew Boatman would be the same. No, this time was very likely going to be his last time and it would be a fitting way to go.

He was going to fight, too, because if he didn't then his brother would die. He tried to push thoughts of Tobias into a box in his mind because to think of Tobias too much quite simply hurt his heart. He loved that man, and it ached not to see him or to hear from him, but he had no idea whether Tobias was alive. Boatman had given him a clue during their video call, but it was a scrap of a clue and gave no comfort or certainty that Maverick's fiancé was safe. He wanted to believe Tobias had managed to elude the Empire but, with all due respect to his boyfriend, Tobias found confidence and comfort when someone else was leading and the two leaders he found most comfort from were about to fight each other to the death.

Maverick had once told Tobias that the only thing or person he feared was Boatman. Now, sitting in a sparse and dimly lit room, waiting to fight Boatman, he realised he was lying; the only thing he feared was losing Tobias. When Tobias had almost died, Maverick ran. He felt ashamed for doing so and his face even reddened whilst sitting alone. He made out he was seeking revenge for what had happened to Olivia and how the situation had acted as a catalyst for Tobias to be injured, but he was deceiving himself. He ran because he was scared of seeing Tobias die. He took the coward's way out and believed if Tobias was out of sight then he would be out of mind and if he couldn't see it happening then maybe it wasn't. He was acting like a child who puts their fingers over their eyes and believes the world has disappeared because they can't see it. His vision went blurry as tears dampened his eyelashes and he wiped his eyes with the back of his hand. By the gods, he missed his boyfriend. He half laughed and half cried as he realised he even missed Tobias's incessant whinging.

"When are you going to set a date?" Tobias had asked Maverick just over a year ago, before Faust had hospitalised him.

"A date for what?"

"Oh, it's great to see you care as much as always."

Maverick was sharpening his sword. "Tobias, before I shove this sword up your ass, you need to be more specific."

"We've been engaged for three years, Mav, I would have thought you would have set a date by now."

"I'm not sure if you've noticed, but we've just got home from killing a patrol of soldiers and tomorrow we're planning on blowing up a Centurion. Excuse me if booking a priest has slipped my mind."

"There's plenty of couples out who work full-time and still find the time to plan a wedding."

"Have you hit your head or something?" Maverick asked his boyfriend. "Because Gallus and Matteus who own a little trinket store by London Bridge selling, 'London Crucified Me' T-Shirts are going to have a bit more time to choose flowers than we are, Tobias."

Tobias huffed. "I bet you don't even know what my favourite flower is."

"Seriously, how did you survive that many years in a gladiator ring?"

"I tended to get scheduled to fight someone you ended up fighting a few days before. The ones I did end up fighting were so shaky, they would have died from being spoken to a bit harshly."

Maverick stopped sharpening his sword. "And you don't see the irony in what you just said?"

Maverick wiped his eyes again as he thought about the silly conversations he would have with Tobias and prayed to the gods, even the God-Carpenter Tobias worshiped, that he would find a way out of this situation and that Tobias was still alive. The fear of losing Tobias motivated him to find a way to freedom. It dawned on him that he was willing to plough through Boatman to get back to the man he loved.

The music in the Colosseum stopped and the beating of drums began. It was time.

Boatman and Maverick made their separate ways to the entrance to the arena.

33

Maverick was standing at an entrance on the east side of the arena and Boatman on the west side. That way when they were announced the drama of them walking toward each other would make the crowd go wild. Which it did. Maverick 'The Beast' Kirabo was introduced to roars of delight and applause. The stadium chanted his name and Maverick felt like he had never left the gladiator game. Boatman King was introduced to much more restrained applause and whistles and boos scattered through the Colosseum. Faust smiled at the crowd's reaction; it meant the work he had done in feeding negative propaganda about the rebel leader was working, that it had made many people cynical of the previously adored Boatman.

Before the men had even entered the arena they had been asked, a couple of weeks before, to choose their weapons. Maverick chose the Gladius sword, which had always been his favourite. The version of this sword that he used though, had been modified to make it more effective as a weapon. It had a double-edged blade and a protective hilt. It meant Maverick was able to inflict damage when swinging the sword either way and at least give himself a chance against Boatman.

Boatman too chose a sword, a Cutlass, which had a thick curved blade and large hand guard. It was effective against heavy blows but light enough for fast movements and intimate fighting conditions like a gladiator match. He also wore metal vambraces that would protect his forearms against the inevitable barrage of blows coming from Maverick.

The two men walked across the large arena floor to the roar of the crowd, with huge screens erected throughout the Britannia Colosseum replaying the trailer advertising the bout. It was a wall of noise and Boatman despised it. He hated crowds and he hated being centre of attention in this way. When he'd married Olivia, he'd said he didn't want to do anything with too many people in attendance and to keep it very subdued. Olivia had initially laughed at Boatman's request. "You're the leader of the most famous rebellion in the Empire, why would you want a low-key wedding?"

"Because that's how I've stayed the leader of the most famous rebellion in the Empire, by not entertaining loads of people."

Boatman was a confident, effective and, at times, scary leader, but he wasn't an entertainer. He wasn't like Maverick, who enjoyed the adrenaline of the crowds and of all focus being on him. Tobias commented when they had been a couple a short while that Maverick was different in the arena to in private. Maverick had replied that to be a gladiator was to put on a mask and give the crowds what they want. He also said, in a quieter voice, that being The Beast in the arena helped him compartmentalise what he was doing so he could separate it from the Maverick sitting at his kitchen table having a coffee. Boatman and Maverick were very different men inside and outside of the gladiator ring and at this moment in time, with the Britannia audience clapping and cheering, Maverick was the one absorbing it with pleasure and enjoying the spectacle.

176

The men stopped when they both got to the centre of the arena and were within six feet of each other. The noise was hitting levels that made Boatman want to put his sword to the crowd. He stepped forward a foot. "I'm sorry it's come to this."

"It was probably always going to come to this."

Boatman frowned. "How so?"

"Because I started in an arena, it's only fitting my life ends in the arena."

"Our lives aren't ending here, Mav, we always find a way."

"Our lives? There's only one life that emerges from a fight like this."

"I'm not going to kill you."

"Yes, you will."

"Maverick, I won't."

"You will, because I won't give you a choice."

Before Boatman could say anything else, Faust spoke through a microphone, calling the crowd to silence. "Welcome to the Britannia Colosseum and the greatest fight in a millennium!"

The crowd clapped and cheered. Faust waited for the noise to subside. "It's an honour to be your host this afternoon for what will be an event to be remembered for years to come. It would not have been possible without the skill and brilliance of your emperor, Caesar Maximus!" More clapping and cheering. Not as fervent as it was for Maverick, noticed Faust. "Please give a warm, Britannia welcome to Caesar Maximus!"

Faust stretched out his hand in the direction of the emperor who was sitting on the balcony with Faust, overlooking the crowd and the stadium floor. He held up his hand in greeting and chants of "Hail Caesar" echoed out. The huge speakers in the stadium were also playing the greeting, making it appear the chanting was more exuberant than it really was. Maximus held up both his hands to quieten the crowd and then his robotic voice said, "Let battle commence." The sound of a shotgun being fired initiated the start of the fight between Boatman and The Beast.

Boatman hesitated. He rarely hesitated, but this time he did. He was used to fighting in battle and he was used to fighting for a purpose related to the rebellion. This was a fight with a good friend in order to entertain the masses. His brain was struggling to process that. Maverick's brain wasn't struggling with the same conundrum, and he rushed at Boatman and brought his sword in an overhead arc, straight at Boatman's head. Boatman was a good half a foot shorter than Maverick, which gave The Beast a ripe-looking target: the top of Boatman's skull.

Luckily for Boatman, even though he had hesitated, his innate ability to counter most attacks meant his muscle memory kicked in and his body reacted before the conscious part of his brain registered it; he crossed his forearms above the top of his head. Maverick's sword connected with Boatman's vambraces, and Boatman went down onto one knee as he absorbed the blow. Boatman then pushed his arms up, driving the sword away. It was Maverick's turn to hesitate as he had put a lot of effort into that blow and most men would have ended up sprawled across the floor. Boatman took advantage of Maverick's surprise that he hadn't caused Boatman's spine to concertina and stepped into the Ugandan's space, bringing his sword up to gut his opponent. As Boatman swung his sword upward, his conscious brain kicked into gear that he was about to gut his dear friend and his arms tensed in reaction to that, trying to stop the momentum. Momentum does what momentum does, and the sword's trajectory was on course for spilling Maverick's intestines all over the arena floor, regardless of Boatman's last-minute change of mind. Even though Maverick had hesitated, he too found his body instinctively reacting to danger because of years of combat, and he grabbed the tip of his sword and brought it down, horizontally. The thin edge of the Gladius sword's blade connected with the thin edge of the Cutlass's blade and the shear force generated from that knocked both men backwards. The crowd gasped as it looked like the fighters had been struck by a surge of electricity with the way they were both floored.

Maverick got to one knee and shook his head, trying to focus, whereas Boatman was already on his feet and raising his sword. Maverick rolled backwards to give himself a fraction more time and then was on his feet again. Their swords met with immense force again, and the metal clanged and scraped as they exchanged blows. Boatman was on the back foot, retreating as they fought. Maverick's strength caused his sword to push the rebel leader back. Even in the midst of the fight, a thought bubbled in Maverick's brain that Boatman wasn't giving it his all. Four years previously, when the men had first met, they had fought, and Boatman had made Maverick look like an amateur. Boatman barely broke a sweat that time, fighting Maverick. This time, Boatman was struggling to contain the ex-gladiator's ferocity and Maverick was sceptical of it. He decided to test his theory and recklessly raised his sword high to do an ill-thought downward strike. The move left his whole body exposed and if his theory was wrong then Boatman would have the opportunity to kill him in an instant. Boatman didn't take the opportunity, as Maverick predicted, and stepped to the side instead. Maverick was surprised at the sidestep, though; he was used to men falling backwards as his giant figure loomed. This was where Maverick was wrong in his prediction because Boatman tripped Maverick over by using Maverick's forward momentum against him. Maverick then rejected his initial theory about Boatman's restraint as Boatman's sword was on the nape of his neck before he had time to get to his feet again. Boatman moved with such speed that Maverick wondered if the man was one of the gods the Romans spent so much time praying to.

The Beast felt the coolness of metal on the back of his neck and for the first time in his life understood what mortality felt like. And the feeling wasn't great. He had convinced himself that he would be okay with dying without seeing Tobias again, but it was a brutal and gut-wrenching hopelessness that spread through his body when the finality of his death neared. Knowing he wouldn't see his fiancé ever again was not okay. He wanted to cry out to Boatman to stop, but his ego would never allow such a thing.

The Beast would never be known to surrender. So he didn't. He started to stand up instead, pushing back against the sword on his neck. Boatman had a choice to push back and, essentially, let Maverick kill himself or ease off the pressure to allow Maverick to stand. Boatman let Maverick stand. He was always going to let his friend stand. It was at that moment both men realised the stadium was almost silent. The two men had been slugging it out, amazing the crowd with their skills, and when it had seemed certain death for The Beast, the crowd had quietened. It truly revealed the mood of the public about both fighters.

Both men stared at one another, breathing hard and wondering how they could continue the match if no-one was willing to kill the other one. Faust could see it too, so made sure there was an incentive and radioed through to the comms team. In a matter of seconds, on the stadium screens, there was footage of Damba being lashed by soldiers. Maverick felt his knees go weak as he was reminded why he had to keep fighting. It was irrelevant if he won or lost, but he couldn't drag the fight out or put little effort in so it was a draw like in the past, because this time, if Maverick didn't fight, Damba would die. If Maverick tried to avoid fighting, Damba would die. Maverick had to fight with all of his might and commitment and not delay, because any stalling meant Damba would die. Which is why he had tried to throw the fight without it seeming like he had, so that at least he would die and his brother would live and he also wouldn't have had to kill his friend and make another friend a widow. Boatman wasn't on his wavelength, though, and now Damba was being tortured again.

"Please finish me," said Maverick.

"What?"

"You need to fight me properly and kill me," said Maverick.

"Why?"

Maverick paced, angry and scared, "Because they'll do that to Damba every day otherwise," he said.

"We can save Damba," said Boatman.

"Olivia once said to me that the only way you were able to be such an effective leader was because you were so naïve. I thought she was talking nonsense because I've seen what you can do." Maverick was still pacing. "But she's right. You are so naïve. This isn't a moment where Boatman saves the day. This is a moment where Boatman realises we're screwed and does the right thing." Maverick pointed at one of the big screens where footage of Damba being flogged within an inch of his life was being broadcast. "There's no clever escape on this one, all our teams have been driven out of London. I can't have my brother tortured anymore. You need to save him," said Maverick and lunged at Boatman.

Boatman parried the blow from Maverick and elbowed the Ugandan in the face with a right hook. Maverick stumbled back but came at the rebel leader again. This time he spun his sword around and used the hilt of his sword to uppercut Boatman, which he then intended to spin the sword back round in his hand and as Boatman stumbled back, head tilted back, he would be able to take Boatman's head clean off. That would have got the crowd roaring with pleasure if it had happened, but Maverick only got as far as spinning his sword round and aiming a shot underneath Boatman's chin when Boatman blocked the shot with his forearm and then headbutted Maverick square in the face. Maverick's vision blurred and as he tried to gain focus, Boatman did what any fighter does to gain control over a man and kicked The Beast in the groin.

Maverick went down on one knee and saw a foot coming directly for his head. His hands went up and managed to stop the full force of the blow and grab enough of Boatman's foot to force him off balance. Boatman fell backwards, but rolled away before Maverick was on top of him. He got to his feet and Maverick was on all fours, just getting to his feet again. Boatman kicked Maverick's temple with such brutality he thought this was the moment he would be killing his friend. Maverick went down, but within seconds was back on his knees shaking his head as if trying to get rid of a nasty thought.

Again, Boatman hesitated as he couldn't go through with what his friend was asking. Yes, Damba was Mav's brother, but he was a complete stranger to Boatman. He couldn't kill Maverick to save the life of a stranger. He was certain there was a way out, and he would find it. Maverick was out of hope so left him no choice but to go at Boatman again. He was terrified that Maximus or Faust would think he wasn't trying to win the fight and would put Damba through more horror. Maverick swung his sword at Boatman and Boatman blocked the attack. Maverick went again, thrusting and slashing, the men's swords clanging and the crowd cheering.

Boatman felt the weight of hopelessness envelop him as he knew Maverick would keep fighting until he was certain Damba would be safe. He also felt hopeless knowing there was nothing he could do to make Damba safe and therefore stop his friend from being on a suicide rampage. Boatman knew suicide wasn't on Maverick's mind, but being willing to die so that his brother could live was effectively suicide.

Boatman admired Maverick for being one of the most ruthless and effective fighters he had ever seen. Maverick's abilities were better than anyone Boatman had known, and some of that was down to Maverick's pragmatic approach to life. Right now, in this ring, Maverick was not being pragmatic and was fighting with fear and emotion because of his brother's safety. It was causing Maverick to make a lot of mistakes, and as he continued to fight Boatman, his style and training were being sacrificed for emotion. Boatman parried a move and then kicked Maverick hard on the side of his knee. He went down, the pain shooting up his leg, making him buckle. Boatman then punched Maverick hard in the face. Maverick saw stars and his eyes rolled back. He collapsed unconscious. Boatman stood over his friend, still holding his sword. Boatman looked up and scanned the Britannia Colosseum. A few people started chanting, "Kill! Kill!" Within moments the entire crowd was chanting for Boatman to kill Maverick. Boatman threw his sword to ground, and the chants petered out.

A robotic voice echoed around the arena. "That's very noble of you, Boatman. But it doesn't end that easily."

"I'm not killing him," Boatman said up to the balcony.

"At this moment, there is a sniper aiming directly for your chest. If you don't kill Maverick, then you will be shot."

"Then shoot me. I'm not killing my friend."

"Your integrity truly is admirable, Boatman, but it's also incredibly boring. Faust, help him to understand."

Faust bowed his head and turned to Boatman. His voice hummed through the speakers. "This isn't like the old days, when gladiators could show mercy. If you don't kill Maverick, then he will be tortured for as long as we deem fit and for as long as we think we can do it without killing him. He will wish for death many times over. And once we have done that, we will crucify him. Trust me, Boatman, he will be crucified but not allowed to die for days. Your act of mercy will open the door for us to take him to hell."

"I'm going to come up there and tear your throat out," said Boatman.

Faust laughed. "You won't need to do that. If you make the right decision, I'll be down soon. Remember, whoever won today would also have to fight me. The question is: are you going to take the opportunity to kill me, or condemn Maverick to untold pain while you receive a bullet in the chest."

Boatman knelt beside his friend and whispered something in his ear. He picked up his sword and stood up. He bowed his head and rubbed his eyes. He weighted the sword in his hand and shook his head, trying to think of a way out. "Tick, tock," came Max's voice through the speakers. Boatman felt his rage build. He couldn't believe he was backed into a corner like this. But he couldn't let them torture Maverick. Boatman gripped the hilt of his sword with two hands and held it above Maverick's chest. A powerful downward thrust, straight through his heart would be painless. "I'm sorry, my friend," he said and lifted the sword high.

A high-pitched screech stopped Boatman in his tracks, and he dropped the sword and covered his ears. Everyone in the Colosseum covered their ears, too. The big screens, which were broadcasting live footage of Boatman on the verge of killing Maverick, went black and then a man's face appeared on all the screens. The face spoke. "Hail, Caesar," said Bjorn Aská.

34

Askå didn't wait for Maximus to respond to his greeting and said, "I'm going to keep this short and sweet because I'm sure your nerds are frantically trying to work out how I have hijacked your signal and are also trying to work out where I'm broadcasting from. It's really rather simple: Boatman and Maverick are going to walk out of the Colosseum and get into a chariot that will be waiting for them when they do."

"That's not going to happen," said Faust.

"Grand Protector, it's lovely to meet you. I wish we could talk in more depth, but time is our enemy. Like I said, both men are going to walk out of the Colosseum and they will, without hindrance, get into a chariot I have arranged and leave without being followed. It's very simple and there's no negotiation on that."

"This is London, Lord Askå, you have no jurisdiction here."

"Oh, this has nothing to do with jurisdiction, Grand Protector. This is me telling you that's what you're going to do otherwise I will kill you."

Faust went to respond but Max held his hand up. "Askå, your lack of respect and disregard for our treaty is going to have your kingdom ripped from you, and I will be there when your insolent tongue is torn from your fucking mouth."

"As terrifying as you think that sounds, Caesar, I don't take threats from a bastard cripple."

Maximus began to hyperventilate with rage and his fingers were unable to type his response. His monitor started to bleep a warning that's his heart rate was too high, and his doctor came running to the emperor's side to try and calm him down. Maximus writhed in his chair, struggling for breath. He started to cough and wheeze and choke and Faust felt a tingling of hope that the emperor was going to go into cardiac arrest. Maximus's doctor wheeled the emperor from the balcony and inside so he could tend to him without the world being able to see Max's complete vulnerability.

Faust spoke on Caesar's behalf. "You've destroyed peace with Rome in a matter of seconds, Askå. It's a dumb decision."

Askå waved his hand. "No delays, Grand Protector. Boatman and Maverick are to walk out of here, unharmed. Or you and the emperor die. I've been talking too long already. I'll leave you with a message." The broadcast went dead, and the screen went black. A few seconds later, Askå's face appeared again and just before Faust was about to speak, he realised it was a pre-recorded stream. Askå proceeded to detail why Faust was going to allow Boatman and Maverick to walk out unscathed and Faust had to admit the Kingdom of Rome and Askå ruler was making his presence known rather impressively.

Faust was also wondering why Askå was burning his truce with Rome so emphatically. Askå was famous, but famous to many for being so mysterious. Hardly anything was known about him and anyone who did know him intimately either died before they could share their knowledge or were as elusive as the man himself. Much like Boatman, Faust noted. Faust had tried to get information on Askå for many years and for the past year and a half, since being Grand Protector, had sent spies into Askå's kingdom, only to receive footage of them streamed back showing them being used as gladiator fodder in a camp in the Aestii region. After three attempts in the space of weeks, Faust gave up. He toyed with sending Delilah and Sebastian into Askå's realm, but they were too valuable for such a risky mission.

Even as Faust wandered his memory palace, he had little to extract on who Askå was. He was certainly feared, and it was rumoured he was once a gladiator. There was no footage of him. He was as much of a mystery as Boatman, if not more. There had been whispers around Rome that Nero managed to keep Askå on his side and quiet by sending new gladiators to Askå's kingdom as a tasty offering, and Faust had personal experience of this being a truth no-one wanted to admit. He knew there was place he could go inside his palace had more information about Askå but he wasn't brave enough to enter it, as this point in time. Speculating about Askå's depravity wasn't going to help figure out not dying from an explosive balcony.

Askå, in his message had described in detail how he had managed to infiltrate the building process of the Colosseum for the past eighteen months and the balcony Faust was standing on had been rigged with explosives. If Faust tried to evacuate then the balcony would blow. If Faust tried to stop Boatman leaving, the balcony would blow. Showing he wasn't bluffing, footage of the balcony being installed and explosives being inserted into the metal frame of the balcony was streamed to a packed Colosseum.

Askå had also ensured a mass panic didn't commence, as he wanted Boatman and Maverick to leave quickly and quietly. The way he did this was to illustrate that he had also hijacked the sniper who had been apparently keeping tabs on Boatman and Maverick. In fact, the sniper was a friend of Askå. To prove it, she fired a shot which lodged itself in the back of the chair Faust had been sitting on only moments before. Akaå also pointed out to the crowd that they would be safe if they would be so kind as to sit very still and quietly watch the proceedings.

He also said that the crowd would find gold in their accounts if they did oblige. If any spectators had toyed with the idea of trying to leave, the promise of gold made those thoughts dance away. To prove he wasn't lying, a few phones in the Colosseum pinged and random people whooped and cheered seeing they were richer. The final part of Askå's message was that he had more than one sniper stationed inside the Colosseum and outside, so it was futile trying to get soldiers to intervene. Faust didn't want proof of this one, as he couldn't be seen to needlessly sacrificing a soldier's life.

During the entire message, Boatman had been waking Maverick up and explaining the situation. Maverick didn't need telling twice and was on his feet in no time. And just as Askå had said, both men walked out of the Colosseum, unharmed. Faust would have been angry if it wasn't for the brass balls of the entire scenario. After the men had left, Faust vacated the balcony and went inside to where the bar was. He ordered a beer and downed it, his hands shaking. He went to the next room and the emperor was in there, in his chair, asleep. Faust felt his skin prickle at the thought of Maximus waking up and discovering what happened.

Boatman and Maverick had got outside and bundled into a chariot. The chariot's bulletproof glass had closed over them and then they sped off out of London.

Bella watched the chariot leave whilst she sat perched on a

rooftop. She was holding a sniper rifle instead of a bow. It had felt strange in her hands when she had first been given it, but as she trained with it over the course of months, it had become as natural to her as the bow. In fact, she felt a bit like she had betrayed her heritage by how easy she found the gun to handle and shoot. She was searching for anyone who might try and interfere with Boatman and Maverick's extraction and was surprised how smoothly it went. She didn't trust these apparent new allies, but they were at least proving their worth at this point. Satisfied there wasn't any threat, she shuffled backwards along the rooftop. She remained crouched whilst she dismantled her gun and then left the gun, safely in its case, besides the bedroom window she was lowering herself back through. She closed the window and walked back into the lounge.

"Did they get away okay?"

"Well, yeah, yeah, they did. I can't believe it. Nothing happened at all."

"He has something else planned. He always does."

"Maybe. But they sped off without anyone following."

"It's not that simple."

"You know him better than anyone but, for now, it is that simple," said Bella.

"I hope so," said Alypia, Faust's wife, and she let herself sink into Bella's arms.

35

"Why did you change your mind?"

"About you?"

"I thought you hated me."

Alypia put her hand on Bella's cheek. "When you lie to yourself day after day, it makes you unwell. It makes you bitter. I've never hated you, Bella. I hated what you represented."

"Which was?"

"An end to my way of life."

"Your way of life?"

Alypia shifted her position, so she could face Bella. "I'm the darling of the Empire, Bella. Faust and I are the golden couple. We're showered with gifts and praise and gold, month after month. Why would I want to give that up?"

"Is that a rhetorical question?"

Alypia smiled. "I'm not sure."

"What's changed?"

"Power. Power changed everything this past eighteen months. Faust always wanted the power, and now he has it."

"But?"

"He's drunk on it. He wants the emperor dead. He told me. He wants absolute power."

"But then surely you'd be the ultimate golden couple?"

Alypia shook her head. "No, I don't think so." She looked at Bella and Bella felt her stare into her soul. "I think he's grown tired of me. Bored of me. I served a purpose to get him into the right circles, because of my father." Alypia held Bella's hand tight. "But he's the most powerful man in the world now, what else can I give him?"

"Alypia, the emperor is the most powerful man in the world."

"You've seen the emperor, Bella. He's on the verge of death every time he wakes up. Faust knows this."

"But you love the Empire."

"I do. I do love the Empire. It's made me rich and famous."

"Then what?"

"There's more to that."

"Such as?"

"You know, after I left you that day, I thought about how horrible I was to you. I thought about how it hurt that you'd lied to me." Bella went to speak, to defend herself, but Alypia stopped her, wanting to continue with her thoughts. "I felt like an idiot, because it seemed like you were yet another person in my life using my influence to access other people. I was the same pawn my father used me as when I was a teenager, and still the same pawn now." She held her hand up. "You don't need to explain, that's water under the bridge. What struck me, after I left you and for the past year and a bit, is how I just haven't been able to stop thinking about you. That's why I'm here."

Alypia tried to speak more, but felt her words stick in her throat and gulped back some tears. Emotions came at her more powerfully than she expected, and she realised it must have been pent up for months and months. She had convinced herself she was okay and convinced herself that the knot in her stomach was normal. Everyone has a constant knot, right? Holding it together for this time, though, it had taken its toll and now the emotions were coming to the front. And then Bella wiped a tear from Alypia's eye and kissed her forehead, whispering it was going to be okay and Alypia allowed herself to cry. She cried those big, heaving sobs that come when you have freedom to feel everything with no judgement and Bella held her, stroking her hair and letting Alypia properly feel for possibly the first time ever in her life.

36

Faust stood on the Colosseum balcony and watched the crowds being dispersed. He walked back inside and grabbed a beer from the bar. One of the emperor's carers was standing at the bar, drinking a glass of water. His hand was shaking as he tried to put the glass to his lips. Faust watched the carer struggle and then shakily put the glass on the bar top. "All okay?"

"Fine, my Lord."

"You don't look it."

"I'm fine my Lord, I'd better get back to Caesar." The carer scurried away, too afraid to speak to anyone. Faust was impressed that a cripple, who almost died when getting too excited, was able to instil so much fear. Maximus was barely able to control his bladder, let alone an Empire, so Faust was finding him more and more insignificant. But *finding* someone insignificant is very different to them being insignificant and Faust was well aware of his vulnerability at the hands of Maximus, even if he was an incontinent, wheezing waste of space. Faust took a deep breath and followed the carer into the room where the emperor was.

"Hail Caesar," said Faust, making his presence known. A carer was wiping the emperor's nose and a second one was putting a dirty diaper in a bag. Faust wrinkled his nose at the smell of shit. Faust waited for Maximus to get himself together and stood patiently at the entrance to the room. He took the moment to absorb his surroundings and all behaviour of the people in the room, to log in his memory palace. He was never complacent about that, as it was the tiniest detail that proved the largest vulnerability for many of his enemies.

Once Maximus was cleaned up, he pulled out his phone. "You know you have to die for this embarrassment, don't you, Faust?"

"I'm sorry?"

Maximus typed again. "You can't survive this. Fucking Bjorn Askå facilitated the escape of the most wanted men in the Empire, on Britannia soil." Maximus coughed his guts up, his emotions making him splutter and gag. When he found composure, he typed some more. "Even Titus didn't screw things up this bad."

Faust found himself resenting Maverick for not swinging that damn hammer hard enough and instead having to listen to this shit. "My lord, Askå has destroyed his truce with Rome, and therefore he will be removed from his throne. And Boatman and Maverick won't get far. Britannia's not that big."

"Not that big, you say? It took you long enough to find Boatman." Fatigue hit Maximus like the hammer that Maverick had once swung, so he dismissed Faust to get some rest.

Faust had escaped Neo's wrath, maybe by luck, so sure as hell wasn't going to find his life shortened by a petulant man who couldn't stay awake longer than a couple of hours. He needed the B-Unit to find Boatman and find him fast.

Faust wandered back out on to the balcony and admired the view of the Colosseum, now that it was empty. He was pleased with the work done to it to make it, in his opinion, the greatest stadium in the Empire. He personally thought it surpassed the Colosseums in Rome and Aquitania, but maybe he was biased. He was disappointed not to see the blood of Maverick or Boatman on the arena floor. He video called Delilah and she eventually answered.

"Yes, my lord?" Delilah was breathing hard.

"I don't care what you're doing right now, you need to focus your energy on Boatman."

"Of course." Delilah swept her hair away from her brow and caught her breath. "Is there anywhere I should be looking first?"

"They must be going somewhere they see as safe. Anything worth pursuing in Caledonia?"

Delilah shook her head. "No, the woman we found up there gave us nothing." Delilah smiled and looked up, reminiscing. "She was tough. I enjoyed her." Delilah licked her lips and sighed. She brought herself back to the present. "Caledonia's a dead end."

"Fine. That chariot they escaped in was stolen or bought from somewhere Empire-approved. Check CCTV and track its origins down. Whoever they got it from might know something. Do whatever you need to get information. Whatever it takes," said Faust.

Delilah squealed with delight at Faust's last sentence. "Thank you, my lord. We'll get on it immediately." A hand came into view and stroked Delilah's hair. Then the line went dead.

Faust wondered what happened to Delilah to be so delighted by the idea of hunting people down. He could tell it wasn't the thrill of the chase, it was more like a sexual pleasure she found in finding and killing people. Regardless of the ecstasy Delilah garnered from killing people, she still had to file reports to Faust. After all, the B-Unit was an official operation of the Empire. The most recent report from Delilah proved Delilah was a sadist, and even Faust felt sorry for the victim, Kiera. It wasn't a report he was going to read twice.

Faust's phone rang again. It was an unknown number, trying to video call. Faust never ignored calls, even if he didn't know who it was from. He didn't believe in hiding. The screen was black when he answered. "Who is this?"

"Hello again, Grand Protector." The screen went white and then came into focus. It was Bjorn Aska.

"How did you get my number?"

"You Romans really need to stop believing your stream security is flawless. I'd find a toddler's account harder to hack."

"To what do I owe the pleasure?"

"I thought it appropriate to introduce myself more officially."

"I must say, it's good to meet you. Anyone who could make the greatest fight in history fall flat on its face deserves some praise."

Aska laughed. "High praise indeed, Herr Faust." Faust grimaced at the title. Aska noticed the annoyance. "Apologies *Lord* Faust, I didn't realise your ancestry was a sore spot."

Faust waved his hand in dismissal. "What do you want?"

"Nothing too difficult, really. Felt like you needed a little more convincing about my influence, even in your city. If I were you, I would step off that balcony you're on and maybe stand near an exit." Faust didn't need telling twice and walked inside. Before he was able to ask Aska another question, he saw flashes of light and then everything became a blur as the balcony exploded and dust burst through the entrance from outside. Faust was knocked on his back and the explosion made his ears ring. Later, after his bodyguard had dragged him away from the blast site, Faust would enter his memory palace and slow down the event. Even though he was used to death and destruction, he would find it difficult to process, until the day he died, listening to the screams of a young boy being crushed by the rubble of the balcony. A young boy who had won tickets to the Britannia Colosseum had not been evacuated from the site as some staff had thought he would enjoy wandering the whole stadium by himself. It was a tragic miscalculation and Faust vowed to take from Askå something innocent in return.

37

Askå leant back in his oak chair and repeatedly ran his fingers through his hair. He arched his back and felt his lower back click and breathed deeply in satisfaction at the sensation of it. He was feeling happy. He had disrupted the pathetic piece of shit who passed for an emperor. He had outwitted the famous Augustus Faust. He was actually disappointed at the ease of outmanoeuvring Faust; he had assumed it would have been much more challenging. Maybe even he had been influenced by Empire propaganda and believed Faust was way more intelligent and powerful than he really was.

"Thank you for that information. It proved very useful."

Titus didn't respond. He knew it wasn't wise to respond.

"I find your friend Faust very, very interesting. I can't decide if he's as intelligent you make him out to be."

Titus remained silent. He was curled up, tight against a wall, trying to remain as inconspicuous as possible. Not that it made any difference. When Askå wanted to indulge in Titus, he would. It was irrelevant if Titus attempted to sink into the background. Askå carried on his one-sided conversation with the Roman.

"I'm pleased Maverick is alive. It would have made me angry, dear Titus, if he hadn't survived. I want to fight him again. Although, it seems he's past his best. This Boatman though, he looks formidable. What do you think my chances are?"

Titus stayed curled up.

"Hmm?" Aską clicked his tongue. "You're right, I shouldn't get cocky. He's killed an emperor after all!" Aską stood up and pushed his giant oak chair away with his foot. It was like he was kicking a bamboo chair, and Titus tried to curl up even further into the corner he was in. Aską cricked his neck. "Do you think he will fight me? I liked his style." Aską walked over to Titus and knelt down in from of the Roman. He stroked Titus's hair, like he was petting a dog. Titus stayed perfectly still, hoping to neither enrage nor engage.

"Maybe I could fight Maverick and Boatman at the same time? That would be entertaining, wouldn't it, dear Titus?" Aską stroked Titus's face.

All Titus wanted to do was swipe Aską's grubby hands away from his face and stop the man from touching him. The trouble was, for Titus, it was almost impossible to bat someone's hand away when you no longer had any hands because your captor had eaten both of them.

38

The chariot Boatman and Maverick were in had sped through London's streets, avoiding major roads, which were heaving with people who had come out to watch the fight. It went weaving through ancient parts of the city and frequently changed direction to lose any potential tail. The chariot was also dressed as an official Legatus chariot, so amongst the commotion of the Colosseum event, it was ignored by any soldiers who noticed it speed past.

They arrived at a disused pteron-port near the outskirts of the city and came to a stop. The driver, a longtime supporter of Boatman, turned to face her passengers. "We're changing vehicles here, sir."

Boatman saw a pteron-chariot, its engine firing up. "Where are we flying to?"

"Nowhere, sir. It's a diversion."

"Then where are we going?"

"Back into the city, sir."

"That makes sense," said Maverick. "No-one's looking for us there."

"No-one's looking for you underground," said the driver in

response to Maverick's sarcasm. "New headquarters have been established. There's another chariot waiting at the entrance to a tunnel, a hundred metres that way." The driver pointed toward the river and Boatman remembered that there was access to the tunnel system here that hadn't been used in years. "The access point has your facial details so will open when you approach," said the driver, anticipating Boatman's next question.

"And where are you going?"

"Someone has to fly the pteron-chariot," said the driver.

"I assumed everyone had fled the city after we left?"

"Not everyone had the luxury of going somewhere else. A few of us decided to stay." The driver exited the chariot and her passengers followed.

"Thank you," said Boatman.

"Some of us still believe in you," said the driver and made her way to the pteron-chariot.

Boatman called out to her. "I'm confused about something." The driver turned around. "How does Aska fit into all this?"

"That's for someone else to explain," said the driver, "but don't worry, friends are waiting for you underground," and then she carried on walking.

Boatman looked at Maverick. "Are you any wiser?"

"I only know that Aska didn't help us out of altruism. We should be very wary of his involvement."

The two men jogged to the tunnel entrance, and Boatman saw the facial scanner. It was camouflaged to look like old brickwork. Boatman stood in front of it and a green light blinked. The brick archway was, in fact, a set of double doors, which swished open. The doors revealed a tunnel twenty-feet high and wide enough for two chariots side by side. Waiting in the tunnel was one chariot, and once they walked through the doors, they swished shut and fluorescent lights blinked into life.

Maverick and Boatman climbed into the chariot and the glass roof closed over their heads, sealing them in. Maverick took the controls and fired the chariot up. It was a fairly new model and had been modified. The standard tracking facility, which allowed each Castrum to monitor where their patrols were, had been disabled and replaced with an electronic map of the tunnel network. It had been preprogrammed with where they needed to go and told them they were only ten minutes from their destination. This particular network of tunnels had barely been used by Boatman at the height of his rebellion effort. It was mainly used to escape the city and either grab a boat on the river or find an inconspicuous form of transport to head north. Boatman had escaped the city nearly two years previously via an oyster boat along the Thames and then headed up the coast until he had got to Meresig. After he had killed Nero and had a showdown with Faust, he had escaped via the tunnel system and disappeared through the Fish borough. With Nero murdered, Legatus Titus missing, and Faust critically injured, the Empire's operations in London were in complete disarray and meant Boatman was able to escape without a trace.

The tunnel network had been raided by Faust after Boatman and his followers had evacuated it. Faust's soldiers had discovered the array of living quarters and main offices of Boatman and his deputies. There was little information to be garnered because explosives were set off, destroying most of the rebels' underground HQ and killing a legion of soldiers with it.

Boatman was ever the pragmatist and had set up a smaller secondary HQ underground as backup if they were ever discovered. The underground network had over 300 miles of tunnels and covered over 400 square miles; it would take the Romans years to navigate it without getting blown up working out which tunnels weren't dead ends. After Faust had found the original HQ and lost a whole legion, he decided it wasn't worth the effort to even attempt to monitor underground. He had exerted all his energies and resources on drawing rebels out through fear above ground. The rebellion's effort was on the verge of collapse on the day of Maverick and Boatman's bout, so although Maverick was scornful of travelling back into the city's underground network, it made perfect sense. No-one would bother venturing into a tunnel system full of booby traps and collapsing tunnels, right?

Maverick scrolled the route with his finger on the screen in front of him. It was a fairly straight journey with only a few twists and turns. The chariot was quietly humming. "Have you considered this is a trap?"

"Everything we do always has that possibility."

"It hasn't been working very well, has it? Maybe we're too old for this shit."

"Speak for yourself."

"Incidentally, how old are you?"

"None of your business." Boatman thought for a moment and looked around the chariot. No weapons. "The driver has always been trustworthy."

"You can't remember her name, can you?"

"I don't see you telling me what it is."

"I'm not the boss."

"Look, whatever reason Aska has decided to align himself with us is, at this moment, irrelevant. It would be strange for him to create an elaborate escape for us, only to kill us."

"Like I said, I'm not the boss. If your gut says we should take the chance, then we take the chance."

"It's settled, then. Let's go."

Maverick obliged and pressed the throttle lever forward. The chariot accelerated from nought to sixty miles per hour in under three seconds. Both men enjoyed the exhilaration of the chariot's power and they sped through the tunnels, Maverick driving it with ease, anticipating the turns like he had driven this route thousands of times before. Boatman sat behind Maverick and tried to analyse the various option available. Ever since his encounter with Faust, his confidence had been knocked. Not that he would ever admit the fact. He didn't trust his gut and he didn't trust his abilities anymore. He certainly didn't feel like a man capable of inspiring an insurrection again and mentally crossed his fingers that they weren't travelling at sixty miles per hour toward their deaths.

39

Maverick slowed the chariot down when they neared their destination and Boatman told him to come to a stop. They only had another left turn and then it was a straight tunnel ride to where they needed to be. They discussed walking the rest of the way so they wouldn't be heard, but spotting them would be like shooting fish in a barrel as there would be nowhere to take cover. It made more sense to them that at least in the chariot if it was an ambush they were inside a bullet-proof chariot and could make a very, very quick escape. As long as the glass was actually bullet-proof, Boatman thought but didn't say aloud. They also decided they had nothing to lose so would arrive fast and loud. Maverick pushed the throttle fully forward and the hydrogen engine roared in the tunnel. Might as well make a grand entrance if they were speeding into a shit storm.

As Maverick raced the chariot down the tunnel he saw a figure in the distance, standing in the middle of the tunnel, underneath an archway, which Maverick figured was the entrance to the new HQ. He slowed the chariot down and said to Boatman to prepare himself as there was someone waiting to either greet them or kill them. Boatman stood up and sat next to Maverick. "Can you tell who it is?"

Maverick squinted and then smiled. "I can tell that poor posture from a mile away." As they drew closer Maverick said, "Did you know he was in the city?"

"I assumed he was far from here."

They came to stop and jumped out of the chariot. Maverick, not known for showing emotion jogged over to Tobias and embraced him. He then kissed his fiancé hard. Tobias returned the passion of the kiss. "I assumed you were dead," said Maverick.

"Nice to know you still think so highly of my survival skills."

"I just guessed if your gladiator skills were anything to go by you would have been toast by now."

"If I'm not mistaken, I'm the one standing in the top secret HQ and you're the one who had to be rescued from Boatman kicking your ass."

"I'll kick your ass in a minute."

"You haven't seen me for nearly two years. I'm a hard bastard now."

"You don't look it."

"And you look like shit, so let's call it evens," said Tobias and put his hand on Maverick's cheek. Maverick reached up and put his hand over his fiancé's. "So have you thought about it?"

"About what?"

"A date for the wedding?"

Maverick rolled his eyes. "I've been a bit busy, if you hadn't noticed, Tobias."

"You were spending a lot of time in a cell. You could have planned a whole wedding in that time."

"I'm wishing I was back in that cell right now."

"Over recent months I've learnt that words can't hurt me, so you can say what you like."

"Your words are hurting my head right now." Maverick huffed, "Can we talk about this another time, please? There's more important things to worry about right now."

"Oh, I'm not important?"

Maverick turned to Boatman. "If you don't mind, I'm taking the chariot back to Faust and getting him to lock me in a darkened room."

Boatman also huffed. "Have you two waited all this time just to bicker as soon as you see each other again?"

"Oh, this isn't bickering, this is flirty banter," said Tobias.

"Did you drop a basket of oysters on your head when in Meresig? Because that wasn't flirty banter." Before Tobias could say anything else, Maverick walked off. "Come on, we haven't got time to be pissing around."

"He's as charming as ever," said Tobias to Boatman. Boatman shook his head and followed Maverick into the HQ.

40

Boatman hadn't been to the secondary HQ in years, so had forgotten much of what had been put in place. He walked onto the main concourse, which was much smaller than what had been built at the original HQ but, Boatman noted, was still very impressive. There were three tunnels feeding off the concourse, which were framed by twenty-foot high archways. Above each archway were stained glass windows, illuminated by spotlights, which were echoes of the designs at the main HQ before it was destroyed. The far-left archway had a window depicting the God-Carpenter, his hands outstretched and fire raining down on a scorched earth. The second window at the centre of the room depicted Mars holding a spear, lighting surrounding him. The third window was of Dante's Inferno with the words *Abandon hope all ye who enter here.* Boatman had decided that if their first HQ was ever discovered and destroyed that meant their crusade had failed and this HQ was about vengeance. The windows reflected that desire for revenge and now, standing looking at them, after so many years, he knew he had made the right decision.

He had believed his mission of freedom for Britannia and

righteous indignation at the Empire's occupation would inspire a nation. Instead, he had ordered and willingly spilled a lot of blood, looked an emperor in the eyes as he drained the life from him and failed to protect his wife from the brutality of crucifixion. Inspiration hadn't been born, but resentment and hatred. And now Boatman wasn't so sure Britannia even wanted to be free of their oppressors. Standing in the Britannia Colosseum, facing Maverick in a potential fight to the death, and the crowd wanted the fight to happen. They weren't rising up in protest, hoping to see the two rebel fighters freed. They were cheering for blood to spurt from wounds. No, the people appeared at ease with Roman rule. They seemed happy to be conquered.

So Boatman was standing on the concourse looking at the windows of revenge and realising how wrong he was. He had believed that if he were to be standing in this position, he would be doing so with many, many civilians, tired of their oppression and ready to fight. He wanted to laugh at his naïvety. No, he was standing on the concourse realising everything from this point onwards was about ego; it was personal. He was going to personally kill Maximus for crucifying his wife. Maverick was going to tear Faust apart for nearly killing Tobias.

This wasn't about the greater good, because the people of Britannia didn't want the Empire stopped or destroyed. They were happy if they were entertained and distracted. Boatman was pulled out of his thoughts. "You managed to dodge death again, then?" He turned to see Olivia and went to her. She kissed him lightly on the cheek and hugged him.

"How did you get here?"

Olivia gently pulled away from her husband. "Your contacts in the RIA also have their own contacts."

"Askå," said Boatman. it wasn't a question.

Olivia nodded. "It seems Askå has never had the money to resist the Empire because the Empire have controlled his kingdom's income. The RIA though, have a lot of money and are very willing to fund whomever to ensure Romans never step foot on their land. Askå has the skills, the RIA has the money, and we have the location." Olivia waved her hand around the room.

"But what does Askå want?"

"He wants Faust."

"There was one of his snipers at the Colosseum, they could have taken Faust out at any time."

"No, he wants him alive. And completely unharmed."

"Why?"

"I don't know, but Askå believes you and Maverick will be the ones who can extract Faust and take him to Askå."

"Olivia, I don't answer to Askå. We're going to kill Faust and Maximus and then leave the country. My plan is to escape to the RIA, and that's why I sent you there, so I could meet you eventually and you would be safe."

"Safe? Safe from pain? How could I feel safe knowing you're at the mercy of the man who crucified me?"

"But that was why I sent you away from Meresig and went to London, Liv, to keep you safe and avenge what happened to you."

"I don't need your heroism, Boatman. I need my husband."

"And as your husband, it was my duty to protect you by sending you to the RIA." Boatman rubbed his face in frustration. "You weren't meant to come back."

"But we did come back, and we came back to save you, Boatman. If we hadn't agreed to what Askå asked for, you and Maverick would be dead by now and I would be safe, but a widow."

"But you're not."

"You know, sometimes I feel like I am, because time and time again you refuse to listen to me. And even after all this time of not seeing you, your attitude hasn't changed. Blundering on, like you're the centre of the universe. I feel like I lost my husband a while ago."

Olivia's words were brutal, but honest. She remembered the passionate, romantic idealist. He thought there was a way to inspire people to reject Roman rule and seek a more inclusive and equal way of life. He chose violence when he felt there were no other options. He would lament the violence, though, when in the quiet of Olivia's arms late at night. He mourned every solider he personally killed or had ordered to be killed by another's hands. Olivia was shocked at how much remorse came from him and wondered if he had the detachment necessary to press on with the rebellion. Now, though, now she was struggling to recognise that man. Now she was seeing a man obsessed with a personal vendetta. It was like debating with a fool, not the intelligent, considered man she fell in love with.

"I'm fighting to get rid of Maximus and Faust. I'm not blundering along. And there's no way in hell I'm trusting or answering to Aská."

"Who else are you going to trust?"

"Myself."

"And that's your problem," said Olivia.

She walked away.

"That went well," said Maverick.

"She'll come round," said Tobias.

"What does that mean?" Maverick said.

"What?"

"What does, *she'll come round* mean?"

"I don't know. That's what you say when a couple have an argument."

"Since when?"

"Since forever. That's what you say. It's comforting," said Tobias.

"Tobias, what do you think you're comforting by saying that? What's she coming round to? Seeing Boatman not be full of himself?" Maverick looked at Boatman. "No offence."

Tobias turned to Boatman. "Boatman, does it make you feel better?"

"I don't even know what you're talking about anymore."

Boatman walked away, going in the direction of his wife.

"See, that's what you do, you scare people off."

"Me? You're the lumbering giant."

"And you're the vocally lumbering idiot," said Maverick.

"It's lovely to see you again."

Maverick smiled. "You're a pain in the ass, you know that, right?"

"And I'm all yours," said Tobias. He leaned in for a kiss and Maverick obliged. "So, do you at least have a year in mind for the wedding?"

41

Boatman had tried to speak with Olivia, but she said she was too tired to talk so he left her and navigated his way to a communal area that, even as a secondary HQ, had a decently stocked bar. He poured himself a beer and slumped on a nearby couch. It was comfortable and he guessed it would be his bed for the night. Before he could get too comfortable, an older man sat down next to him. "Sorry for the intrusion, but I thought it best we got properly acquainted." They shook hands and Boatman was impressed by the grip.

"Thank you for your help."

"You're welcome. We're concerned about the fractured nature of the Empire. It's dangerous."

"We're?"

"The 35. We're concerned about how volatile the Empire is becoming. Losing you was too dangerous."

"Dangerous to who?"

"Us, of course."

Boatman shifted his position to look properly at the older man. At first sight, the American looked in his seventies. He had deep lines across his forehead. Lines which looked like he had been engrossed in thought for decades. His skin was leathery and tanned and his stubble was as white as snow. The more Boatman looked at him, the more he wondered if the man was nowhere near as old as he looked. It was his eyes. They were bright like a man half his apparent age.

"I'm surprised the 35 are as interested as they are. Surely the Empire imploding is a good thing?"

"Empires imploding can cause chaos. Like a nail bomb going off. You don't know where the damage will be done, but you know there will be significant damage."

"But to get rid of Maximus and Faust would be to everyone's benefit."

"Would it? Would a destabilised government be beneficial?"

"They have the Senate."

"Ah, yes, the famous Senate. Bureaucrats who have been nodding along to emperors for as long as it guaranteed their wealth and safety." The old man shook his head. "With Maximus and Faust gone, there would be yet another power vacuum and Aská would seek to fill it."

"Not if I filled it first."

The old man squinted at Boatman's words. "No offence, Mr King, but Aská has resources way beyond yours to march into Rome if the throne is empty. You have some very loyal, and powerful, sidekicks but that's very different to political might."

"So your solution is to keep them where they are?"

The older man shook his head. "No, not at all. Faust needs to be extracted and given to Aská. It's part of the deal we have with him. Maximus needs to stay in power, for now."

"Why?"

"Because a crippled, dribbling emperor will effectively grind the Empire to a halt and give us more time to work out how we fill the void once we eliminate the archaic traditions of Caesars."

"We have the opportunity to kill him now."

"I appreciate all the years spent trying to destabilise the Empire, but the 35 needs more time."

"I don't answer to the 35 or to Aská. I appreciate your help getting me out of the Colosseum, but I'm going to kill Faust and Maximus, Mr… sorry, I didn't catch your name?"

"Omaha."

Boatman was mid swig with his beer and stopped completely when he heard the name. He lowered his beer. "You're Omaha?" Omaha nodded. "Why would you personally come to London?"

"That was another part of the deal with Aská. Something about delivering a personal service." Omaha yawned. "Look, it's late, and I need rest. But you need to work with us, Boatman." He held his hand up. "You don't need to explain yourself, just sleep on it and let's talk more in the morning." He stood up. "But, trust me, leaving Maximus alive, for now, will help your cause. He's obsessed with what Maverick did to him and his days are filled with recreating when he crucified your wife. But instead, there's a different ending. He's distracted. It's causing problems for the Senate."

"He still managed to catch Maverick."

"More luck than judgment. The general workings of government are creaking along."

Boatman understood. "And as long as they creak it means the Empire isn't looking at you."

"Or you," said Omaha. "If Faust is extracted."

"Let me sleep on it," said Boatman.

Omaha bowed slightly in agreement and left.

Boatman didn't sleep on it, though. He stayed up through the night playing various scenarios in his head. He was being caught out again and again by either the fact that he was far more stupid than he had thought, or he really was as arrogant as his wife suggested. He was leaning toward a mixture of the two where his arrogance was making him stupid. And ignorant. The thought of making a deal with Bjorn Askå made him uneasy; the rumours about Askå were unsettling and made Maximus and his father, Nero, seem like angels in comparison. But if Askå created a way to get rid of Faust then maybe there was something in it?

The more he thought about it, the more he didn't know, and as the hours drew on he realised the most glaring problem he had wasn't from Faust, Maximus or Askå, but from himself. In all his mental wrangling, he had barely thought about Olivia. And that was a problem. She had gone through hell and for a time he thought his rage and desire for revenge was about avenging what had happened to her, but here he was, thinking about everyone else but her. His heart ached at the guilt of not thinking about her, but he also acknowledged the flicker in his mind that maybe that was the most honest he had been with himself in a very long time.

42

Delilah kissed him on the lips and then gently bit his bottom lip. She bit slightly harder and he winced. She moaned at his discomfort and bit hard enough to draw blood. He tried not to react. He knew better than that. She drew away and dabbed his blood that had transferred to her lip with her finger. She sucked the blood from her finger and smacked her lips, enjoying the bitterness. The man didn't move. He was too scared to move because the last time he thought he could knock the crazy bitch out, he hadn't anticipated the crazy bitch's brother behind him. And behind him, again, the crazy bitch's brother stood, and then leant down.

Sebastian kissed the back of the man's neck, and the man thought his heart was going to stop from the fear pumping through him. Sebastian gently kissed the man's neck and then pulled the piano wire ever so more tightly. The man involuntarily breathed in and then found breathing out the most terrifying thing he had ever done. Delilah moaned. The man moaned again. Pleasure and pain were sparring with each other.

"Peter, you taste wonderful by the way, but you need to be honest with me."

Peter was trying to focus on breathing, but he could feel a panic attack crawling its way up his body, and he didn't know if his heart was going to make it. He scorned himself because his doctor had said he needed to take his health seriously, but who really does? He was only 47, so who would take a doctor seriously about health warnings when they're so young? He didn't expect being garrotted as something he should be looking for in regard to looking after his health. He knew he had let himself go over the years. Everyone does when they hit their forties, right? By letting himself go, he would have been more honest if he had said that if his body was a temple, he had filled the entire temple with beer and deep-fried chicken and then stuffed that bulging temple with cigarettes, poured fat all over the temple and then moaned at everyone around him about why the temple looked like shit. Whatever his excuses for why he had never done anything about slowing the buildup of fat around his heart, he was now faced with his heart potentially stopping because some psycho was threatening him with piano wire whilst another psycho was kissing him.

Delilah could see Peter was on the edge of a full-blown panic attack. She enjoyed torturing people and would get people close to paralysing fear and then calm them down again. The constant fear and hope of freedom was brutal and destructive to a person's mind, and Delilah loved it.

"Peter," said Delilah, softly, "it's okay." She stroked Peter's leg and indicated for Sebastian to remove the piano wire. Sebastian obliged. "Peter, I need you to take some deep breaths and try to calm down. Sorry to have startled you like that, but if we don't get any answers, then Faust will nail us up on London Bridge." She kept stroking Peter's thigh, talking gently, just above a whisper. "We just want to find this chariot and then, hopefully, Faust will let us go. You understand, right? Help us and we get out of Faust's sights and so do you."

There's a thing about shock, when you experience it, you can become completely disoriented, like Peter was. In the back of his brain, instinct was telling him he needed to run. His internal dialogue was also telling him he was going to die. Those voices were being drowned out by the shock he was experiencing so that he couldn't remember how moments before Delilah had been taking pleasure in drawing blood from him. All he was able to focus on was how gentle and soothing Delilah's voice was, and therefore he should help her with whatever she needed. "I just need to focus," said Peter, "and then I'll tell you what you need to know."

"Take your time, sweetie," said Delilah and glanced up at Sebastian, who was standing a few steps back, piano wire at the ready.

"Sorry, my head's a bit of a blur."

"You were talking about how you came to the point of selling the chariot?"

Peter started to hyperventilate again. "Please, I'm sorry. I needed the money." Peter was struggling to hold it together.

"Sweetie, it's okay. Ssh, it's fine." She kept stroking his thigh with her thumb. "We don't care about the chariot, just who you sold the chariot to and anything you might have done to alter the machine."

Peter took a few moments to calm down again and then spilled the beans. That part of his brain which told him that confession was a terrible idea was being drowned out by the comfort of his leg being stroked (as it had been a very long time since a woman had done that) and the relief felt by confessing. He'd watched a lot of crime dramas and would get frustrated when someone confessed quickly, like they were weak, but now he understood. It was cathartic to confess.

And confess is what he did.

Peter worked for the Empire as a technician, specifically programming the navigational systems on chariots. He was a clever man and had designed not only the software which helped Castrums all over the Empire keep track of where exactly their chariots were, but he was also involved in designing the hardware the software was used on. Peter understood how accessibility and usability are key, especially in fast-paced, high-pressure work places, like a 300bhp chariot. Peter had commendations galore and even personal messages from Augustus II and Nero II congratulating him on his fine work with innovating chariots in the Empire. He had been in Britannia for a number of years because the Empire was hoping Peter would be able to adapt his software to be able to navigate the tunnel system in London. Operating deep underground made it much, much tricker to write software that could navigate in real time.

Peter had designed something capable but had kept it secret from everyone he worked for. The reason he did was because he felt they didn't deserve it because they didn't deserve him. He had designed and built innovation beyond anything rebels were doing but was never paid accordingly. As lauded as he was, even by Caesars themselves, he was never paid enough. He was praised by software engineers throughout the world, Empire and not, because he was a talented man, but he never received the renumeration to match the applause.

When he was approached about providing not only a chariot but a chariot equipped with navigational software for underground, he was shocked that the rebels knew. He was also shocked at the amount of gold being offered for his services. It didn't take much for him to make a decision because he wanted to have a moment in his life where he could say, "Fuck it," and do a last-minute trip abroad or even just blow some gold on something excessive and pointless. The Empire had the chance to pay him what he was worth, but never did. At the end of the day, pay pittance and receive zero loyalty. The rebels were willing to pay handsomely, the Empire was willing to stay cheap. He did the math.

A woman from the rebellion who had come to him about the job came back when Peter had finished modifying the chariot. She had looked at his work, satisfied, and paid him a large amount of gold plus a tip for finishing early and being so efficient. Peter had been flattered and asked if he could join the rebellion. The woman had said, "You're already part of the rebellion. And you're much more effective destroying them from within with your set of skills." Peter was flattered again in a matter of minutes and said he was available as often as the rebellion needed.

"This is all very interesting," said Delilah as Peter mind vomited everything that had happened in recent months. "But who was the woman?"

"I never got her name."

Delilah was reaching the point where torture was going to be her favoured method of interrogation on Peter. She stopped stroking Peter's leg and looked up at Sebastian. Sebastian tensed the piano wire in his hands. "Peter, we need to know where this woman went."

Peter had his head down and was still sniffling. "That's easy."

"If it was easy then I wouldn't be asking you."

"But you didn't ask where the woman went. You asked who the woman was. That's a big difference."

Delilah struggled with being patronised and Peter's words grated on her enough that she imagined taking great pleasure in tearing Peter's throat out. "Then tell me if it's that easy."

Peter asked if he could get his phone out of his pocket and when Delilah gave permission, he opened up an app which showed the exact location of all the Empire's chariots in London. He pressed on the sidebar and then scrolled through until coming to a halt and clicking. The app then dissolved a map of London and instead was replaced by a map of the tunnel network underneath London. Peter turned his phone to face Delilah and she could see a yellow dot moving rapidly along the tunnel systems. "That's the chariot I modified." Delilah stared at the screen, transfixed by the yellow dot whizzing on the screen.

"May I?" Peter nodded and she took the phone from him and zoomed in on where the chariot had stopped. "Thanks, Peter." Delilah had a thought. "One other thing; is the access to the tunnel network monitored by CCTV?"

"Only at the tunnel entrance."

"Can it be disabled?"

Peter motioned for Delilah to give him back his phone and she obliged. The technician opened another app and found the cameras. "I can just switch them off whenever I want."

"Do the rebels know you can do this?"

"By the gods, no. I just thought it would be handy if I ever got taken there, then I could switch the cameras off so no-one could trace my whereabouts." Peter went a bit red. "I know I'm not important or famous, but I needed some insurance."

"Anything else?"

"There's a facial recognition scanner to open the entrance to the tunnel."

"Can you override that too?" Delilah put her hand back on Peter's leg. Peter blushed.

"I can't override it," Delilah frowned at those words, but Peter continued, "But I put my face into the system to make sure I always have access."

Delilah smiled. "Have you ever been?"

"No." He seemed disappointed. "I thought they would have wanted to meet me once I modified the chariot."

"Well, Peter, I have good news: you'll be visiting their HQ tonight."

Delilah stood up, and before Peter could say another word, piano wire was round his throat.

43

"Any guards?"

"Not that I can see," said Sebastian.

"You're sure?"

Sebastian took the binoculars away from his eyes. "Have a look if you don't believe me."

"I believe you."

"Really? Because your tone suggests otherwise."

"Sebastian, don't start. Now's not the time."

"You just need to trust me more."

Delilah grabbed Sebastian's ear and twisted it; Sebastian whimpered, "I'll trust you when you stop being such a flakey imbecile." She leaned in close to her brother and licked his cheek. "Now, are you sure there's no guards?" Sebastian nodded. "Good." She let go of his ear and said, "So if you are so sure, make your way to the entrance. Because if you're wrong then you might have The Beast rip your head off or Boatman knock you out again."

Sebastian held the binoculars up again and said, "You're so mean to me."

"Be thankful Mother isn't here," said Delilah.

Sebastian made a point to scan the whole area for much longer than necessary and confirmed again there was no activity around the pteron-port. Delilah stood up and said, "Well, let's go then."

"What about CCTV?"

"Were you listening earlier?"

"No, I wasn't, I was busy making sure you didn't get attacked."

Delilah knew her brother was angry and that had the potential to interfere with operations if he was sulking, so she moved closer to him and ran her fingers through his hair. She drew her nails down the back of his head, and he murmured in pleasure at the feeling. "And I'm always thankful to you, Sweetie, for looking out for me." She carried on stroking his head, thinking her brother was more like a dog than a human. "Peter told us about the CCTV and we've disabled it, so we can go through the tunnel and find Boatman and The Beast and dispose of them."

"Then maybe we can get what we want at last."

"Maybe." Delilah took Sebastians's hand. "But let's not worry about that right now."

They jogged down to the hidden tunnel entrance, finding it as Peter had advised and stopped in front of the facial recognition panel. Delilah told Sebastian to turn around, and she opened the rucksack on his back. She pulled out Peter's now decapitated head. Blood still dripped from the neck, and she swore as some drops stained her shoes. She held Peter's head up to the panel and the light went green. The doors swished open, and the B-Unit grinned as they were granted access to the rebels' secret tunnel network.

Delilah pulled out Peter's phone and looked at the map. "It's a good hour and a half walk from here."

"We're not just going to walk straight into their HQ, though, are we? Putting aside the fact Boatman and Maverick will be there, surely a bunch of other rebels will be too. We need more soldiers." Sebastian stepped away from his sister as he spoke and put his hand up to his ear, instinctively protecting it. He was offering an opinion but knew she would take it as criticism.

Delilah stared at her brother and took a while to say anything. "You're right," she said and it took Sebastian all the will in the world not to cry with joy at those two words coming from her mouth.

Sebastian had grown up craving praise but being fed abuse instead. He had yearned for adoration but received resentment. He used to pray at night, when hiding under his bed, as he listened to men tearing each other apart and hearing his Mother laughing at the horror. If he ever called out to his Mother, she would call him a pathetic waste of space and then his older sister would beat the crap out of him for drawing attention to themselves. He eventually learnt how to keep quiet and even when things became so scary he would feel dampness and his bottom lip trembled, he wouldn't make a sound. He used to feel so proud of himself when he stayed dry and didn't cry and thought Delilah would praise him for keeping it together. Instead, she would use his silence as a reason to smack him about because he wasn't shouting out to protect their Mother.

Sebastian was always trying to work out the right formula to not only make his sister praise him but also make her respect him. All he wanted was her respect and for her to say that he was doing a great job. Hope sprung eternal each and every day and each and every day he didn't receive his sister's praise he would try harder the next. Even when she told him he had to do 'what those other men did' and he thought he couldn't, but still managed to, and still no praise passed her lips, he still believed praise would come.

So, standing there, in the tunnel, after all the years of an absence of recognition, to hear his sister tell him he was right, it was like the gods had reached deep into his soul and blessed him with joy directly from heaven. "Sorry?"

"You're right."

"Really?"

"Absolutely," said Delilah. She walked a bit closer to Sebastian and lowered her voice. "You're right. If we walk into their HQ, they'll kill us. We need to let them take us in."

"What?"

Delilah did two things. She spun Sebastian around so he was facing back down the tunnel from where they had come and then she pulled out his gun, which was in his chest holster and aimed it down the tunnel. Sebastian also did two things, which were to attempt to ask what the hell his sister was doing and then cough because he couldn't get his words out.

He wasn't able to get his words out because an arrow was protruding from his chest, stopping his body from functioning the way his body should. His brain was telling him that he should be scolding his sister for, yet again, manipulating him, but the sum total of how he was expressing that disappointment in his sibling was to be gasping for air as the arrow had pierced his lungs. He collapsed, but his sister didn't help break his fall. She remained standing, hands in the air, crying and begging for her life. Sebastian went into panic mode as he tried to breathe because his lungs wouldn't give him the air they should have been. Panic meant he tried to gulp in air faster, but the air he wanted to gulp wasn't there.

Before Sebastian died, his brain did a terrifying thing in a matter of milliseconds: it showed him his life. It showed him the horrors he had experienced as a child, and it showed him the horrors he had performed as an adult. It also showed him how little his sister cared for him and as his synapses fired their last, to Sebastian it seemed like an age, but in reality it was a blink of an eye. He saw that his sister only ever saw him as an object. A very disposable object. And as death came and wrapped its arms around him, hate and sadness pulled him down into nothingness.

44

"Give up the act."

"Please! Please don't kill me," sobbed Delilah. She howled in the tunnel.

"By the gods, shut up." Bella strung another arrow, "Or I'll shoot you in the throat." Delilah shut up. "I've seen your handiwork back on Meresig, so please don't patronise me with this little performance." Bella moved forward, slowly, arrow ready to go.

Delilah wiped her nose and breathed out. "I've seen you."

"And I've seen you."

Delilah squinted. "I'll be able to get you a pardon. Directly from Faust."

"You seem to think I give a fuck about Faust."

"He gives a fuck about you." Bella's arrow dipped slightly but she corrected it in moments. Delilah noticed the falter and decided to bluff. "If you help me, Faust will go easy on you. In spite of what you've done."

"I don't need Faust's forgiveness."

"Maybe not. But you need his mercy."

"I'm the one with an arrow aimed at your chest and your

boyfriend dead on the floor."

"He's not my boyfriend, he is my brother."

"Was your brother."

Delilah sneered at the past tense.

Bella warned, "I'd be very careful about lowering those hands, because I guarantee I'm a faster shot than you." Delilah carried on sneering but kept her hands aloft. "Kneel down and put your hands on your head." Delilah obliged and then Bella called HQ and a chariot arrived in moments. She cable-tied Delilah's hands, and the chariot whisked them back to HQ where the Roman was escorted to the concourse. She was told to kneel down again. Her hands remained tied behind her back. Boatman arrived after what Delilah believed to be a disrespectful amount of time. Her joints ached from being in the sitting position. She had tried to loosen the ties around her wrists, which had made her even more uncomfortable but no closer to escaping as the ties had barely moved.

"I'm sorry for your loss."

"He knew the risk," said Delilah.

"That's cold," said Tobias, who had followed in behind. "Your boyfriend not buy you enough flowers?" Tobias glanced over his shoulder at Maverick. "I know the feeling." If Maverick's sigh wasn't heard across the entire HQ, then it was simply because they had hearing difficulties.

"He wasn't my boyfriend, he was my brother."

"Wow, okay." Tobias looked at Boatman, "And you thought your family life was messed up."

Boatman ignored Tobias and asked Delilah another question. "I spoke with Bella about earlier. Why sacrifice your brother like that?"

"There's always a bigger picture."

"Which is worth killing your brother for?"

"That bitch over there killed my brother, not me." Bella stayed silent, not rising to the bait.

"I emulate Tobias's feelings, you don't seem too upset about the recent departure of your boyfriend," said Boatman.

Delilah screeched that Sebastian wasn't her boyfriend, but her brother and Faust was going to crucify everyone in the room.

Boatman knelt in front of Delilah and raised a hand. "Okay, okay, I'm sorry, I'm being facetious. I'm genuinely sorry for your loss." Boatman meant it, too. He was suffering the loss of his wife, and she was still alive.

Delilah looked up at Boatman and, for a second, Boatman thought he saw sadness. Her face changed though, and she said, "Like I said, he knew the risk."

"And you know the risk." Boatman looked over at Bella and said, "Kill her."

"Wait. Just wait a moment. Faust will do a deal."

Boatman laughed. "No he won't. He won't do any deal. He will try to kill me with every chance he has."

Bella pulled an arrow.

"Okay, okay! Wait. Faust won't do a deal. I have an offer."

"Which is?"

"I'll give you Caesar."

"And how would you do that?"

"I'm part of the exclusive B-Unit. I can get close enough to kill him."

"And who says he needs to be killed?"

"Why wouldn't you want him killed?"

"Sometimes it's better to keep your enemies close," said Boatman. Delilah went to speak again, but Boatman held his hand up. "What are you trying to offer? It's not access to Maximus. Don't bullshit me with that. Even if you did manage to kill him, you'll be dead too. I'm pretty sure you're not some martyr for the greater good, considering only moments ago you gave your brother up just to get close to me."

Delilah laughed. "You're not as dumb as I thought."

Boatman spread his hands out, "So?"

"Maybe I just wanted to get close to you."

"Maybe you did. I'll say it again, So?"

"Because maybe I can see more benefit being on your side."

"I'm sure your current pay is way beyond what I would be able to offer," said Boatman.

"It's not about pay. It's funny, I thought you would be asking me about the most relevant thing to you in all this. I thought that would be the reason why you haven't killed me."

"And what would that be?"

"Olivia's mother, of course."

"I'm sorry?"

"Olivia's mother. I assumed you wanted to save her?"

Boatman felt his stomach turn. He'd forgotten about her in the chaos of recent months. He wished he could say he had thought about her and ensuring she was free, but he hadn't. Yet again, his wife was forgotten. "Faust said he would free her once I gave myself up to him."

"And you believed him?"

"Let's cut the shit, what do you want?"

"I want Faust's job."

Boatman laughed. "You can't be serious?"

Delilah didn't laugh. "Do I look like I'm joking?"

"It's hard to tell with that strange psycho look plastered on your face," said Tobias.

"I was asking the engineer, not the oil rag," said Delilah.

"Wow, really looking forward to working with you," said Tobias and went to walk off. Maverick grabbed Tobias's arm and shook his head.

Boatman hadn't taken his attention away from Delilah. "Why would you think we would give you Faust's job? Aside from it not being part of my job description to assign Empire roles and, of course, that small issue of the fact that it's bat-shit crazy to even think you're worthy or capable to take over from Faust, why even ask me?"

"Because I watched you, that time, when you fought Faust, and nearly killed him. I was one of the soldiers ordered to guard the pub so no-one entered. I watched you fight him. I saw you beat him, and then I saw you run. So I know you know how to take Faust out."

"Beating him in hand-to-hand combat is different to removing him from his throne in some kind of coup."

"When you beat someone physically, you also beat them mentally." Delilah looked around the concourse. "And, if I'm not mistaken, you lot aren't down here for some drab social club."

"Who's she calling drab?" Tobias said.

"You don't need to comment on everything like a word vomit machine," said Maverick to Tobias.

Boatman smiled. He was surprised how much he'd missed listening to his friends bickering. "Look, Delilah, even if our drab social club does have a plan to deal with Faust, there's no reason to risk everything by trusting you."

"I can get you to Faust without breaking a sweat, but he is weirdly prophetic and taking him out is a different matter, because it's like he predicts it. And would somehow predict me trying to usurp him."

"If he's predicting you, then he'll certainly be predicting me."

"But not the information I can give you. He won't predict that."

"How can you be so sure?"

"Because even Faust has blind spots, and his is that he sees me as an instrument of death, who takes delight in that death and therefore doesn't wasn't anything more than that. Which he was right about."

"So why the change?"

Delilah smirked. "You killed my brother. Death isn't so enjoyable without a companion to share it with."

Boatman grimaced and shook his head. "No deal. I don't want you anywhere near what we're doing."

"You're such a prude!" Delilah laughed and threw her head back. As she did so, a small blade fell out of her hair and into her hands. The blade was razor sharp and cut her fingers as it did so. She didn't care. It was normal. No-one noticed the blade, it was tiny, and if Boatman was next to her, people tended to relax as being in Boatman's presence usually meant no-one was dumb enough to try anything on. Delilah was dumb enough.

Her wrists were restricted by cable ties, but Delilah's blade sliced through the plastic. She waited for Boatman to ask her another question. Delilah knew that if you stayed silent someone would feel an innate need to fill the silence and speak. Boatman obliged. "What happened to you and your brother?"

"I don't need some bullshit psychotherapy, Mr King." Delilah swung her right arm out from behind her back, blade in hand. Her swing was arched in a way that it was going to slash Boatman's throat so he would have been dead before he even knew he had been cut. And Delilah's swing was fast. What Delilah didn't know, even having met Boatman before, was that as fast as she was,

Boatman was always faster.

There were rumours about Boatman and where his speed and strength came from. Some whispered it must be supernatural and maybe he was gifted with powers from the gods. Arguments in bars usually ensued because why would a man empowered by the gods fight against an Empire ordained by the gods? Others argued he had been trained by a supreme gladiator. Maybe Bjorn Askå himself. But no-one could verify. Maybe he used mind control to mess with his opponents before killing them so they weren't able to fight properly?

That last theory was put to rest for everyone in the room, because as Delilah swung her arm, blade in hand, moving swiftly toward Boatman's throat, most people saw a blur and then the blade was no longer in Delilah's hand but protruding from her neck. Blood splattered Boatman's shirt. Delilah slumped on the floor and Boatman stood up. He muttered that he needed to change his clothes and stepped away from Delilah's dead body. Those standing on the concourse remained in stunned silence for a few moments. Most of them had seen plenty of death, but Boatman's merciless and swift execution of Delilah still managed to shock. Even Maverick was staring at the body of Delilah as if he didn't believe what he had just seen.

Boatman stopped walking and turned to face the rebels. "Tobias, can you clean up my mess, please?" Tobias nodded. "Sorry, I didn't have a choice."

"No problem, boss. We'll put her and her brother to rest."

"Thank you. I need to get cleaned up. Bella, Maverick? I need you to meet me in my office in an hour." Maverick and Bella nodded and then Boatman was gone.

45

There was a knock at Faust's door and Faust said for the visitor to enter. It was a soldier from the surveillance and communications centre.

"Hail, Grand Protector."

"What do you want?"

"It's about the B-Unit of Sebastian and Delilah; their trackers have gone dark."

"How?"

"I don't know, my Lord."

"This is what I find interesting. I'm the Grand Protector of Britannia, and when I ask questions about a very well-funded part of operations that I'm funnelling gold to, I tend to expect a better fucking answer than, 'I don't know.'" The solider looked down. "Keep your eyes straight when in my presence soldier, or I will find a reason for you to have a private audience with the Emperor." The soldier looked ahead again. "I'll ask again, how did their trackers go dark?"

"I don't know, my Lord, but the most logical reason would be they went somewhere signal could be lost."

"Like where?"

"There shouldn't be anywhere. The trackers can be traced nationwide."

Faust thought a moment, "What if they were underwater?"

"If they drowned, then yes, the trackers would short themselves out. But the last known location was half a mile from the river. That's a big margin of error for both trackers."

"What if they went underground?"

"Into the tunnel system? How? The rebels kept access very tight."

"I got in there before," said Faust.

The soldier stayed silent.

"You're free to speak your mind, soldier. I won't punish you for it. Call it a sharing of ideas between equals."

The soldier coughed. "Okay, no offence, my Lord, but your access before was more luck than skill. You gained access through a tunnel Boatman had blown up, but not blown up as effectively as he thought. But you treated that tunnel like it was the only way in."

Faust smiled. "I appreciate your honesty, soldier." Faust wrote a couple of notes. He didn't really need to as he was storing it all in his memory palace, but sometimes he felt he needed to appear normal. "So there's another area underground Boatman has snuck into? And Delilah and her brother have followed them?"

"Indeed sir, but the last known location from the tracker shows a location on the outskirts of the city. The tunnel network is huge; without their trackers activated, it will be hard to find them."

"Why haven't we been sweeping the tunnels as standard?" It was a genuine question from Faust. He had a bigger picture approach to crushing the remnants of Boatman's rebellion. But some operational tasks weren't on his radar as he did not have the time.

"Resources, sir. We've been sweeping houses and streets for nearly two years now. We haven't had the capabilities to explore three hundred miles of tunnels."

"Four hundred."

"Sorry?"

"It's four hundred miles. Plenty of space for Boatman's cult to hide in." Faust was getting bored of the conversation. He hated debriefs. He tended to know what was going on and didn't need meeting to regurgitate what he already knew. He registered a micro expression from the soldier. It was an expression of disdain. He didn't like being corrected. Faust understood the sentiment. Still, he didn't like it. It was disrespectful.

Faust wasn't satisfied about his weakness in regard to searching the tunnels in recent months. Losing so many soldiers because of explosive traps made him feel stupid because he should have swept the tunnels first. He needed to treat the rebels like rats and drive them out of the tunnels, not follow them in. Like, it seems, Delilah and Sebastian had done. He dismissed the soldier and pondered how he could flush Boatman out. He also retreated into his memory palace to try and find any snippets of information he could use to not only protect himself but go on the offensive with Bjorn Aska. That man had managed to completely undermine his efforts in his own city.

He was used to fighting enemies coming from multiple directions, but Boatman and Aska possibly in an alliance was the most formidable threat against Rome in centuries. And a crippled, perverted Caesar didn't make Faust confident Rome had the capabilities to deal with such a threat.

46

Bella and Maverick walked into Boatman's office and saw Omaha was already sitting on the only sofa. He stood up and shook their hands and sat back down again to resume drinking a coffee that was steaming on the small table in front of the sofa. Bella and Maverick sat on chairs in front of Boatman's desk.

"I'm here on a purely relational basis."

"Which means what, exactly?" Maverick was cynical.

"Call it international relations," said Omaha.

"Like I said: which means what, exactly?"

"The RIA believes Britannia needs freedom from Rome, but patience as to when that freedom should come."

Maverick didn't exactly growl, but a displeased noise came from his throat. "And why should you decide when we get our freedom?"

Omaha smiled. "And why should you?"

"Because I've been here, pulling nails out of victims' wrists for years. And I have records of every one." Maverick was telling the truth; he did have a record of every person he had saved from crucifixion. On his left arm were dots. Maverick had a tattooist draw a dot on his arm every time he saved someone. Three hundred and seven dots adorned his arm.

"Then maybe you're not in the position to decide what Britannia needs, as you're too involved."

Maverick looked at Boatman. "Who the fuck is this guy?"

"This is Omaha."

Maverick looked surprised and Boatman tried to remember how often he had ever seen Maverick genuinely stunned. "You're Omaha?" Omaha nodded. "Why risk coming to London?"

"Call it a personal service to prove we're genuine in our support for what you're doing."

"I thought you just said we need to delay getting our freedom? I don't care if you are Omaha from America, why would we avoid the opportunity to be rid of Rome's toxic presence in this country?"

"If you don't get to the root and try to tear the problem out, you might end up adding strength to the problem."

"Maybe sitting in America and having nice peaceful debates about what could happen gives you room for this vague, philosophical bullshit, but back here in reality I see it clearly: kill the crippled Caesar and kill the psycho Grand Protector. Then I'll happily patrol the streets and chop down every soldier I see until they flee Britannia."

Omaha sipped his coffee, listening to Maverick's rant. "Your blunt instrument approach is certainly welcome at times, Mr Kirabo, but maybe there's a time and a place."

"Don't patronise me. I trained with your partner in crime, remember. I'm not some naïve teenager looking for his first kill."

Omaha held his hands up. "I apologise, Maverick, I honestly don't mean to offend. I just don't believe obliterating Faust and Maximus will necessarily bring you the freedom you want."

"Why?" Boatman spoke up.

"The Empire has a Senate, which has become very rich from regions their Empire controls, including Britannia. The Senate might not like the current Caesar and some might even quietly say to each other that they would like to see Maximus dead, but that doesn't mean they won't want someone else to take his place, to continue the status quo."

"Like Faust."

"Exactly. Faust is clever and a great strategist and therefore I think the Senate was hoping Caesar Maximus was going to die and then Faust would slide into an Emperor role." Omaha thought for a second. "But an Emperor role with maybe a more democratic spin to it."

"Hence the Grand Protector title," said Boatman.

"That's right. The Senate thought they could stay rich with a leader of Rome whose ascension was the start of phasing the Caesar dynasty out."

"But why would they want to phase the dynasty out if they were having such a profitable time?"

"It's a poorly kept secret in Rome that the son and grandson of Augustus are seen as the most despicable Emperors since at least a millennium ago. Fear only keeps people submissive for a limited period of time."

"Then they start to get pissed off for always being afraid."

"They do. May I?" Boatman nodded and Omaha opened an app on his phone and bounced a presentation onto the screen on the office wall. What was being projected was video footage of violent protests against Roman soldiers.

"Where are these happening?" Bella had stood up to look more closely at the footage.

"A number of provinces in Africa and the Aquitania region."

"We haven't seen anything about this," said Bella.

"Propaganda is a powerful thing."

"And so is greed," said Bella. "If the Senate were starting get afraid their funds were going to be cut off."

"It still makes no sense to me." Boatman was staring at the screen. "What?"

"We extract Faust and give him to Askå, leave Maximus alive and then have another psychopath take Faust's place? And why leave Maximus alive if these riots are happening? The way I see it, kill Faust and Maximus and the riots stop. And then the Senate can rule the Empire like the 35 rule the RIA."

"True revolution takes time. A dramatic change in power structures might, in theory, be good, but the people tend to find it unnerving." Omaha looked at the screen and pre-empted what Maverick would say. "Yes, there are riots, which prove people are fed up with fear, but dramatically shift things the other way and people become even more afraid. Most people don't like change. Gradual, creeping change that tends to go unnoticed is a much more effective tool of ruling. If we get rid of Faust, install a known ruler, like Askå, and then fade Maximus away into nothingness, that, I assure you will lead to greater things than a mad killing spree."

"Britannia is different, though," said Maverick.

"Is it?" Omaha asked the Ugandan. "Do you remember a politician named Corbyn from the early forties?" Maverick shook his head.

"I've read about him," said Boatman. "He promised some radical things to improve Britannia."

"He did indeed. Britannia wasn't ready or interested. Although the Empire wasn't in Britannia, their legacy was, and it permeated through the politics of the British. And the main aspect to that permeation was the belief in being ruled. Corbyn had suggested instead of being ruled, why don't people share society together? It made sense to quite a lot of the population, but then fear set in. For many, such a radical diversion from how things had been for centuries was too much. His campaign came to a rather violent and abrupt ending, as I understand it. So, no, I don't think Britannia is any different to other provinces."

"But you truly think Aska is the right man to transition Rome away from its Caesars?" Boatman wasn't, by any stretch of the imagination, convinced.

"It's not just what I think, it's what the 35 think, and together, yes, it seems the most plausible route to freeing Britannia and some provinces in the coming years." Omaha added, "But your help is vital in that."

"But Aska seems a big risk; I've heard the stories about him. The things he's done."

"And I've heard the stories about you and the things you've done." Omaha looked at Bella and Maverick, too. "What you've all done. No-one's morally superior when it comes to leading this nation, or even this Empire."

"Like I said, I've met Aska," said Maverick, "I'd say we are morally superior to that fucking lunatic."

"A lunatic who saved your life yesterday."

"I didn't ask him to."

Omaha put his cup down and leant forward. "Look, I'm not here to convince you of Aska's moral character, more remind you of his credentials. But even I can see I'm failing on that front. How about you speak to the man himself?" Omaha closed the footage being looped on the screen and instead brought up a screen showing a video call going out to Bjorn Aska.

47

"Dear Boatman, how very good to meet you in far less of a frantic situation," said Aská.

"I'll reserve the pleasantries until I understand what it is you want."

"But lovely Omaha here explained it all?"

"He explained what you want us to hear. But all this kindness and building for a better future sounds like the same old shit the Empire has vomited out for decades. Why should we believe you're not yet another megalomaniac?"

Aská laughed. "But my sweet Boatman, I am a megalomaniac! Of course I want to rule the world. And let's be honest here, you do too. If you didn't, why do you bother with this rebellion nonsense."

"Rebellion against oppression isn't nonsense."

"But of course it is. Most people need oppression because they're too dumb to know how to live their lives unless they're being told. Tell me, how many of those fawning idiots, cheering for you and Maverick to hack each other up, were singing your praises a couple of years ago?"

Boatman had thought the same thing but wasn't going to say it. "That's not the point."

"Oh, Mr King, but it is. You're trying to free people who don't have the first clue what true freedom is."

"And I suppose you know?"

"Of course I know. I've been free for decades. And it's hard work, I can tell you that."

"Free, but relying on Rome's gold?"

"All freedom comes at a cost."

"A cost of what? Integrity?"

Askå grinned. It seemed false to Boatman. "Integrity is a subjective thing, Mr King, which you must be painfully aware of."

"I've never sucked the Empire's cock for gold, if that's where we're going when talking about integrity."

Askå wasn't grinning anymore. "You're alive because of me."

"Maybe. Don't expect gratitude. If working together achieves what I want, to be rid of the Empire from Britannia's shores, then that's fine." Boatman got up from behind his desk and stood in front of the screen. "But that doesn't mean I won't come for you. I've heard about you and what you do."

Askå managed to plaster the false grin again. "Has poor Maverick still not gotten over his time training with me?"

Maverick growled. "I'll repay the scar one day, Bjorn."

"Maverick hasn't said a word to me about what he experienced with you, but I've heard you're a sick fuck and I'm bored of sickos sitting on a throne in Rome."

"Is that a personal challenge, dear Boatman?" Askå looked excited. "It is."

"Well, I look forward to meeting you in person."

"Indeed."

"Anyway, enough of this testosterone-filled nonsense. I can get you the freedom you so desperately desire if you deliver me Faust."

"What about Maximus?"

"Maximus? That pathetic excuse for a functioning human is one diaper change away from going into cardiac arrest. He won't make it another month."

"And if he does?"

"He won't. Like I said, we'll fade him into the background with little effort. He's irrelevant."

"Again, stop me if I'm being dumb, but why don't we get rid of him now?"

Omaha cleared his throat. "Sorry to barge my way in to this conversation, but it's getting repetitive." Omaha looked at Boatman. "With all due respect." Omaha bounced an image on to the screen. Aska was able to see it too. It was polling information from the previous week. "Look, when asked about Faust, polling is in the high eighties, which means the real figure is twenty points below. When asked about Maximus the figures show polling of only fifty percent. Which means he's actually polling at about thirty percent, and I would dare to suggest that thirty percent is from coercion. My point is, Maximus is toxic for the Empire so a transition to a new and exuberant leader will likely slow the riots down. But a natural death will keep stability. Another coup will create instability."

"How many people being crucified were polled at the time?"

"You can stand on that self-righteous pedestal all you want, Mr King," said Aska, "but facts are facts. Work with me and you'll get your city back. Fight me and, well, I will enjoy it very much, but I doubt you'll see another six months before you're in the ground."

"Is that a threat?"

Aska laughed. "Really? I thought you were more mature than that."

Boatman wasn't backing down. "I've seen men like you, drunk on power, believing you have the answer to bringing peace and balance.

But all you really bring is chaos and confusion. I'm old enough to remember when that twerp named Orban tried to usurp you."

"He didn't do a very good job."

"Maybe not," said Boatman, "but I'm pretty sure you have a lot of dead bodies of his supporters scattered around your kingdom."

"I don't comment on insurrections."

"Then why comment on mine? Stick to your kingdom and I'll deal with mine."

"Yours?"

"You know what I mean."

"Hmm, yes, I think I do, dear Boatman." Askå sniffed. "We seem to be at an impasse and I'm bored. Omaha, for your sake, find a way through this or the 35 might not hold you in such high esteem." Askå cut the call.

48

Askå closed his laptop and found it took a lot of will not to throw it across the room or even use it to bludgeon Titus to death. He composed himself. "I understand why you hated Boatman so much when you were in London."

Titus didn't answer.

"Yes, that's true. A man like that has to be belligerent in order to defy an empire. How did you not go crazy dealing with his arrogance?"

Titus remained silent.

Askå laughed. "That's true, it takes one to know one when it comes to arrogance." Askå got up from his chair and kicked it back. The chair tumbled and crashed, and Titus tried not to flinch as he cowered in his corner. "I want to meet this Boatman. I want to meet him more than I want to meet Faust." Askå knelt beside Titus and stroked Titus's hair. "How do I meet Boatman?"

Titus froze.

"Hmm?"

Titus stayed still, like you would when approached by a predator.

"Ah, yes, if you can't beat them, join them. You're right my tasty pet, I need to go to him. No point in moaning unless I see him face to face and physically pluck out his eyes, hey?"

Titus was straining with all his might to stay as still as possible so as not to entice the monster.

"Right! Off to Britannia I go!" Askå stood up and walked away from Titus. As he got to the door he stopped. "I'll make sure you're fed while I'm away. Can't have my dinner going off." And then Askå was gone.

Titus stayed frozen for another thirty minutes until he was certain Askå had gone and wasn't playing a game. He had made that mistake before and thought Askå was no longer in ear shot, sobbed and then found the giant next to him, licking his tears from his cheeks. The last time Titus had cried, it had caused Askå to be so enamoured Titus feared that was the moment he would finally die. He didn't though, and now he allowed his body to relax and now he allowed himself to cry.

He would have called out in his angst, but it was impossible as he no longer had a tongue, because Askå had eaten it.

49

Askå strode across the large lawn area where his outbuilding was and toward his main house. House was an understatement, as it was a mansion, consisting of twelve bedrooms, six bathrooms, an indoor pool, private cinema and a games room. Askå was a huge fan of snooker, a quaint English sport, and he loved watching it when the national championships were streamed. He had gotten good at playing it because the twelve-foot table seemed small in his more-than-seven-foot presence. He was able to lean over the table and pot balls from any angle without too much difficulty from having to stretch, like most snooker players needed. He hoped when he became the new Emperor, he might be able to host a snooker championship in Rome and even decree it as an Empire sport. He corrected himself; before he got to that stage, he needed to get rid of Faust. And possibly the rather belligerent Boatman. He would need to go to London and meet the situation with full force.

"Uncle Bjorn?"

The quiet voice pulled Askå back to the here and now. "Yes, my dear girl?"

"Is it okay if I watch a film in the cinema?"

"Of course! This house is yours to use as you please.

"Thank you, Uncle Bjorn."

"You don't need to thank me. It's an honour to have you with me." Bjorn knelt down so he could be at a more even level. "I think you will do great things."

Molly smiled. It was nice, she thought, to be somewhere so kind and welcoming. She didn't see or experience the stress and uncertainty she had felt being with Boatman and Olivia. Molly hugged Aská and began to run off toward the cinema room. Aská called after her and she stopped and turned. "Yes, Uncle?"

"What film are you going to watch?"

"The Gladiator," she said, grinned, and ran off.

"Of course she is," said Aská.

"It's a strange thing to have brought that girl in," said Aská's General.

"She's given me more intel than most of my spies."

"And tactical information?"

Aská made his way toward the kitchen and the General followed. "Her innocent observations about Boatman and what he does every morning will be as useful as a spy's report."

"Any observations already?"

"Judging by what she's saying, Boatman is an arrogant, selfish man." Aská smiled, "Much like his father it seems."

The General huffed.

"Oh come on, old man, is that a surprise? I made you General because of your selfishness and arrogance."

The two men had arrived in Aská's kitchen, and they sat down at a large, marble island. It was their custom each afternoon to sit and drink vodka together. Ira didn't need to ask permission and grabbed the bottle from the freezer and a couple of tumblers from a cupboard. He poured two generous drinks, sat at the island and slid a glass to Askå. They raised their glasses in silence, downed the vodka and then Ira refilled and they began to talk, sipping this time.

Ira spoke first. "What's your plan?"

"I'm going to Britannia."

Ira sipped his drink, slowly digesting the vodka and the information. "To what end?"

"Dear Ira, I would have thought that obvious."

"But Boatman should bring Faust to you. It seems too risky going there. That's surely the whole point of saving him?"

"There's no point to anything, Ira. If your son is anything like you, which he very much seems to be, then he won't extract Faust, he'll kill him. Which is most certainly not the goal for me."

"So you get to Faust first?"

"Or eliminate Boatman."

"You're considering killing my son?"

Askå laughed. "Ira, you are amusing. You say that like you care about your bastard son. I don't recall many tears shed over Nero's death."

Ira knocked his vodka back and refilled his glass. "I don't give a fuck about them dying, I give a fuck about my seed carrying on. Maximus is a useless freak and Boatman doesn't have any children. He's the only hope I have for my legacy. An old man like me needs to see his children carry on who he is."

"By the gods, Ira, that's one out of control ego you have there."

"It's about legacy," said Ira.

Askå held his hands up in a mock surrender. "Okay, okay. What are you suggesting?"

"Let's bring Faust and Boatman back. I'm an old man. Boatman, my blood, could replace me as your General. Carry on my legacy."

"That's incredibly ambitious of you, dear Ira, to think Boatman will happily fill his old man's shoes."

"You're mocking me?"

"I mock everyone. And I mock the idea Boatman King will abandon his cause to help me run my kingdom."

"Your kingdom will include the Empire."

"An Empire Boatman wants to destroy."

"The Empire or the people running the Empire? A promise of absolute power and I guarantee his ideology will change."

"You sound very confident, my friend."

Ira sucked his teeth as the vodka hit his taste buds. "My genes are strong. I know the apple doesn't fall far from the tree."

Aská waved his hand. "Fine, fine. We'll bring Boatman to us if that makes you happy." The Aestii giant stood up and stretched his back. At his height, sitting down, even on stools, meant he still had to lean forward. "Are you hungry? I have some freshly butchered offcuts in the fridge, which I was going to make a stew with if you wanted?" Ira's stomach turned, but he had enough experience not to express his disgust.

"I'm fine, my Lord, thank you. I need to carry on planning the strategy for marching on Rome. Even if we have the Senate's blessing, there will be loyal soldiers waiting."

"Imagine being so deluded you still believe Maximus the Cripple is somehow a god, chosen by the gods." Aská went over to the fridge and pulled out an object wrapped in brown paper. Ira didn't need to ask what it was and made his excuses to leave, as he had lots to be getting on with in preparation for the coming mission. He also needed to get out of the kitchen before his stomach turned too much and he ended up puking on the kitchen floor. Ira had seen and done horrible things, he knew that. He was at an age where reflection on past sins became as frequent as blinking, but Askå's delight in the taste of human flesh was something even he couldn't digest.

When Ira closed the door behind him, the last thing he heard was Askå murmur in delight as the brown paper crinkled as it was unwrapped to reveal its contents.

50

Faust retreated from his memory palace and opened his eyes. He felt sweat around his top lip and wiped it with the back of his hand. He hadn't expected to see what his palace had stored away, and part of him wished he had left those memories undisturbed. Faust usually enjoyed visiting his memory palace because it allowed him to explore nuances of a situation that would be missed in the moment. The times he had seen death or destruction and it seemed like it had come out of nowhere, but he'd then visit his memory palace and see that everything has a reason and nothing happens in a vacuum.

Once, the rebels in London were accessing sensitive information and it appeared impossible for them to have been able to; so many heads were being scratched. The most obvious reason, as always, was a human one and a soldier must have been leaking to the rebels. Every soldier potentially involved was interviewed and passed, and it confounded Centurion Atticus, one of Faust's equals at the time. Atticus had asked Faust to assist in the investigation. Within hours the reason for the leak was found. Faust had watched all the interviews on replay and then went into his memory palace to analyse the soldiers' behaviours and mannerisms. All the soldiers', in Faust's mind passed with flying colours. No-one exhibited any guilt, and no-one appeared unnecessarily nervous beyond being interviewed for potential treason.

The benefit of Faust's memory palace, though, was that he could be very specific about people's behaviour and look for tics, specifically. So, Faust had ventured into his memory palace and one of the soldiers gave a slight tic to a rather innocuous question about the soldier's girlfriend. Faust noticed the slight eye twitch and then walked through his palace highlighting moments he had encountered that soldier before. He brought forth a memory where the solider had been in a bar that Faust and Alypia frequented. The soldier was in the bar having drinks and enjoying a merry, intimate evening, kissing and flirting. The thing was, the soldier had been kissing and flirting with a man and not his girlfriend.

With that passing piece of information, it took no time to break down the soldier to admit he had been having an affair with a male escort. A little more digging revealed the identity of this escort; he had been a spy for the rebellion. The soldier had given the escort valuable information during post-coital pillow talk, mixed with too much alcohol. The soldier and his lover were consequently crucified together, on one cross. Their final, macabre embrace.

Faust, therefore, found it oddly unnerving to be visiting his palace out of necessity to uncover more information but to wish that there were another way. The reason for his sweaty top lip was that he was accessing memories associated with Askå and Faust's dealings with Askå decades ago. And those memories had been suppressed for good reason.

Faust's father, Goethe, was a Roman Legatus often compared to Scipio Africanus, arguably the greatest Roman general in history. Just like Africanus, Goethe Faust had never lost a battle and, as some argued, his defeat of advances from a tyrant named Stalin in the Aestii region were comparable to Rome's greatest victories. Because of Goethe's defeat of Stalin, in some of the most inhospitable conditions, it was assumed the young Augustus Faust would follow in his father's footsteps and there was no more appropriate a way to do this than be assigned to the Aestii region.

Faust was eighteen when he was posted in a small town on the Dvina River, in the heart of Aestii and bordering with Askå's kingdom. Faust had arrived at the village with his Centuria, seventy-nine other newly qualified soldiers. Faust recalled the reasons behind their posting to be vague apart from being promised it would teach them how to be fearless soldiers for the fruit of the Empire.

The first night in the village was brutally cold, and the young soldiers shivered in their bunks. Faust was used to the cold, having been trained by his father to withstand the cold because, as his father had repeatedly said, "If you can fight when your fingers are throbbing and numb and every punch feels like agony, then you can fight anywhere." Even so, Faust wasn't used to the cutting severity of the Aestii cold. The young soldiers had been warned their sleep would be a fitful one because of the cold, so had been offered vodka to warm their bones. Nearly all the young men and women had gleefully taken huge swigs of the alcohol to try and help numb the cold. Within a couple of hours, almost all the new Centuria had passed out, drunk.

Faust though, Faust had remained sober. His father had conditioned him to withstand the cold and made a point that drinking alcohol only made the cold worse. It thinned your blood and made it even harder to get warm. So, on the first night of staying in that little village on the Dvina River, Faust lay on the top bunk, shivering and sober whilst nearly all the other members of the Centuria were snoring.

He had managed to nod off into one of those weird types of sleep where waking and sleeping were so intertwined, dreaming and waking were muddled. When he thought he was awake he was asleep and when he thought he was asleep he was awake. And everything in-between. On that first, bitter night, in the midst of snoring and shivering, Faust had heard footsteps clonking on the floorboards of their dormitory. Faust had wrapped his blanket round him so tight; he was scared to move in case it created a gap and let any biting cold in. He was almost too afraid to open his eyes in some irrational fear of the cold freezing his eyeballs. Nevertheless, he did open his eyes and saw a man, a very large man, almost a giant, walk into the dormitory and pick up a snoring soldier like he was picking up a rolled up sleeping bag. Faust was trying to work out if he was waking or sleeping and assumed he was sleeping when the almost giant put the sleeping soldier on his shoulder and then sniffed the still snoring newbie like he was smelling the cork of a freshly opened bottle of wine. The almost-giant turned to walk away, but paused, as if disturbed by something in the room and spun gently on his heels (which was a terrifying sight to Faust, considering the man had a fully grown man on his shoulder), until he was facing Faust's bunk. Faust still had no idea if he was dreaming or awake but knew one thing: he shouldn't move even a millimetre. With that in mind, he was too afraid to close his eyes as he feared even that movement, in the darkness of the dormitory, would be like setting off a flashlight. So he stared straight ahead at the terrible figure of the almost giant, who was twitching his nose, like a famished predator. The predator took a step in the direction of Faust's bunk and Faust was surprised at his self-control to have not let out a whelp. The clonking boot rattled the floorboards again but then the almost-giant stopped. He too heard something that made him tentative and then he was gone, clonking off, snoring soldier on his shoulder.

For another hour, Faust refused to close his eyes in case he would be attacked and flung on to the shoulder of a giant in the night. When day came and some began asking where the soldier was, Faust's stomach knotted, realising it wasn't a dream. He wanted to warn the other young soldiers of the danger in the night but couldn't speak. His voice became even more absent when one of their commanding officers said the missing soldier had died of hyperthermia in the night and everyone needed to remember to drink plenty of vodka to keep them warm through the night.

Before the second night's call to bed, Faust approached another soldier and asked if he wanted to swap bunks, as he hated sleeping on a top bunk. The soldier, who looked like the youngest in the Centuria jumped at the chance as, he said, he had never been allowed a top bunk at home. When they went to bed, most soldiers had drunk their fill so were snoring in a cacophony of a drunken chorus. Faust though, Faust kept his eyes wide open, wrapped tight in his blanket and didn't look away from the entrance to the dormitory.

No-one came that night and no-one came the next night, or even the next. Faust had tried hard to stay alert in the night in case the giant came again but fatigue is much more powerful, and Faust woke one night just before dawn, relieved he was still in his bunk but petrified someone else had been taken. No-one had been abducted and Faust had that flicker of doubt about his own reality. Maybe the dead soldier *had* died of hyperthermia? Maybe he had been hallucinating? No-one else in the dormitory uttered a word about an almost-giant coming like a phantom. Faust had been dumped into wilderness in the Aestii region, subjected to extreme cold. He was sleep deprived and hungry. It was possible he had imagined the whole thing and dreamed what he thought he saw. As the sun came up and light crept its way into the dorm, Faust felt his fear pushed away by the light and he smirked to himself that he must have been imagining the whole thing.

On night eight, Faust and his fellow soldiers went to bed. They had all had a skinful of vodka, but Faust, again, had resisted. His father's words were more potent than peer pressure, and he knew he would sleep better and wake better not having consumed shots of vodka. After the lights had gone out and the dormitory was covered in a blanket of snores and snuffles, Faust rolled on to his side, made sure his blanket cocoon was tight and stared at the doorway out of habit. He had done it every night for the past week and after a few minutes, allowed himself to relax completely and within moments he too had joined the sleepy chorus. Faust had felt his eyes getting heavy and, like the previous night, the phantom giant didn't appear. Faust closed his eyes, convinced he had invented that first night's horror. He was starting to enter that dozy stage where your body starts to find the wonderful embrace of sleep when a dull thudding noise wormed its way into his consciousness. The dull thud turned to a clonking noise as he was pulled from slumber.

Faust opened his eyes and saw the legs of a man who must have been over seven feet tall. Faust felt fear bolt through him, so much so that even if he had wanted to move or cry out, he was too frozen to be able. The terror of the giant man in the room snapped him out of any tiredness he was feeling and he then knew what he was seeing was real. The giant strode across the dormitory, and Faust kept as still as possible, hoping not to draw any attention. Faust was in the far-left corner of the dorm and could therefore see most of the room without needing to move. His former bunk was two rows ahead of him and the giant walked straight to that bunk. The young soldier Faust had swapped bunks with was out cold. He didn't even stir when the huge man stood over him, because he was tall enough to stand over someone asleep, even on the top bunk. And like he had done a week previously, he picked up that young soldier, flung him over his shoulder and took a deep sniff of the young man's neck. And like a phantom he was gone again, another man gone in the night. Faust quietly pulled the blanket up to his mouth and whimpered.

The next day, commanding officers said the same as before: that the cold had got to the seventeen-year-old. Faust had pulled an officer aside and questioned their explanation. A lashing and video call from his father put a stop to him questioning them again, even as each week, more and more young men and women disappeared. After thirty-five weeks and only forty-five soldiers remaining, commanding officers had called the now terrified young soldiers together. They had said that their training in the Aestii region was done. In that time, the soldiers had learned to survive each day in extreme conditions and learn how to strategise when everything seems futile. The surviving cadets had gone to bed each night, drinking more vodka than ever before, willing the unconsciousness, because they were too afraid to confront that there might have been another option other than dying of natural causes from being in the cold. Any talk about the deaths in the night brought lashings and the soldiers were reminded their posting was about training them to withstand all pressure because they would eventually be Rome's next leaders. Faust had resisted going to bed drunk because after multiple weeks of terror and seeing the giant man come for his prey, he had vowed he would fight with all his might if he happened to be the chosen one.

All these months later, he was never chosen and then they were shipped out of Aestii, scarred, scared but apparently Rome's next leaders.

Faust left his memory palace, pleased to be rid of the terror he felt all those decades ago. His hands were clammy, and he had a headache from reliving his time in that encampment. It was vital he relived it, though, because all these years later it was now useful to wean small details. One obvious detail was it was Bjorn Askå who had come in the night to take those thirty-five soldiers. Why? Well, he wasn't sure he would get an answer on that one unless he met with Askå in person. He wondered who in the Empire knew of what happened and, he assumed, still happened on the border with Askå's kingdom. He was sure his father had known.

Still, he was able to pinpoint other details he missed when he was a terrified teenager. One was the fact Askå had entered the dormitory with no shirt on. It was below freezing outside, and yet that appeared not to bother the giant man. It had never crossed Faust's mind before because he was so scared. Another detail was the direction Askå had travelled when he left the encampment. One night, Faust had felt brave enough to leave his bunk and see where the monster had headed. On the night Faust had failed to see anything of substance, but since walking through his palace he was able to break down the night and was able to see that Askå had walked away from the encampment toward the river. If Askå had driven, he would have walked in the other direction, which made him think Askå had arrived by boat.

It wasn't much to go by, and even Faust had to admit his palace had limitations, especially when it was used to access memories from his teenage years when he had barely begun to understand what his mind could do, but Faust knew it might be enough. The fact that Askå was topless and likely travelled by boat meant Askå, at that time, must have been based close to the river. The Empire had never worked out where the base might be because any spies sent in never came out, or only parts of them returned. The Empire had also officially agreed to stay out of the kingdom as the long-term benefit of their truce outweighed trying to know the house Askå resided in.

Things had changed, though. Askå had torn up that truce and Faust had been belittled by him. Faust decided that just as Askå had invaded his home, he would invade Askå's. Boatman had been in Faust's grasp and had slipped away. The Emperor somehow still held on to life each day. Faust felt impotent and craved a battle. Faust had been terrified of Askå, like he was a bogeyman; it was time to show that fear misplaced and make Askå experience that crippling fear when you realise you're powerless. He would go to the Kingdom of Bjorn Askå and Rome make that insolent man respect the title of the kingdom he lived in.

After all, Faust was trained in Askå's realm. It was time to put his training back into practice and leave the desk in his office to gather dust.

51

Faust tried again to video call Delilah, but the phone just rang out. He tried Sebastian also, but his phone did the same. He called the Communications department and asked them to send him the pinpoint of Delilah's last known whereabouts. They told Faust her phone was tracked to a disused pteron-port on the outskirts of the city and then it was like her phone disappeared into a blackspot. He asked for a map of the area Delilah had been in to be pinged over to him. He also asked for a map of the tunnel system beneath London. "It's a very limited map, my Lord. It's only twenty percent complete." Faust insisted it be sent to him anyway. Once he received the map, he bounced the overground map onto his office screen and then overlaid the tunnel map. He changed opacities and even though the tunnel map was almost useless, it did show a possible entrance tunnel at the pteron-port. It was marked in red because no time or resources had been spent on trying to establish the existence of this entrance. Since the mass casualties caused by Boatman rigging the tunnels the Romans had found, Faust decided it a fool's errand to keep going underground. It seemed, though, this fool was going to be drawn back. Delilah and Sebastian had to be underground. Faust sat back and thought: he was more and more convinced he needed to go to Aska's realm to bring the man to his knees in contrition.

But.

Aska had orchestrated Boatman's release for a reason. He was sure it wasn't just out of a desire to see chaos and revenge tear through London; Boatman was a weapon for something else in Aska's mind. Faust was going to pre-empt that and use Aska's weapon against him. Maybe that was the key. Get Boatman and then get Aska.

Faust called his bodyguard and instructed him to gather together a dozen soldiers and then meet in the foyer of the HoC in twelve hours. He also instructed his bodyguard to ensure the fastest chariots were brought round the front of the building ready for their departure at that time. Faust needed to freshen up first. Get some sleep and analyse his tactics for going in a way that many would think recklessly.

He stared at the incomplete map on his screen. If Delilah had entered a tunnel system, then it wasn't boobytrapped. For one, her phone wouldn't have rung if it had been obliterated in an explosion and secondly, an explosion would've been registered. No, there's an intact tunnel that leads to somewhere or someone interesting, thought Faust. And knowing Boatman and his obsession with London, Faust was willing the bet the rebel leader was there.

He called the Communications for a third time and asked if they had access to any CCTV in the vicinity of the pteron-port. After being put on hold for a few minutes, the team leader came back on and said there were cameras not only around the pteron-port but, strangely, two were positioned over an archway that was a solid brick wall. The tunnel entrance, thought Faust. The Grand

Protector asked if the cameras were in use and the team leader said that was the other strange thing: the cameras had been recently disabled. There was footage going back years, but two days ago the cameras stopped recording. The cameras being disabled at the same time as Delilah being there made him guess it was Delilah's handiwork, but he couldn't figure out why she hadn't reported any of this back to him if she was on a decent scent of Boatman. It made it all more the reason for him to go and see what was happening himself.

Faust decided he would go in fast and furious and maybe the sheer audacity of it would be unexpected enough for Faust to get close enough to Boatman. He saw an opportunity to rid the Empire of two men arrogant enough to think they were better than Rome. Two men who treated Rome like a piece of shit on someone's shoe. No, it was time to show these men why Faust was the Grand Protector and also why Rome remained the centre of the world and still ruled the world. It was time for these men to show some damn respect and Faust was willing to go to the frontline to do that.

52

The next day, refreshed, rested and energised, Faust jumped into the lead chariot, which was waiting outside the HoC entrance and the bulletproof glass closed over his and the driver's heads. The driver put into the navigation the address for the pteron-port and then they were off, hitting sixty miles per hour in seconds. They headed east, speeding over the Castrum Bridge with three chariots in convoy behind. As they travelled, Faust tried to get a better guess at what the tunnel system offered. The diagram he had was woefully incomplete and showed a few tunnels that ran off the entrance at the pteron-port, but it didn't give any clue as to where rebels would have the opportunity to set up base. He felt as ill-prepared as he had ever been, but hoped the advantage he had was no-one, including Boatman, would expect the Grand Protector of Britannia to abandon the safety of the Castrum to storm a tunnel network. Surprise made people react weirdly. It made them panic. It made them forget the basics and then it would snowball into major mistakes. He'd seen Boatman make mistakes before, so knew he could get under the rebel's skin. It was just whether this time was too ambitious.

Fifteen minutes later his chariot came to a stop on the runway of the pteron-port. The driver had asked if it was wise to get so close and Faust said the driver should shut the fuck up with his questions or wisdom, unless he wanted his tongue torn out as he clearly could not stop it from wagging. The soldier bowed his head and didn't move, even as Faust climbed out of the chariot. The other chariots had parked up and the other twelve soldiers, including Faust's bodyguard, Cassius, climbed out.

"My Lord," started Cassius, "as I have already said, I strongly advise against this. We have no idea what we might be coming up against."

"Neither do they," said Faust. Unlike the driver, Faust was willing to listen to Cassius, as Cassius was a fine tactician and very capable fighter. Cassius was the brother of the now deceased Aloysius, Nero's former bodyguard. Boatman had killed Aloysius as a decoy to get to Emperor Nero and Faust had failed to predict it.

Cassius had been the bodyguard for Grand Senator Frigus but requested to be posted in London to guard Faust and also help get to the bottom of how Boatman had managed to kill Nero with such ease, considering Aloysius was regarded as the best of the best. Cassius's own investigations couldn't find any fault with security and only confirmation that Boatman had managed to dupe Faust. Which, again, seemed strange to Cassius as Faust was never easily duped. In the time he had been his bodyguard, Cassius noted Faust seemed to remember everything, even the tiniest details, which seemed supernatural and a gift from the gods. Cassius felt a tension within him, as if Faust's loyalties were clearly for the Empire, but a niggle of distrust, that maybe, just maybe, Faust had somehow been involved in the death of the Emperor. He couldn't prove a thing, but his gut told him something was off.

Whatever he felt about Faust, he had to put it to one side and dedicate himself to protecting the Grand Protector. And in protecting, he hoped it would lead him to Boatman, or Boatman would come to him, and he could kill the man who killed his brother. He felt shamed and impotent that he wasn't able to do something when they had Boatman in their custody. He felt rage at Boatman's mocking, but now, in this situation, heading into Boatman's lair, as tactically stupid as it seemed, he had the chance to avenge his brother and make the rebel leader suffer. He would advise Faust against entering the tunnel system, because that's what a good bodyguard would do, but he secretly hoped Faust would ignore him. Which he did.

"We're going in," said Faust. "If they're in there, they won't expect us."

"As you wish, my Lord," said Cassius. "I would suggest that I go first, as your protection?"

Faust gestured Cassius to lead the way. Cassius, Faust and the other soldiers guarding the rear walked toward the hidden tunnel entrance and for a moment stood, staring at the apparent brick wall in front of them. Faust clicked his tongue analysing the archway and then he saw a slight difference in coloration on the wall to the left of the arch. He walked over to it and saw an electronic screen, covered in a plastic cover made to look like brickwork. He stood in front of the screen and a small light blinked red. No entry. He stepped away from the screen and looked around. The tunnel entrance was surrounded by junk and debris from the abandoned pteron-port. It helped disguise the entrance and avoid any scrutiny. Faust had to admit Delilah and her brother had been exceptional in tracking it down. His only questions were had they gained access, and if facial recognition was needed, whose face was used?

He scanned the surrounding area, looking for anything that might give him a clue. Old suitcases, trolleys and other artefacts from the operational days of the pteron-port were scattered everywhere. Everything was mouldy and damp. It perfectly summed up London, thought Faust. Then it caught his eye. It was out of place with everything else. It was a rucksack, but it was clean and bright. It hadn't faded. It hadn't been here long. Faust went over to it and picked it up. It was thick material, but rodents had tried to get into it, with gnaw marks around the base of the bag. There was more weight to the bag than Faust expected. He opened the bag and the eyes of an unknown man stared back at him. The key to the tunnel entrance, Faust thought. It also fitted with Delilah's MO. She had a flair for the dramatically macabre. Faust reached into his jacket pocket and pulled out some gloves. He pulled the head of Peter out of the bag and a couple of soldiers made some noises of disgust. Cassius said, "What the hell is that?"

"I believe this is our key to getting into the tunnel," said Faust and walked back over to the facial recognition scanner. He placed the head in front of the scanner and the small light blinked green. The doors to the tunnel swished open.

"Should we take the chariots?"

"No, the sound will let them know we're here a long time before we find them." They entered the tunnel, the doors swished shut, and it was then illuminated by ceiling lights.

"I don't have any information on the layout, so it's complete guesswork," said Faust, "but I'd like to think there's some breadcrumbs along the way."

Breadcrumbs was an understatement because after walking for fifteen minutes, feeling very vulnerable in the brightness of the tunnel and no cover at all from attack, they came across the body of Sebastian. He had an arrow protruding from his chest. "Sebastian," said Faust, almost as if he was greeting the dead man. "Well, that confirms the rebels are down here."

One of the soldiers asked, "What shall we do with his body?"

"Nothing," said Cassius. "Unless you want to carry him?" The solider blushed. "We need to keep moving."

The soldiers carried on their journey into the unknown network, hearts beating a bit too fast, sweat beading foreheads a bit too much. Faust, though, Faust wasn't scared. He was pumped. He was fed up with Britannia and its crappy weather and bland food. If he was offered another oyster, he would shove it down the waiter's throat. If he had to drink another drop of locally brewed ale, he would drown the brewer in his own beer. He welcomed the thought of this being an opportunity to kill Boatman and maybe get a seat back in Rome. He'd had his fill of this green and pleasant land. Alypia, his wife, had grown weary of it too. She still wowed the public with her public appearances and graced the billboards of London as the most beautiful and popular woman in the Empire, but Faust saw her eyes had gone dull in recent months. He wondered if her eyes were dull from being in London or from being with him. He'd never dared to ask because after the last time she left him for a short time, and then returned, he felt he was lucky and didn't want to rock the boat again. He was surprised when a spy of his told him that his wife had been having dinner with a woman. He was also surprised that somehow, after his wife had left the restaurant with this mystery woman, they were able to lose the spy. It was like Alypia was seeing a rebel. Faust enjoyed knowing every little detail, but he couldn't bring himself to know every little detail about the woman who had seduced his wife. If he knew that, then he would have to confront his own inadequacies and possibly confront the fact that he would have to crucify his own wife. He wasn't even going to look into his memory palace to confirm that scenario. So the chance to propel himself out of Britannia and into Rome seemed like the perfect solution to the stagnation he saw in his marriage. Killing Boatman could make him the hero of the Empire and possibly a hero to his wife.

The soldiers came to a fork in the road, so to speak. The tunnel split in two, and this was where Faust needed a bit of luck. The wrong direction and they would be wandering the tunnels for hours and never find Boatman or his companions. It wasn't luck, though, it was attention to detail. Cassius was the one with that attention. "My Lord, look." Faust went over to Cassius, who was bent on one knee. "These chariot tracks, going off that way." Cassius pointed toward the righthand fork, which, to Faust, made sense when he put some thought into it. They were close to the river, which had been running parallel to the tunnel for the best part of two miles. The left turn would most likely have taken them to some sort of outflow or dead end. Going right was the most logical choice, so that's where they went.

As they travelled the tunnel, it stayed illuminated, which was making them all nervous. There wasn't much chance of finding cover or taking anyone by surprise, but as they drew closer, it became apparent no-one was paying any attention to the tunnels. There were no sentries or indications the tunnels were being watched. Faust held up his hand and they all stopped. He spoke quietly. "We're close. Look." Faust pointed up ahead and at the end of the tunnel and at the very end, about a hundred metres away, was a spotlight, pointing toward what must have been an entrance. It wasn't a turning to another tunnel.

"Where are the guards?"

Faust shook his head, "There's a chance there's no-one up there or they don't expect anyone to find them."

"Or."

"Or what?"

"Or they're distracted. If Delilah's in there, then they'll be extremely distracted by her. She's like a mosquito in a dark room."

"Or it's a trap," said Faust. "But, whatever the reason, there's no point going back. Keep your weapons drawn and remember, shoot to kill. Any of them. All of them. They've been a disability to the Empire long enough. Whoever *they* might be in there."

The soldiers kept tight against the wall, in single file and edged to the end of the tunnel. They took their time, Faust listening for anyone coming or any sign they were about to walk into a trap. Nothing. He was confused. It seemed sloppy to have no-one posted. Boatman wasn't sloppy, but it was too late to turn back now, so on they went. They reached the end of the tunnel, and it was an entrance. The entrance had double sliding doors, which were closed. It looked like another facial scanner to access. Faust clicked his fingers and one of the soldiers brought the rucksack to him. In all his years of seeing crucifixion after crucifixion, holding a man's head to open some doors was the most gruesome. Before he held Peter's head to the scanner, Faust said, "Remember your training, fast and low and fan out." Everyone nodded. Faust held the head to the scanner, two doors swished open, and they made their move.

53

As Faust was edging up the tunnel, Maverick and Tobias were in their quarters bickering. "It's good to know you've missed me," said Tobias.

"Like a hole in the head," said Maverick.

"You know, someone with a more fragile heart would be upset by the way you speak."

"You had two years to think of a reason to ditch me, or find someone else, but no, here you are getting your panties in a twist."

"There's no way I'm ditching you."

"And why's that?"

"Because I will see us get married. Even if I have to drag that black ass down the aisle."

"We haven't seen each other for two years and you're still banging on about the same stuff as when I left," said Maverick.

"I just want you to make an honest man of me."

"Marriage doesn't work miracles, Tobias."

"I don't know why, but I thought Rome would make you softer. All that culture to soak up."

"The only thing I soaked up was betrayal from my brother."

"He had no choice, Mav."

"There's always a choice."

"For you, maybe. But we're not all the fearsome Beast Kirabo, are we? Choice is sometimes an illusion."

"When the fuck did you swallow a philosophy book?"

"I've just had time to reflect whilst you were away."

"Reflect? More like hit your head on something."

"Luckily for you, no matter what this head hits, it's all for you," said Tobias and walked over and wrapped his arms around his fiancé. Maverick let Tobias sink into his arms and kissed his forehead. "Tell me," continued Tobias, "did you learn anything whilst sneaking around Rome?"

"Yeah, we're nowhere near ready to topple an Empire."

"How does Boatman feel about that?"

"I wouldn't know; I'm not stupid enough to tell the man leading a rebellion to topple an Empire that he probably needs to think about a career change."

Just then a gunshot was heard, echoing off the tunnel walls. Tobias and Maverick were out of their quarters in a flash and running toward the sound.

54

Faust was half-right when they stormed onto the concourse of the second HQ. It seemed deserted, bar a couple working on laptops. If Boatman had laid a trap, then the two rebels hadn't received the memo as they weren't quite sure how to react to a dozen Roman soldiers bursting into their apparently secret HQ. One rebel went to put his hands in the air whilst the other went for her gun. Neither got very far in their respective actions as Cassius fired two quick shots, making the rebels crumple. Then complete silence. "What the hell is going on?"

"He's here," said Faust. "I know it. Stay alert and split into pairs. We'll have to explore each tunnel leading off from this room. No prisoners. Understand me?" The soldiers said they understood.

As they started to fan out, though, the silence was broken by the faintest creaking, then a thump. The soldiers looked around, trying to work out where the sound had come from and that's when one soldier turned to his partner to see his partner was no longer standing next to him, but splayed out on the floor with an arrow in his chest. "Shit!" The soldier raised his gun and scanned the semi-circular balcony above him. It was dark up there and so the solider fired blindly, hoping to hit whoever had fired the arrow. The bullet hit brickwork, creating a puff of dust and if he needed confirmation he wasn't close to hitting the assassin, then he received a rather solid answer when an arrow struck him in the chest, kicking him off his feet and killing him instantly.

"We're like fish in a barrel down here," said Cassius. He had followed the trajectory of the arrow and then fired into the balcony. He missed the attacker but heard footsteps running away and fired again in the general direction. Some of the soldiers followed Cassius's lead and fired, whilst some kept their guns trained on the tunnel entrances. Faust had retreated into the shadows of the room and watched the situation unfold. He wasn't going to get involved in some pathetic recreation of a final shootout.

Cassius thought the same and had found cover too awkward for the archer to get a decent aim. One of the soldiers had a similar thought but the thought was as far as he got before an arrow took him out. The remaining soldiers concentrated their gunfire on the balcony and managed to find cover before any more arrows sliced through the air.

"What now?"

"We've made our entrance, they'll come to us," said Faust. And Faust was right. The room was dotted with pillars, which the Romans had managed to use as cover, and they watched as out of the tunnels came a handful of rebels, including The Beast (which made nearly every Roman gulp) and Boatman King himself. Bella also appeared and let another arrow off. It whizzed past Cassius's head and stuck itself in the wall behind. Bella knew it wouldn't hit him but act more as a welcome to the party gesture.

"Whatever you want, Grand Protector, I think you've overestimated your ability to get it," said Boatman.

"I just want you, dead."

"Like I said, you've overestimated your ability."

"Give yourself up, Boatman, and save the torture of us killing everyone down here. Your followers can scatter through the tunnels like rats of London."

"I can confidently say even if you had the opportunity to kill everyone down here, you wouldn't."

"And why would that be?"

"Because even you wouldn't kill your own wife."

Faust frowned and looked over at Cassius. Cassius shrugged. Cassius had been told, by Alypia, she didn't need or want extra protection on top of the bodyguards she had. Also, nothing suggested the rebellion had any way of getting close to her. She was too high profile to have been abducted in plain sight and her protection would have alerted Faust of any immediate threat. "I didn't take you for desperate, Boatman, but playing that card is verging on it," said Boatman.

"He's not being desperate," said Alypia. She emerged from behind Boatman and stood next to him.

"Alypia? Are you okay? Have they hurt you?" Faust didn't give his wife a chance to answer which, Alypia thought, summed her husband up and therefore highlighted his blindness to her disappearing in the plain sight. Alypia had ditched her bodyguards days ago. She had told them that if they reported to Faust about her new instructions then her father would ensure they were shipped to Aestii to be trained as gladiators. The bodyguards didn't resist and had been spending the last few days 'guarding' her living quarters, as if she was still in there. "You're a parasite for abducting my wife, Boatman. There's rules."

"Your esteemed Emperor didn't abide by those rules when he

took my wife," said Boatman.

"I'm still alive," said Olivia. Everyone's attention turned to Boatman's wife. "You arrogant pricks. When were you going to tell me my father had died?" Olivia's eyes were red. She was shaking from anger. "And you've been using my mother as a negotiation tool?" Boatman went to speak, but Olivia cut him off, "Fuck you."

Olivia turned to walk away and then a number of things happened. A soldier thought he had seen an opportunity to assassinate the wife of the rebel leader and drew his gun to fire. Alypia had stepped forward to get Faust's attention and Boatman had turned away from Faust to try and placate his wife. The soldier had fired his gun, but as he fired his gun he was hit in the back with an axe, which had originated from the tunnel entrance to the concourse. As he fell, his gun had still fired and instead of hitting Olivia, the bullet spun Alypia like a bottle top and she collapsed. Faust saw his wife go down, turned to the soldier who fired and paused moment to try and understand where the axe had come from.

Boatman had instinctively dived in front of Olivia to protect her and as he got to his feet, realising she was okay he realised neither Faust nor the now dead soldier were going to be the problem. The men standing in the entrance to the concourse were the problem. Faust had glanced in Boatman's direction and seen the rebel leader was no longer interested in him, so had followed his gaze and that's when he saw Bjorn Aská standing there, grinning. Faust saw this as the opportunity he needed and aimed his gun at a running Boatman. Before he could get a shot off, he felt a sledgehammer blow come down on him and heard a crack as his arm was broken. He fell down and cried out at the pain of his broken arm, with Maverick standing over him.

Cassius saw his leader go down and went to his aid. He drew his gun to fire at Maverick, but Maverick saw it coming and rushed at Cassius, creating no room to fire and then Maverick grabbed Cassius by the wrist and violently twisted. The Roman yelped and dropped his gun. The bodyguard was well trained, and as he went down he aimed a punch a Maverick's groin. Maverick was used to this move as he had performed it loads in the arena so was able to move just enough so the blow hit his thigh instead. Even so, Maverick had to let go of Cassius as the punch gave him a dead leg. Cassius felt invigorated and his adrenaline pumped through him seeing The Beast looking vulnerable having gone on one knee in pain. No-one he knew had ever seen that and Cassius saw his moment to be famous for killing Maverick Kirabo. So he took his opportunity and pulled his sword from his back sheath and swung it in a high arc to come crashing down on the kneeling Maverick's head. Maverick wasn't an amateur though, who'd never been in tricky situations and when Cassius drew his sword and swung it over his head, to Maverick that was like performing a move in slow motion. Maverick could have wandered off and made a cup of coffee and still had to wait for Cassius to finish his deadly move. That was how slow and obvious the bodyguard was being, so all Maverick did was thrust his own sword upwards and into Cassius's belly.

Cassius was mid-thrust so still had his hands in the air and had to drop his sword. Maverick's sword was in Cassius up to the hilt. To prove to the bodyguard that the dead leg was nothing, Maverick put both hands round the handle of the sword, stood up and then lifted Cassius off his feet. Cassius gasped and died in seconds and Maverick dropped him. Maverick wiped his sword on his leg and looked over at Faust, who was on the floor, clutching his arm. Maverick noted that Faust wasn't crying out in pain but was perfectly still and almost serene. Mav had heard rumours that Faust was able to retreat into his head and was impressed at the man's ability to retreat away from the pain a broken arm would bring. Nevertheless, it was irrelevant as Maverick was now able to kill the Grand Protector and at least take another step toward ridding Britannia of the Romans.

Maverick stood over Faust and said, "I wish I'd punched you harder when we last met." Faust didn't look up or respond. Maverick shrugged and gripped his sword in both hands to bring it down on Faust. He raised his hands but before he could execute the Roman he was knocked off his feet from someone tackling him to the ground. He still had hold of his sword and went to impale whoever had the audacity to attack him. He stopped when he realised Tobias had tackled him. "What the fuck, Tobias?"

Tobias pointed at the pillar behind Maverick. Maverick turned to see a battle-axe lodged in the concrete. Mav stared at the axe and looked round to thank Tobias for saving his life. Tobias wasn't by his side anymore, though. He was aiming straight for Bjorn Akså, his own sword drawn.

55

Bella cradled Alypia and put pressure on the bullet wound. Alypia had been hit in the shoulder, the bullet passing through but tearing flesh out of the top of her left shoulder. Bella clamped down on the wound and then called for someone to go grab some medical supplies. She reassured Alypia it would be okay and asked if she had the strength to get to her feet. Alypia tried but fell down, the shock paralysing her. Bella looked around the concourse, but it was carnage. She hoped to see Tobias in close vicinity to help her, but all she saw was Tobias marching toward Aská, with his sword drawn and an angry face. She cried out to him, and he paused a microsecond at the sound of her voice. It barely impacted his stride, though, and Bella hoped she would see her friend alive again.

She urged another rebel to help her pull Alypia from the concourse and into a tunnel. They managed to get Alypia to her feet and stumbled into a room just off the concourse, which was also a medical room. Bella assured Alypia that she would get her sorted and touched her comms piece in her ear. She called for Doctor Silverman to hurry. Silverman had treated Olivia after Maximus had attempted to crucify her. He'd also been at Tobias's side after Faust had stabbed him. Somehow, in spite of the main players of the rebellion being driven out of London, Silverman had stayed under the radar and kept looking after rebels who kept going. He'd done what Boatman, Maverick, Bella and Tobias had failed to do: he'd stood his ground.

Silverman arrived in minutes and took a look at Alypia's shoulder. He assured her it was a superficial wound and she'd be okay. He gave her a shot of painkiller and dressed her wound, stopping the bleeding. It'd knocked Alypia for six though and she was struggling to walk. Silverman advised she be taken to the farthest sleeping quarters from the concourse and hoped to the gods that Boatman was able to get control of the situation.

"If he wants to get control of the situation then I need to be out there helping him," said Bella.

"Your friend here isn't going to bleed to death, but she might go into shock if no-one is there to keep her calm. She's not entirely sure where she is right now, think of when you wake up from a dream and are completely disoriented. Now think of that with a bullet hole in your shoulder." Bella understood and, with the help of another rebel, got Alypia out of the medical room and away from the fighting and carnage. As they stumbled away and toward relative safety, Bella was terrified that her final moments, if Boatman and her friends were overpowered, would be underground like a rat and that she would never be able to share a meal with Alypia in the restaurant where they first met. After all this time, and all the fighting, had the desire for freedom resulted in dying in an oversized coffin deep beneath London?

56

Before Boatman got to Askå, a number of Askå's men got to him. Their instructions were to disable for extraction, but if the resistance was too much, his life wasn't worth more than theirs. Boatman might have been a legend or phantom in the Empire, but in Askå's kingdom, he was another splinter causing irritation.

So Askå's men went at Boatman with that view: a splinter that needs extracting. What they didn't realise was Boatman wasn't a splinter but a force of nature, and he wouldn't be dealt with like an unruly teenager or stray animal. No, he wouldn't be extracted, but exact his vengeance on anyone who not only doubted his abilities but patronised him, too. Two of Askå's goons went at Boatman with batons. They were going by the instructions of not only Askå but Ira, too, that they should at least attempt to take him alive. If the batons failed, then so did mercy. Both men thought, like any typical fighter, that rushing Boatman before he had time to think would work. One aimed high and one aimed low. Double blows, quickly, with maximum effect. Attacking Boatman, though, was bit like trying to hit water vapour. The goon swinging his baton toward Boatman's head thought he'd done a good job as Boatman raised his left arm to deflect the blow. The vambrace Boatman was wearing took the brunt of the force and Boatman dropped to one knee. The change in height of the rebel put the second goon off and he decelerated with this baton swing, which was meant to hit Boatman's shins. Instead, Boatman caught hold of the baton with his right hand and pulled it from the goon's grip.

The first goon raised his arm again to take another shot, but instead of connecting his baton with Boatman's skull, he felt a baton connect with his ankle, and connect hard. The goon heard the crack as his ankle bone splintered and the pain came microseconds after. Boatman got up from being on one knee and grabbed the other goon by his throat. As he stood up, he brought Aska's man with him and when the goon's feet were barely touching the floor, Boatman slammed him to the ground, shattering the man's windpipe. He stepped over the goons and made his way toward Aska.

Aska had been looking on with mild amusement. He knew his fighters wouldn't be able to nullify Boatman, but it was fun watching them try. He'd also been clear that if they didn't try their best to take Boatman alive and relatively unscathed, then they would be at Aska's mercy on their return home. It was a no-win situation for Aska's soldiers. Before Boatman could get any closer to the giant man, two more goons came at him. Aska wanted to watch how Boatman would handle them, to get an even better understanding of how this phantom man fought, but he was faced with Tobias coming at him.

Tobias was engulfed by the rage coursing through him. For months, he'd felt tired of the fight and tired of the running and hiding. When Tobias boarded the pteron-chariot with Olivia, he was relieved to get away from Britannia, and especially London. He had been missing Maverick so much, his chest hurt from wondering if he would see his fiancé again, but when he felt his stomach drop when the pteron-chariot left the runway, tension seemed to fall away, like it had been left on the ground. He hadn't realised how knotted up he was inside from living a life as a rebel, and flying to the RIA was a glimpse of freedom. So when he and Olivia agreed to return to London, the fear and anxiety returned. He wasn't sure if he would see Maverick alive again, in the flesh, or have to hold some memorial service with no coffin to weep over. When he saw, via a live stream, Maverick in the arena, being beaten by Boatman and watched as it looked like Boatman was going to execute the man Tobias loved, the tiredness dissolved and rage took its place. He had never been an angry man; he'd always found the funny side of even diabolical situations, and being a former gladiator and part of Boatman's rebellion, there had been plenty of diabolical situations.

When Tobias was a gladiator, he had been billed to compete against one of the top fighters from the Aquitania region. It was predicted to have a lot of viewers streaming it from all over the Empire, with a prime-time slot, but as the fight drew nearer, streaming sales were underperforming. Unbeknownst to Tobias, organisers decided to spice things up and when Tobias stepped into the arena, in front of thirty thousand spectators, he saw that he wasn't fighting just one elite gladiator from Aquitania, but three. Even when Tobias barely survived the bout and needed a dozen stitches, he still found it funny, because he didn't understand how he'd ended up killing people in front of sell-out crowds, and even in front of sell-out crowds the Empire weren't satisfied, so they tried even harder to get him killed. For some reason, that was funny to him, because it was absurd to be standing over three dead gladiators whilst thousands were chanting his name. It was so ridiculous, it had to be funny.

Seeing Maverick about to die, because of the Empire's desire for control and revenge, it churned in his gut and the humour couldn't be found. When he reunited with Maverick, the rage subsided and, for a moment, Tobias forgot he was so angry. Seeing Aska almost take Maverick's head off with an axe proved he was still angry as hell, and he was ready to tear Aska's throat out.

Tobias swung his sword at Aska, seeking to hit the man in the throat. Aska stepped away from the potential blow and pulled his own sword out from a scabbard tied to his back. He brought the sword over his head and down on Tobias. Tobias held his sword up to parry the shot, but Aska was holding a longsword and the weight of the sword and power of the Aestiian combined meant as Tobias blocked the blow, he heard his wrist crack. Tobias's sword went clattering on the floor and Aska brought his sword down again, looking to cut Tobias in half. Before the sword hit Tobias, he was pulled backwards by Maverick.

"We need to get out of here," said Maverick in his boyfriend's ear.

Aska said, "Hello my dear pupil," and swung his sword again, this time aiming to hit Maverick. As his sword came down, it stopped in mid-air as Boatman was underneath Aska, holding his arms up.

Boatman turned to Maverick, "I'm right behind you. Seal the doors to the God-Carpenter and Mars tunnels, I'll go through the Dante one. Get everyone to fall back. Go!" Maverick obeyed instructions and got everyone off the concourse.

Boatman strained under the power of Aska, so he punched the Aestii giant in the stomach. Aska let go of his sword and it fell into Boatman's hands. Boatman gripped the sword, weighting it and looked over his shoulder to see Maverick dragging Tobias away. He looked back at Aska and said, "I knew I was right about you."

Aská sucked in some air. He hadn't been expecting such a heavy blow. "In what way, Mr King?"

"You don't want peace or a partnership. You just want absolute power."

"It's possible to have all three."

"Not with you."

"You know, I know a man, very similar to you and, yet, he agrees with my politics."

"I'd like to see what he says about you when he's not kissing your arse."

Aská laughed. "You British really have no social filters." Aská had his hands in the air. "Look, I'm not interested in your overcast city."

"Then why are you here?"

"I'm more interested in the people than the places, dear Boatman," said Aská.

Boatman glanced around him and saw he was alone on the concourse. Maverick, Tobias and Bella were nowhere to be seen. His followers were dead or also disappeared into the tunnel network. He was on his own and surrounded by a group of Aská's fighters. Boatman clenched his jaw, spun the sword in the air and then lunged for the Aestiian. Aská jumped back and his fighters all dove on Boatman. Boatman was not going to die without taking a few with him, and he cut down three men as they tried to pin the rebel leader down. In the midst of the blood and chaos Aská came over, baton in hand, and struck Boatman hard on the head. Boatman went from growling in rage to everything going black.

57

Maverick had sealed the doors to the medical tunnel entrance and another rebel had sealed the second tunnel. He was helping Tobias to where Dr Silverman was. "Why didn't you try and stop Aską?" Tobias was confused.

"I needed to get you out of there before he killed you," said Maverick. "You heard Boatman, we needed to get out of there."

"You had your sword on you, you could have taken him out."

Maverick shook his head. "No. No, I couldn't."

Tobias stopped walking, making Maverick stop, and looked at his partner. "You're terrified of him, aren't you?"

Maverick avoided the question. "We need to get to Silverman. He needs to look at your wrist."

"I can't believe it. The Beast is scared of someone."

"I'm not scared of Aską, I'm realistic about the fact he nearly took your head off."

"You're avoiding the subject. You never avoid subjects. You're scared." Tobias wasn't mocking his partner, he was just surprised.

Maverick dropped his head. "Can we please get you to Silverman?" He held up his hand to stop Tobias from saying anything else. "And I'll tell you everything about Askå, okay?"

"Promise?"

Maverick squeezed the bridge of his nose in frustration. "What are we, ten-year-old girls doing pinky promise?"

"Mock me all you want, you're the one who ran away."

"Fine, I promise."

Tobias nodded in satisfaction, and they made their way to Silverman.

58

Maverick and Tobias walked into the medical room, where Silverman had finished treating Alypia. She was asleep on a bed, with a saline drip and heavily bandaged. Bella was sitting by her side, holding her hand.

Olivia was in the room, too, and when she saw Tobias she walked over to him and slapped his face. "Did you know?"

Tobias blushed. "Olivia, I'm sorry, I thought we could fix things quickly."

"Like my dad being murdered? How were you going to fix that?"

"We just needed a bit more time before telling you about your mum and dad."

Olivia laughed. It was humourless. "Time? Time for what?"

Tobias flustered. "Boatman had a plan. He allowed himself to be caught by Faust. He was going to get rid of him once and for all and then save your mum."

"Oh, that worked amazingly well. Like all his plans," said Olivia. "Where is he?"

"He went down the Dante tunnel, he'll be here soon. We need to blow the concourse once we know he's away from it," said Maverick. He touched his ear and asked Boatman to respond. Static. Maverick contacted a rebel who had sealed the other tunnel, asking if Boatman was with them. They said that was a negative. He ordered the rebel to take some support and go to the Dante tunnel. If it was still open, then they were vulnerable to another attack. "I need to go find him. Bella? Come with me." Bella nodded and let go of Alypia's hand. Silverman assured her Alypia would be okay. Bella and Maverick ran down the tunnel. Both their earpieces went off with news that the tunnel entrance was still open, and also to hurry. The rebels picked up their pace.

Bella arrived ahead of Maverick and saw there were no rebels in the tunnel and the entrance was, indeed, wide open still. She waited for Maverick to fall in step with her and they drew their weapons and stormed onto the concourse. When they saw the scene, they understood why they needed to hurry. The area was deserted. No Romans, no Aestii soldiers and, crucially, no Boatman.

"We need to follow," said Bella.

"Follow who, though?"

"Faust was down and out when we evacuated. Aska must have Boatman." Maverick looked around. "And possibly Faust, too. There's a lot of dead soldiers here."

"We need to go now," said Bella and ran over to the entrance to the tunnel network they'd originally arrived through. As Bella got close, she paused.

"What is it?"

Bella pointed, "Look."

Maverick followed where Bella was pointing to and saw tiny wisps of smoke crawling under the door. The door was sealed, but even smoke finds a way. And if smoke was managing to get through the door, then there was a lot of smoke in the tunnel.

"They've torched the tunnel. If we open that door, the backdraft will kill us all."

"Let's get out of here," said Maverick. As they jogged away from the potential inferno, Maverick had a thought. "Why don't we let them think we opened the door?"

Bella nodded. She didn't need him to explain. She ordered everyone to get into the Dante tunnel and start making their way to the emergency exit hatches. She and Maverick then stood at the entrance of the tunnel and Bella pulled an arrow laced with explosives from her quiver. "How long do the doors take to close?"

"About a second."

"You need to make sure you push that button as soon as the arrow leaves my bow."

"I was a gladiator, my reflexes are great."

Bella arched an eyebrow, "We'll soon find out if they're not." Bella loaded her bow and said, "After my count." She counted down from three and then loosed the arrow. Maverick hit the emergency close button and the doors slammed shut. As the doors closed a deafening roar and intense heat hit their faces for a millisecond before everything went quiet. Bella and Maverick instinctively put their arms up to their faces and lowered them when they realised the doors would hold out.

"And just like that, the rebel resistance is no more," said Bella.

59

Askå was watching as the unconscious figures of Faust and Boatman were being carried onto his pteron-chariot when the explosion rocked the ground beneath him. A brief inferno exploded out of the tunnel, bright orange flames and smoke shot out of the tunnel to about fifty meters. Then the smoke and flames were sucked back into the tunnel like they were being swallowed. It was an incredible sight, and Askå made a mental note to get someone in his team to hack any nearby CCTV camera so he could watch the footage.

"Looks like they opened the door," said Askå to no-one in particular. He turned away from the brief spectacle of the explosion and climbed aboard the pteron-chariot. Grand Protector Faust and Boatman King were strapped onto beds and remained unconscious. Within minutes, a doctor had injected both men with an anaesthetic and hooked them up to an ongoing drip feed. Askå wanted them out for the count for the entire flight and then the journey back to his HQ. He'd found it easy to find Boatman's hideaway, but he wasn't going to leave any breadcrumbs for Boatman or Faust to use if they managed to contact their followers or soldiers. Boatman had left too many clues after he fled London and then returned. He'd failed to keep things watertight in regard to information, and Askå was disappointed by how easy it was to track the rebel down. He had expected a much more formidable force when it came to covert operations. In fact, he had expected a greater challenge when they faced off underground. Yes, Boatman had caught him off guard and he was surprised at the raw strength of the man, but it wasn't a true reflection and Askå felt Boatman had been taken down too easily by his soldiers to pose any kind of threat that would make him nervous.

Askå looked at the sleeping Faust and wondered about him, too. The smartest man in the Empire, apparently, and yet he wandered into Boatman's lair with no real plan it seemed. He was rumoured to be the only man who would be able to dispose of Boatman and the following he created, but Faust seemed naïve and stupid to have walked into that situation like he did. Maybe he had nothing to lose? Whatever the reason, Askå was left underwhelmed by Faust, the greatest soldier in a millennium and disappointed by Boatman, apparently the most fearsome rebel in history. If this was the current quality of leadership in Rome and in rebellions, Askå was feeling much more confident that instead of planning it for two years' time, he would be able to march on Rome in a matter of weeks. The cripple Emperor wasn't going to do anything. The Grand Senate would plead for their lives, and the general public would probably welcome someone with a vision. And Askå had a vision he couldn't wait to share with not only Rome, but across an Empire he could truly expand and improve. The 35 appeared excited for Askå's vision too with how much money they were pumping into his operations.

Askå went and sat down near the front of the pteron-chariot

and stretched out his legs. The chariot had been adapted to deal with Askå's size so that he wasn't cramped and uncomfortable on any journey. He leant back and closed his eyes. Before he nodded off, he called over one of the soldiers who had been underground. "I hope someone recovered both my axes from before, because if they've been left, I will send you back to London and make you dig for them. And I promise, you will have to dig with your bare hands until those axes are in my possession again. If not, your family better hope the gods are merciful."

The soldier nodded and assured Askå that his battle-axes were safe. Once Askå was snoring, the soldier went into the toilet at the back of the craft and puked his guts up.

60

Omaha sat in a tavern in the Fish Borough, eating a dozen oysters with lashings of lemon and pepper and drinking a Germanic beer that had been smuggled in. His phone rang but he ignored it. He was going to savour these oysters as they were the first ones from Britannia he'd ever eaten. The tavern landlord also said that they were oysters from Meresig, which made them even more special and worth savouring.

Once he finished, he picked up his phone and video called back. Dakota, one of the 35, answered. "You were meant to create allies, not enemies."

Omaha swigged his beer, and licked the froth from his top lip. "No-one sees us as enemies."

"Because there's no-one left alive."

"Don't believe everything you read."

"Omaha, Askå was meant to align himself with Boatman, not abduct him. You know what that means will happen to him."

Omaha had to concede Dakota's point, but made another. "It all works in our favour."

"Go on?"

"Everything is a mess in the Empire. We'll be nowhere near their plans for quite while."

"Unless Askå storms Rome."

"He needs our financing to be able to do that."

"He has Faust. Faust is like a direct line to the Senate Bank."

Omaha had to concede their point again. He thought about the situation. "Askå isn't interested in us, apart from the money and potential trade. He won't see us as an opportunity to invade."

"He's just swept into London, without telling us, and completely destabilised Britannia without breaking a sweat, Omaha. Your naïvety is astounding because he'll be thinking he can do that to the RIA. Either get it sorted or get back here and we'll send someone else." Dakota cut the line.

Omaha had to admit Dakota was right to feel threatened by this turn of events. He had thought Askå was satisfied with the idea of Boatman having Britannia as an isolated, Empire-free outpost, but now he wasn't so sure. Which meant Askå had every potential to decide to try and achieve world domination and possibly the funding source to do that. He turned the glass in his hand, finished his beer, and then ordered another.

He would need to find some allies and work out next steps, and the only ones potentially alive would see Omaha as part of the problem. Omaha was famous for his bravery across the continents but even he wasn't feeling so brave when thinking about trying to convince Maverick Kirabo that the 35 were friends and not foes after the mess of the past few hours.

He decided Dakota was half right about sending someone else and sent a message asking for extra help. He knew Maverick's only intention would be to follow Askå, and Omaha certainly wasn't going to do that without some of the RIA's best trackers. If they were going to walk into the gates of hell, at least they'd do it with a semblance of a fighting chance.

61

Boatman woke up, and his arms were cable tied above his head. He did the obligatory twist of his wrists to see if they had any give. They didn't. He blinked slowly a few times to adjust to the light of wherever he was and saw it was a large, stone-walled room, with high ceilings and, it seemed to him, a thatched roof. The floor was also stone. There was a huge fireplace to the right of Boatman, which was blazing out heat, so the room was comfortably warm. The room was sparse, apart from a large, wooden table in the middle and an equally large chair at the head of the table. It didn't take much effort to work out he was in one of Askå's residences. He looked to his left and Faust was also cable tied and awake. He hadn't said a word. He was staring straight ahead.

"How long have you been awake?"

Faust didn't answer.

"Faust, look at me. Faust?"

Faust stopped staring and looked at Boatman. In all his dealings with Faust, Boatman had never seen fear, but for the first time fear was dancing in the man's eyes. Boatman again asked the Grand Protector how long he'd been awake and this time received an answer. "About half an hour."

"You look like you've seen a ghost."

"It feels like I have."

"For once in your life, stop speaking in riddles," said Boatman.

"Over there," said Faust and raised his chin toward the other end of the room. Boatman's eyes had adjusted. He looked over and saw there was someone else in the room. From what Boatman could tell, it was a man, and he was grotesquely emaciated. Boatman called out to him, and the man scurried into the corner like a spider that had been disturbed.

"Who the hell is that?"

Faust was now staring hard at Boatman. "Whatever happens, we need to make a promise to each other."

"Faust, if I had a hand free, I would punch you in the face right now. Like I said, stop talking like life is a riddle."

"You're right," said Faust. "There are no riddles. Life is just an endless hell."

"Remind me to make that quote an uplifting screensaver for my phone." Boatman tried to free his hands. "Look, Grand Protector, I'm guessing that guy over there has freaked you out, but I need to know what's going on with you. We're strung up like hogs waiting to be slaughtered and you're acting like a young recruit who's just joined a legion."

Faust shook his head. Boatman could see his body was shaking, too. "Absolutely, there's no time to panic. Firstly, we need to promise to each other that when one of us gets the chance we will kill the other one."

"I made a promise about killing you a long time ago."

"That's fine, then. However it comes, that doesn't matter, but I promise you, if I have the opportunity, I will help you by killing you."

"Help me?"

"Help you, that's right. That thing over there, scuttling around, that's the reason you will be pleased if I kill you."

"Have you been here before?"

"No. But I met Aská a long time ago. When I was first recruited by the Empire. Back then I knew, deep down, what Aská was doing, but now, seeing him over there." Faust trailed off.

"The rumours are true."

Faust nodded.

"But what's happened to him?"

"That wretched creature is our fate, I'm afraid."

"Who is it?"

"Former Legatus Titus."

"Titus? I thought he'd gone AWOL to the RIA."

"So did I. Aská must have contacts everywhere and picked him up."

"Are you sure it's Titus?"

"I'm sure. He came over to me."

"What did he say?"

"Nothing. He couldn't."

"Why not? Surely he has some information."

"The poor bastard can't talk because he's got no tongue. And he can't write anything down because he's got no hands."

"Sorry, you're telling me Aská has been removing parts of him?"

"And eating them."

Boatman's mouth opened.

"You told me not to talk in riddles anymore," said Faust.

"How has he not died from the shock?"

"I guess Titus is much more resilient than Nero or myself ever gave him credit for."

"We need to get ourselves free and do something for him," said Boatman.

"Oh, you'll be free, soon enough, dear Boatman. You'll be taking Titus's place," Askå's voice came from behind the prisoners. An area of the room they couldn't see.

"Feel free to come and try to take my tongue. I assure you, there will be a lot more resistance than Titus gave."

Askå was now in front of the men. "I'm sure there will be, Mr King, but that's part of the fun." He grinned and walked over to where Titus was hiding. He stroked Titus's hair and whispered some things in his ear. He came back to Boatman and Faust, "I'll miss Titus. He's been a pleasure."

"What exactly do you want?" Faust asked.

"What we all want. Infinite knowledge and power," said Askå, "which is why you're here."

"You'll need to elaborate," said Faust.

"Have you ever realised how many nutrients you get from fruit or vegetables? How much protein you get from a juicy steak?"

"There's easier ways to do dietary advice," said Faust.

"You're being far too diplomatic, Faust. Why even entertain this psycho?" Boatman said.

Askå walked up to Boatman and got within biting distance. He spoke in a low growl. "There's nothing to entertain, dear Boatman, it's about drawing the goodness from *everything* around you." He stepped back, "The lovely Faust here, has a very big brain. Much bigger than mine. Which is why I want to harness the power from his brain." Askå licked his lips. "You, dear Boatman, have such a hugely fiery heart, which I want to share in." Titus, in the corner of the room let out a weird tongueless cry. Askå looked over his shoulder at Titus and laughed. "Titus has fulfilled his quota." He stepped toward Boatman again, "That's why you're here."

62

Ira had poured two cups of coffee as Askå walked into the mansion's kitchen. The General handed his boss the coffee and let him have a few sips before asking any questions.

"So?"

"He's definitely your son," said Askå.

"What makes you say that?"

"The way he looks at me." Askå smiled as he took another sip of coffee. "The way he looks at me is how you look at me when you think I'm not looking."

Ira never shied away from his Lord and said, "How I look at you isn't the problem. It's when I become indifferent to you, that's when you might need to watch your back."

"Threatening me whilst we drink coffee together, General?"

"No, my Lord, just careful advice about the people you keep around you. Julius Caesar was arrogant enough to think his circle was safe."

"You're comparing me to Julius Caesar?"

"No. You're not so easy to kill."

Askå snorted. "I feel like I'm one cup of coffee away from

being poisoned."

Ira got up from the stall. "When do I get to talk to my son?"

Aska shook his head and waved his hand. "Not yet, Ira. Not yet at all. We need to get an understanding of what he was conniving in London. Your presence will distract him."

"Or the emotional impact will make him spill his guts."

"Let's not play the abandoned-child card just yet. After all, he's only your son because you raped his mother."

Ira had nothing to say.

"Exactly. You can airbrush your past all you want, but I highly doubt Boatman will be running into your arms like the prodigal son from that story you God-Carpenter followers read to each other."

Ira stroked his beard. "So, what? You're going to eat him, like he's of no use?"

"Of course not. He's very useful. I want to bottle his vengeance. But you're naïve if you think he's going to find some sort of paternal forgiveness. We need him. He doesn't need you."

"Then what do we need him for?"

"Taking Rome is easy. Maximus will probably die in his sleep. We don't need Boatman for that. What Boatman will do for us is infiltrate the 35 of the RIA and then create a gateway for us to walk in."

"He won't do that."

"He will."

"If you try to force him, he'll resist."

"He won't when I remind him that unless he does what I say, his mother-in-law dies and so does his orphan stepchild, Molly."

Ira looked up from his coffee. "You love that girl."

Aska laughed. "Like hell I do." He leant forward, "Look, Boatman failed his wife when she was crucified, he failed his wife when she was free. He's failed his wife, and her family, every step of his journey to getting his childlike idea of freedom. He'll do anything to redeem himself."

"You could march in on the RIA yourself. Why use him?"

"Why use your queen when you have a bishop?"

Ira pursed his lips and shrugged. "I guess so."

"Also, I encountered Boatman briefly in that tunnel. He is abnormal. He is pure rage. If I can march into RIA's capital with him by my side, then the whole world is mine."

Aská got up from his stall and left the kitchen. Thinking about domination made him hungry, and he knew just the meal he wanted.

Epilogue

Maximus was in-between sleeping and waking. He wasn't sure if he had slept in months. The saline drips protruding from his arms made it impossible to ever relax because with every slight movement there was a pinch at his skin. The only respite he got was when he was allowed another dose of morphine, but he had been counting down the hours until he was due another shot and, by his calculations, he was going to have to wait another hour.

He'd stayed in London as the shit had hit the fan since the farce of the gladiator match between Boatman and Maverick. Then the explosion at the Colosseum had nearly caused his heart to stop forever. He'd been in and out of consciousness for days and tonight was the first time he was starting to get clarity again and work out how to avenge the embarrassment Aska had caused him. He would call together every legion across all continents and march on Aska's kingdom. He would instruct his Centurions, Faust at the helm, to drag Aska from whatever primitive cave he was hiding in and bring him to Rome, where Maximus himself would drive nails through that bastard's hands.

Thinking about what he would do made his heart rate spike and the door to his quarters opened. In walked a nurse and Maximus fumbled for his phone to instruct the nurse to go away and that he was fine. The nurse didn't walk over to his bed immediately. After closing the door, she didn't turn the room's light on, but went to the closet. Maximus was still trying to find his phone as he had fallen asleep for longer than he realised, and it had slipped down the side of the bed. He was hoping to type in his phone, so that his speaker translated it, to tell the nurse to go away and he would call her if he needed. She looked new to him, so guessed she was one of those who would fuss over him, scared of not doing enough to look after the Emperor of the world.

As Maximus fumbled, the nurse closed the closet door and walked over to the Caesar's bed. She was holding a pillow. Maximus was still searching for his phone with his left hand because he wanted to say that he didn't need another pillow. He tried to say it, but his mangled brain only allowed him to utter garbled noises.

The nurse leant over him and said, "Now, now, love. Don't get yourself in a tizzy."

Maximus then recognised the nurse and wanted to cry for help. But it was too late, and the nurse placed a pillow over the Emperor's face.

Olivia was surprised how much effort and time it took for Maximus to die, but it felt good, nonetheless. When she was sure he was dead, she removed the pillow and put it back in the closet. She walked out of the room, pulled the door closed and ambled down the hallway of the Castrum like she was part of the furniture. As she walked, she realised: for the first time in years, the buzzing had stopped.

Milton Keynes UK
Ingram Content Group UK Ltd.
UKHW031856260824
447474UK00004B/64

9 781962 308137